TITO'S DEAD

DERMOTT HAYES

To Hannah, Holly, Brody and Fionn
To Jessica, my daughter from another continent
To Marty, the storyteller
To Eamon, who encouraged me to pursue my dream
O Brave New World, that has such People in It

TITO'S DEAD

DERMOTT HAYES

FOREWORD

No-one was surprised when we heard Tito was dead. For what we knew of him, he was dodgy. You wouldn't trust him with your mother, one of his own pals once grumbled. There was little else to be said.

Or was there? Everything about him left you feeling uncomfortable. I didn't know him that well but I felt he knew my secrets.

It's been a year since the whole Tito thing and it lasted less than a month but the reverberations are still felt. It's not as though he was mourned and missed. His disappearance barely raised a question. Maybe there was a joke or two because he was colourful and weird and that was a perfect combination for some speculative analysis from the committee of experts who reserved squatters' rights in one corner of the bar.

Tito might be dead or sitting on the terrace of a house in Albania, sipping a cold beer and watching the sun set on the Adriatic. In the nature of these things, I'm prepared to believe either story.

The thing that bothered Tito was his invisibility. He knew, considering his legal status, he needed to be invisible but it was not in his nature. Tito raged against the anonymity.

There were other things he hated, like missing his family and particularly, his younger sister. In the days before he disappeared, he mentioned her to a few people. Himself and Deare, the journalist, were close. They often spoke together in a quiet huddle and occasionally you would hear Tito sob or roar. He couldn't just cry.

I told him invisibility protects us but he couldn't see it. 'It is all very well for you to say this when you have people you can talk to, who know who you are and can bless you and curse you…' he lashed back at me and only for it was more words than he'd ever directed at me in one sentence, I might have had a profound and witty reply.

I didn't though. He never let anyone close enough to understand his anger. So all we could do was resent him. When he refused to work, the work got done by someone else. Whether he left when he left, his days in the pub were numbered.

Anonymity is good for a bartender because all you have to do is sell drink. But that means standing in a confined space for eight hours pouring drinks for strangers while you listen to their stories and watch them get drunk. You're anonymous because the customer doesn't see you. Drinking is a performance art and you are the audience. Sometimes it's about a celebration but more often than the celebrants will admit, it's about contrition and regret and you are the priest confessor. Conspiracies and intrigues are hatched in drink and the players forget the stagehands are watching and listening.

I have seen unfaithful wives and philandering husbands spin webs of deceit for their companions or, on any night, their chosen and often complicit quarry and all this without a thought for who might be listening on the other side of the bar.

Most of the time, you couldn't give a damn and mark it all down as part of life's so-called rich tapestry, just another cliché to be stored away for future use. A good bartender, I've always said, should have as many of those in his or her head as cocktail recipes.

'You don't know me,' was one of Tito's favourite, dismissive phrases. 'And you don't fuckin' know me,' I'd bark back at him. And though there was more meaning in what was left unsaid than the empty banter we exchanged, neither of us understood the other.

I wanted him to know you can never know someone who doesn't know themselves; that everyone makes up their own story and there's not a living person on this planet without a secret. I wanted him to know a thousand things I thought about trust and friendship but I couldn't, because I didn't know if I believed them myself or if I wanted to share them with him, either.

He may have felt the world had abandoned him and his kind and you could forgive him for forgetting there were other people hurting. I hope he knew when he was handed the postcard from the pigeon, that that was his recognition. At least, as far as anyone in the pub was concerned but if ignorance is bliss, it's no excuse and certainly, no solace for its victims.

It was Peter Cahill's idea and it was a good one. It surprised me at the time that Cahill, a high flyin' Special Branch man, would even bother his arse. But right then it was the perfect antidote for Tito's gloom. We didn't know then it was his death warrant

The way I think it went, is this: Tito thought he was a player but he was just someone else's pawn. Beneath all his bravado beat a wounded heart. He craved recognition, not for any reasons of vanity but because he wanted to love and, I suppose, be loved and there was no-one who could acknowledge it.

He wasn't unlike anyone else, whether their name was Tito, Mick or Mary. That's why I'm breaking my own rule of anonymity although this is the last you'll hear from me, because this is Tito's story.

SARAJEVO

Peter Cahill wasn't happy staying in Sarajevo's Holiday Inn. He wasn't too happy about being told what to do, either. Particularly when the orders come from a jumped up American spook without the manners to take his mirror shades off throughout their meeting.

It's all very well for this creep to stand there shouting the odds, he thought, *but I'll be the one whose arse will be on the line if the whole thing goes pear shaped.*

'Are you confident everything is in place?,' the eyeless Yank was asking, 'and there'll be no hitches?'

The Holiday Inn was a pig ugly, yellow building that became one of the best known landmarks in the city, only because it managed to stay standing when all about it was getting blown to bits. Smack dab on 'Sniper Alley', on the main route from the airport to the city, it was the headquarters for every foreign war correspondent during the bitter ethnic conflicts in the '90s.

War with fucking room service, he heard himself grumble. The brochures said 'grand' and 'majestic', he figured, because it was still standing. He didn't like it because he felt exposed. He was an Irish policeman meeting an American spook in a Bosnian hotel.

The hotel was fine, he conceded, Holiday Inns were Holiday Inns, the Mickey D's of hostelry. It was central but he wasn't there to see the sights. He hardly left his room since checking in apart from a visit to a café on the corner for a cup of Turkish coffee. Even that put the fear of God in him.

The hotel was stuffed with tourists and carpetbaggers: the first, attracted by the cheap prices and the ghoulish thrill of walking in the shadows of ghosts; the second, the kind who thrive on the carrion of a fallen city.

There were too many Irish people in Sarajevo, in his estimation, as police, soldiers or civilians. If it had been his choice he would have done this somewhere else.

The U.S.'s 'War on Terror' knew no boundaries and America's allies were swiftly finding out if you weren't with them, you were against them, as far as they were concerned. 'Get with the Plan' was no longer an invitation, it was an order.

He studied the face of the man who asked the question. He was square jawed, broad and black. His hair was cut in what Americans referred to as 'crew' style. It looked as though it had been chiselled and finished with a precision laser. The eyes (or, at least, the shades) were impenetrable.

Agent Powers wore the regulation, reflector style, aviator sunglasses they gave him when they broke him out of his mould. He didn't like him but they weren't there to get to know each other.

He concluded his operational briefing and answered, 'we've already set the wheels in motion. Contact has been made with a young Kosovan woman. She has given information about our target's associates, here and in Dublin. We have set in motion a series of events that should draw our man out of hiding to protect his investment and keep control of his operation.'

'Good. Are you confident of your intelligence in Dublin? Are you sure the target will be there?'

'Absolutely, he'll be there, alright. He visits Dublin and keeps a house there. But he's unpredictable but our plan should draw him out of cover.'

'Does your man in Sarajevo know about these plans?'

'No. The operation is 'need to know' only and that clearance goes no further than this room. Everything will be completely deniable in the event of a cock up.'

He stared at his own reflection in Agent Powers' sunglasses. *Christ,* he thought, *I look really pissed off. Calm down, for fuck's sake. Don't give this wanker the satisfaction.*

He knew he was far less confident than he sounded and he hoped Powers was convinced. The job was shaky from the word 'go'. The target was 'untouchable', which was why, he guessed, the task had been handed to him.

Powers appeared to hold his gaze for longer than was needed in the tension filled pause that followed their exchange. He turned to the third person in the room and spoke to him for the first time.

'Are you clear about the details and satisfied with the plan?'

The third man hadn't spoken since he'd arrived, half an hour before, even as they'd gone through the logistics of the operation in detail. He was dressed in a neat, beige suit with an open necked blue shirt, exposing a deeply tanned body. His hair was a blue steel, gray but as thick as a teenager's. He wore no shades but his eyes were a liquid blue and seemed to float about in his head. He considered

Powers' question for a time before answering. Cahill and the American waited. Old Blue Eyes was in no hurry.

The Irishman had already met him, unofficially. Blue Eyes introduced himself as 'Abe' when they met in the hotel foyer, earlier that day. It appeared to be a casual encounter as Abe stepped into the elevator with the Irishman right after he'd registered and collected his room key.

Abe came straight to the point. 'I don't trust Powers,' he said. Cahill feigned ignorance but Abe said, 'I know your name and I know why you're here.' And before he could protest, he continued, 'when they ask us to do something they'd think twice about doing themselves then you have a right to know how to protect yourself. We must do this job together and I like to know who I will share danger with.'

Cahill wasn't sure how to react but he warmed to Abe's direct approach. He couldn't place his origin or accent and Abe never volunteered any information. He appeared Mediterranean in that lifelong tan and his 'cool in the heat' manner, but that was as close as he could call it.

Abe smiled and shook hands with him before he got out of the lift. He didn't see him again until he turned up for the meeting. Now they were sitting in this hotel suite and they were hanging on this man's answer. Abe's silence had shifted the power base in the room.

Finally, shrugging and with pursed lips, Abe said, 'it's a crazy plan but what option do we have?'

Agent Powers wasn't satisfied. 'Have you picked a man to do the job?' he asked. Blue Eyes looked at him as though he was seeing him for the first time. 'If he's happy,' he said, nodding at the Irishman, 'then I am happy. We have the perfect man for the job.

IRINA

Bernard Nolan was surprised to see his breath in a cloud of vapour as he stood on a street corner, waiting for Irina. *It's uncommonly cold for a September night*, he thought.

The evening sun had begun to fade into soft focus and a steady downpour had cleared the streets. The bars and cafés of Grbaviĉa were as busy as ever but everyone had moved indoors from the night chill and the noisy tattoo of the rain on the sidewalk canopies.

Perfect for my purposes, though, Nolan thought, *at least I'll draw less attention*. Not that the sight of a middle aged man - even a foreigner - meeting a young woman on any corner of this Sarajevan suburb would attract more than a fleeting glance. That would change if he waited any longer in this deluge.

Christ, Irina, get your finger out, he wished again if only to dispel the other thought that was jostling for space, *fuck it, she's not going to turn up*.

Nolan was fond of the city that was his home from home. It was both familiar and exotic and, for some odd reason he struggled to understand, it reminded him of Dublin.

The people were friendly and open when you bothered to show an interest in their lives. But beneath their friendly curiosity they could, as Dubliners would say, buy and sell you. Sarajevans were fond of a drink and they loved to eat and talk and dance. You could almost chew their coffee and their food was spicy but simple.

There were times he'd've given his right arm for the taste of a pint of Guinness and a toasted ham and cheese sandwich in a quiet Dublin pub and listen to the murmured hum of quiet conversation.

He'd met Irina half a dozen times. She was working as a bar dancer just three streets from where he was standing. She sat with him one night while the customary cheap bottle of Montenegran sparkling wine arrived at the table with two glasses and a champagne price.

He was surprised to find she was fluent in English and she was fascinated to discover he was Irish. The bar was full of foreigners and dancing girls. It was like many similiar bars lining the streets of this district that was the focus of bitter fighting and bombing during the war.

Much of the suburb had been rebuilt and was now part of Novo Sarajevo, the drab, functional, cityscape of the former Yugoslavia's socialist era. It bore the curious, uneasy mixture of old and new - the buildings that survived the war were pockmarked with bullets and shrapnel, the rebuilt sections made it look all that much more shabby and decrepit. The narrow laneways and alleys remained no-go areas for foreigners at night, where muggings and robberies were common.

He sat with her that night and enjoyed her company but she lost interest in him when she knew he wouldn't pay her to dance and the high rollers began to arrive.

On subsequent nights, she sought him out. One night they got through two bottles of that sickly concoction and she stayed in his company, despite incurring the obvious displeasure of her employer. She said he improved her English and he laughed.

Bernard Nolan knew these bars well and he was a familiar face to their owners. Not just because he spent at least one night a week in them, but because he ran a popular Irish bar in the old city, in the shadow of the Katolica Katedrala and on the fringes of the city's 16th century Jewish quarter, El Cortio. For that reason they were deferential, even polite, but never outrightly friendly.

They left Nolan to his pleasures but paid particular attention to the girls he spoke to, after he left. Nolan had learned the steps of their tune. He was a tolerated, if not entirely favoured, frequent foreign visitor. It kept his face in their minds while he kept in touch with what was moving and shaking.

That night, as the cork popped lamely on their second bottle, Irina told him of her brother, working in Dublin. Then, as she drained more glasses of the wine than was customary for these bar girls, she said something that made him sit up and pay attention.

She told him she had come to Sarajevo to find her brother, only to discover he was in Ireland and working for the same 'pit of snakes' to whom she'd become 'indebted'.

He was familiar with the term, a euphemism for the indentured predicament she and many like her, found themselves in and that amounted to slavery. He made no comment and let her speak. She laughed bitterly at the irony of her plight. What made Nolan sit up was her mention of the man who employed her brother in Dublin, a man called 'The Pigeon'.

Nolan hardly touched the third bottle of plonk while Irina grew more maudlin. She leaned on the bottle in the crook of one arm while waving her other about and spilled more than she drank.

When it became obvious she was too drunk, even in the shadowy gloom of their booth, Nolan could see they had drawn too much attention. He made his excuses to leave but not before tipping her generously and slipping her a card with the name of his bar and his cell phone number, printed on the other side. He hoped his custom and the tip would assuage their curiosity and she wouldn't pay too dearly for her intemperance, but he doubted it.

He reported her discussions in his weekly communication to his boss in Dublin. Although they had long suspected a link between the Dublin criminal and the Balkan trafficking gangs, suspicion never secured a conviction the way hard facts could.

He hadn't seen her for a month when she contacted him. Although their movements were restricted, she caught a tram to the Old City and wandered in to Nolan's one morning, her face hidden by a burkah and a pair of cheap sunglasses.

He didn't recognise her but her appearance would have been enough to cause an uproar if they'd been busy. She walked straight up to him and handed him a slip of paper. Then she turned and left as swiftly as she'd entered.

The note said he should meet her on this night and on the very street corner where he now stood in the rain and the gathering dusk. But she never showed.

IVAN

Ivan hitched the collar of his black leather overcoat round his neck. He sniffed at the rain as he stepped out of his car into the gloom of the alley, lit by the flashing light of a patrol car. A sullen drop hung from the tip of his nose.

Four shadowy figures stood around the crumpled heap on the ground, silhouetted by their own cigarette smoke. *They might have been digging a hole*, he thought, *and had stopped for a break to talk about it*. Rain was everywhere. It eddied in pools and potholes. Ran down the walls. Splashed and spattered off every surface. This was rain that soaked to the bone. Inspector Ivan Toscic of the Sarajevo Municipal Police felt the chill. '*Another fucking dead one*', he thought.

His own cynicism startled him like an unwanted guest at a party. The body lay hunched in a dark, dimly lit and rain soaked back street of Sarajevo. A single bullet hole in the back of the skull had made sure the young man would never worry about the weather again. There was no decomposure. They'd found a fresh one. Here was the body of a young man, possibly in his mid-twenties, fashionable, even expensive clothes, stylish hairstyle, good shoes. Dead. Toscic thought he looked peaceful. Take away the sticky hole in the back of his head and he'd be sleeping.

He had seen worse. Bodies maimed, tortured, burned or blown up. He had waded through the aftermath, his socks and shoes so regularly seeped in gore and burnt tissue he'd taken to storing a pair of gumboots in the boot of his car.

So it began, again. His job was to find the killers. But war turns a policeman's job into farce. He becomes merely part of the process, supervising the production line. Violent death is routine. Someone gets killed. A body is found. The police record and investigate. The paramedics mop up the blood and shovel the body parts into bags. The police tag the body bag. The rain and the City sweep the memory away.

Ivan felt nothing and worried about not feeling regret anymore. Never get involved, was the policeman's mantra. Yet Toscic believed the reverse was true. *Were he not to feel something*, he thought, *then he would be as bad as this young man's killers*. Yet he felt nothing. He might be investigating a traffic violation. This young man had been clamped for life and he could never talk his way out of it.

Toscic thought through the scene – an alleyway, darkness, the body of a young man, a single bullet, a look of easy contentment, the rain. The location was remote so there would be little chance of witnesses The rain would obscure whatever forensic evidence might be gleaned from the scene, footprints, tyre prints, even saliva. The bullet would offer nothing in a country where everyone carried guns and no-one had a licence.

This was an execution. The motive, he guessed, was

commercial rather than some passion fomented in Sarajevo's seething ethnic cauldron. Just some tit for tat partisan killing that went on every day and night, even in a ceasefire. The war is over and the UN wants to go home. But the killings continue as the hate seethes beneath the surface calm.

There were no signs of a struggle or restraint. Death was sudden and precise. There were no placards of denunciation, no hastily discarded, half destroyed clues. Someone was taking care of business and they had no interest in anyone else knowing. An anonymous caller reported the death. That was not unusual. No-one wants to get involved. Not even the team of street cops, paramedics, SOC forensic investigators, or anyone in this circus called to another crime scene. It was wet and dark and cold and no-one, least of all the poor crumpled stiff being stuffed and zipped in a body bag, wanted to be there.

Sarajevo, like any border town in a war, like all the war torn cities in all times and down the ages, had its own war town economy; a thriving underworld that would supply you with anything from Stinger missiles to AK47s, hashish to heroin, bread to caviar, passports to people. The gangs who ran this underground criminal network were the flotsam of conflict; ex-soldiers and partisans, full time criminals, opportunists and the organised terror gangs from the east, the so called Russian and Albanian mafia who ran everything from sex to guns, drugs and refugees. Life is simply another commodity. If it's served its purpose, get rid of it.

Toscic stood for a moment in the mouth of the alleyway, silhouetted by the street light and the cold shroud of rain. He stared at the only thing the dead man was carrying. Carefully wrapped in a sealed Jiffi bag for fingerprinting purposes, was a crumpled postcard of a bar in Dublin, Ireland. In the dim light the rain had already taken possession of the bag in his hand. A beaded mist of damp clung to its surface. The bar in the postcard looked cheerful and inviting. Death had dried his throat. Ivan felt his own thirst rise at the thought of standing among the living in a warm bar.

He stared at the hand written message on the back of the card but didn't recognise all of the English phrases and made a mental note to check it out with the mad Irishman. He put the card in the inside pocket of his sodden overcoat, cast one final glance over the murder scene as the twin doors of the ambulance were slammed shut. Then he turned and walked to his car.

BERNARD

A gunshot whip cracked in a crowded Sarajevo bar. Glasses smashed, beer spilled and everyone scurried for cover. A woman screamed. Men cursed and shouted. Tables were upturned. Two strangers by the door dove into the downpour outside. The bar was in uproar.

There wasn't time for a second shot. Radovan felt the steel barrel of a handgun at the base of his neck. The gunman, steam already rising from his sodden raincoat, could smell Radovan's fear and his mint and garlic breath. He whispered in his ear, 'produce that gun in my bar again and I'll serve your brains for lunch, ye bollix.'

Radovan, 'the madman', as he was known, lowered his raised weapon slowly until it reached counter level. Tiny hairs on his neck trembled. Beer cold sweat beads erupted on his flush face. He uncocked his weapon and carefully returned it to his shoulder holster. The commotion in the bar subsided. The silence, the anticipation resounded in the bar's smoky fug. 'Now get up out of your fucken seat and out the fucken door,' the voice whispered.

Radovan rose and pushed his seat back from the bar. His companions moved their seats avoiding his eyes. Bernard Nolan was looking after business and no-one interfered with that.

Outside in the alley Radovan, suddenly sodden, turned to face the big Irishman who had dared to pull a gun on a militia commander and in front of his own men, too. Nolan's big hand grabbed a death hold grip on the other's neck and hoisted him to his toes against the wall on the opposite side of the alley.

'You've done more damage to my bar in three months than a MiG could do in an afternoon. You've terrified my customers and you're scaring them away,' Nolan hissed at the struggling Radovan, 'if you pull that gun out again in my bar after you've had a skinful, I swear to Jaysus, I'll fuckin' kill ye meself. Now fuck off home, you mad Serb.'

Nolan watched the slowly receding silhouette of the militiaman as he splashed his way, unsteadily, down the street. He heard him thump the roof of his waiting staff car and bark an angry command. A driver leaped from the car and leaned down to open the door for the waiting Radovan who grunted and flopped inside. The door slammed. His driver scurried to his own door, the engine spluttered to life and the vehicle slipped out into the sparse Sarajevan night traffic.

Bernard Nolan leaned back against the rain soaked alleyway wall. He felt his body's tensed muscles relax and slowly, he released the breath he'd held as he watched Radovan's receding figure. *Christ,* he thought, *that fucker'll be the death of me yet,* and then, *what the fuck am I doing here?*

It wasn't the first time the thought had occurred to him. *I'd like to corral the lot of them in a football field and let them at it. It's not my fucking war.* But he knew, in the same breath, he

21

couldn't let go of the danger. He thrived on the intrigue.

Composed again, he stepped into his own doorway and slowly checked the length of the street in the opposite direction. Then he flipped the safety on his pistol and slipped the Glock 9 semi-automatic into the waistband of his trousers.

NOLAN'S BAR

'A pid-jun? What is this 'pid-jun'?' Ivan asked.

' A pigeon, p-i-g-e-o-n, a bird like you'd see in the street. It's a postcard from a pigeon. Somebody's taking the piss...'

Bernard Nolan strutted his giant frame behind the bar, jutting his head back and forth, making the throaty, purring noise pigeons make. He quaked with laughter that rippled his enormous girth. Ivan Toscic was not amused.

He was staring at Orla, the barmaid, who was talking to him but he wasn't listening or, he couldn't hear. His mind was a blur of dead bodies, mystery postcards and the mocking Nolan as well as the jeering twinkle he saw in the eyes of the young Irishwoman .

'Will I get you a pint, Inspector?' she asked, grinning.

'Please,' blurted Toscic. Nolan laughed some more at his young friend's embarrassment. Orla clasped a glass from the shelf beside her while executing a provocative twirl. Ivan felt his neck and ears burn.

Bernard Nolan had come to Sarajevo as an Irish

policeman on United Nations duty three years before. Crime detection was his business and he had no problem fitting into life in a town where the only crime was getting caught. Nolan got to know the city. He knew every operator in its thriving underground and black markets. A Dubliner, there was a no nonsense street smartness about him that kept him alive and thriving in a city where foreigners were treated at best, with suspicion .

After the war 'ended', in the UN definition of the word, he stayed in Sarajevo with the SFOR peacekeeping force. Nothing had ended, it just returned underground. When the UN prepared to leave he stayed on and bought a café he transformed into an Irish pub.

'This is a postcard from a pigeon thanking this fella, Tito, for looking after him and wishing him well… Someone's pulling your leg…What's the story, anyway, pal? You've a face on you like a wet week?'

The pub, 'Nolan's Irish Bar' as the gold lettered sign on the front said, was noisy and packed. Just two blocks from the SFOR headquarters, soldiers from every corner of the globe made it their base from home. It was a regular haunt for the local militias too. One night one of their stray mortars took a hole out of the front of the building. Bernard threatened to bar them from the pub so they apologised.

'They found an exhausted pigeon in the grounds of Dublin Castle once. It had flown all the way from Alabama,' Nolan remarked.

'That's ridiculous, how did they know…?' Ivan knew by the grin of anticipation on the big man's face he had fallen into his trap.

'It had a banjo on its knee,' Nolan exploded in a fresh fit of giggles.

Orla, the raven haired Irish barmaid, danced behind the beer pumps as she lined up pints of Guinness on the tray before her. Ivan watched her sinuous, rhythmic movement and wondered, as he always did, if she was a typical Irish girl and if he could dare to ask her out.

Bernard, the giggling subsided, waited patiently for Ivan, his friend, to spill the beans.

'There y'are, Inspector, get that into ye.' Smiling Orla planted the pint of creamy, black beer before him and was gone before he could say a word, leaving only a faint trace of lavender in her wake.

Toscic raised his pint of Guinness to his mouth and sank his upper lip into the thick creamy head, tilted the glass and felt the black Irish beer lubricate his throat. Satisfied, he put the glass back on the counter, staring at it all the time and slowly licked the creamy moustache off his face. Then he smiled.

Nolan liked Toscic and knew they shared a mutual respect. The big Irishman's image belied his flytrap mind for facts and details. Those sparkling blue eyes missed nothing. Behind them worked a mind fired by a sharp wit and a considerable cunning. Ivan knew Nolan had the local uniform police in his pocket. More precisely, they had his bulging brown envelopes in their pockets. 'This place is worse than the Wild West,' he used to say, only half joking.

Ivan glimpsed too the iron in Nolan, the iron promised by his presence that said, 'don't fuck with me.' They had common ground together as policemen and Ivan used the big Irishman to work on his English. Bernard's knowledge of the city could be as good as the local police files and they had found ways to help each other out in the three years since they first met. As well as UN personnel, foreign military, spooks and journos and the local militias, Nolan's clientele included the movers and shakers of the Sarajevo underworld, drawn by the lure of foreign currency.

'There isn't a corner of this civilized world that doesn't have an Irishman,' Nolan joked to him, 'and a corner isn't civilized without an Irishman.' In the patriotic blur of their occasional after hours boozing sessions, Nolan would turn poetic.

'The British may have colonized Ireland and used the Union as a blueprint for the empire that followed. They stole our land, they crushed our religion and killed our native language…and how did we reply?' he roared rhetorically one night, swinging and slopping his mug of beer, 'our religion grew stronger, we colonized their langauge and we took our land back off them…then we built their roads and their railways and their cities and their Chunnel tunnels .and far from feeling hard done by, we fought and continue to fight their wars.'

And where they went, they drank. An Irish pub drew them all. It was their refuge. They had money to spend and nothing to spend it on except booze and singing. They drew the hangers on, the people who enjoyed their joie de vivre. They breathed life back into a city shook by war and death.

Nolan grew up working in pubs, his uncle's pub in Sligo as a boy and then the student bar in Dublin before he took off for six months to work in London. There he worked in strip bars, knocking shops, fancy pubs and even worked a sideline serving chilled champagne to City investors at garden parties in Chelsea and Mayfair. There are two things a great pub makes, talk and booze.

The big Irishman chose his spot well. He knew everyone. He knew the fags and the dykes, the forgers, the thieves, the dippers, the pimps, the pushers, the Ivans and the Igors. He knew every heavy in the street because sooner or later they all drank at Nolans. For whatever he was, Nolan's was the perfect window into the dark festering pit this city had become.

'We found a body…' Ivan began.

'Jaysus, there's nothing new in that…' Bernard commented.

'He was shot in the head. Once. There was nothing in his pockets except this postcard,' he finished.

'Jaysus,' Bernard repeated. He picked up the postcard in its sodden plastic bag again and looked at it with apparently renewed interest. ' I know the pub,' he said, hesitantly, nodding at the picture side of the card, 'Coogan's, …it's a city centre pub full of mods and rockers and street traders and every other headbanger you can imagine. Your man, Tito, if that's the name of your stiff, must have been there sometime. In Dublin, like, because the note was written by a local…er, pigeon,' he concluded, suppressing another fit of giggling.

'Laugh as you wish, my friend, but this is serious,' Toscic responded. He could see the funny side of it but he wondered why the Irishman had hesitated? Had his friend seen something…? Aah! The suspicious mind of a policeman! He raised his pint again and drunk as though it would wash his thoughts away with his thirst. Orla swept by.

Emboldened and enervated by the night's events, Toscic threw caution to the wind, 'Orla, please, may I have a word with you?'

'Yes, certainly, Inspector,' she replied twirling in the narrow space behind the bar. Was it his imagination, his insecurity, which made him feel there was something mocking in her voice?

'How can I help you?' Orla said, leaning towards him and resting her chin on her arms. The fragrance of lavender was almost intoxicating. Or was it just her proximity. Once more he was at a loss for words.

'I have something to ask you,' he said, stiffly, immediately regretting his tone. Orla, assuming a demeanour of mock alarm, stood up on her feet, bunched her tiny fists and reached her arms out straight towards him as though she expected him to 'cuff her, 'shouldn't you read me my riots first, Inspector?' Her childlike tone of fear and apprehension knocked him off guard.

'You..you…your riots?' he stuttered. Then he realised Bernard Nolan was standing watching this tableau, his giant frame quaking with laughter and he knew the Irish had 'pulled his leg' again.

'Sorry, Inspector, but you were asking for it,' said Orla, 'I'm all yours.'

'Please? …please,' he said, confused again, the courage he had found was gone, 'please call me Ivan.'

He turned for the door and called, 'I must go… goodnight.'

The rain had stopped and the hot, humid summer night reeked of damp. As he walked to his car thoughts of the young man lying in the rain soaked alleyway made him shiver despite the heat.

Nolan watched his young friend leave. He knew the young Bosnian thought he had the measure of him. They first met when he opened the bar. Toscic was no fool and there were no flies on his boss, Chief Inspector Loe, either. Nolan suspected Toscic was dispatched to check him out, a former cop among the circus of foreigners and so-called peacekeepers.

Outside, Ivan's thoughts returned to the lonely death of the man in the alley. Maybe he cared more than he wanted to admit to himself. Bernard's translation of the postcard only deepened the mystery. If he had made it to Ireland and escaped the war, why did he return? Do people have a homing instinct?

PADDY THE PIGEON

Paddy the Pigeon got the phones hopping the following morning. Inspector Toscic circulated an e-mail to Interpol with the dead man's photograph and a description of the mystery postcard. Within hours there were responses from five European national police forces and another from Interpol requesting further information. One of the national police forces was the Republic of Ireland's Garda Siochana. They had a particular interest in the postcard and its author and requested to be kept up to date on developments. There was a name and a phone number attached; Tommy O'Brien (Detective Superintendent), Garda Siochana International Liaison Office, Harcourt Square, Dublin. Interpol wanted fingerprints and more photographic evidence before they could help with identifying the corpse, the email said. A postscript attached suggested there might be a swift and positive response. Toscic responded by forwarding the relevant autopsy report information.

The Irish message intrigued him and he wondered, in passing, if it bore any connection to Bernard Nolan's muted reaction the previous night. There was no time to dwell on it. There were other things to do and his first priority was to identify the shooting victim.

An email, from the Italian police bureau for the investigation of asylum seekers and refugees, suggested the dead man could be one 'Tito DeLillo', a figure of indeterminate origin wanted for questioning in Italy on charges related to using false papers, passing himself off as an Italian national and aiding and abetting the illegal transport of foreign nationals. When Ivan put the photo of his corpse alongside the Italian identity of 'Tito DeLillo', the response that had been a trickle turned to a deluge. 'Tito DeLillo' or a person fitting his description, if not his exact identity, turned up on the suspect lists of police forces throughout Europe including Scandinavia. In every case the Tito character - a young man in his mid to late 20s, average height, brown hair, brown eyes, well dressed, several aliases, facility with languages - turned up in relation to suspected refugee smuggling activities in each country.

A profile of Tito DeLillo, the Pigeon Man, began to emerge. No charges had ever stuck and, in most cases, Tito had disappeared before the investigations went any further. The last sighting of him alive, according to reports, was in Dublin less than six weeks earlier. The Irish connection again, he thought.

Toscic's ruminations were interrupted by his superior, Chief Inspector Lukas Loe on the telephone. 'Toscic... where is the report on the body found last night? Have you identified the corpse? What's this pigeon bullshit?,' he barked. 'You mean birdshit?' Ivan thought, but he dare not voice it. Under enormous pressure from militias and politicians, Lukas Loe saw his job as 'keeper of the lid' as he once told Ivan in an unguarded moment. 'My job is to keep the lid on this cesspit but that's impossible when the real slime is above ground, protected and in control.'

Loe was a young detective when Toscic joined the police force. He was a dogged investigator who had risen in the war ravaged ranks to make it to a secure desk job, safe from the streets.

Ivan knew another side of his boss as the two forged a trust. Loe made fun of the younger man's moral dilemmas. 'I, myself,' he would say, 'am a cynical realist.'

Word of Toscic's 'postcard from a pigeon', mystery corpse, had spread. It reached the ears of a local journalist who figured the angle was good enough to interest his editor, jaded as he was by the daily death reports. The journalist, after talking to a friend from the ambulance service, put in a call to police headquarters and asked to speak to the officer investigating the unidentified corpse. Such calls were automatically directed to the Chief Inspector's office. And that was why Loe was calling Toscic.

'What the fuck is going on? Half the world appears to know something about this mystery man but your Chief Inspector remains in the dark! Where's the fucking report, Inspector Toscic?'

'Well, that's just it,' Toscic spluttered, 'there is no report….yet. We haven't made a positive identification but we have had responses to some routine e-mails circulated, we have a suspect in the frame and we may have a name soon.'

' Toscic. Can you explain why journalists are calling me and asking about 'the pigeon man'? What, in hell's name, is that about?'

Ivan updated his boss. Loe's rage subsided as he listened. He became distracted, as though his mind had moved on to something else. Reassured Toscic had the situation under control and his arse was covered, Loe was now prepared to let his young protégé handle the case.

'I want the report on my desk first thing tomorrow morning,' he announced, interrupting, then waving his hand in dismissal, he returned to the papers stacked on his desk.

'Inspector…,' Loe called just as Toscic grasped the door handle. Ivan turned, 'remember one thing. Once you give me the report that's the end of it. You put the lid back on the bin and let's not have any more foreigners digging around in our rubbish.'

THOUGHTS OF DUBLIN

Bernard Nolan had been thinking of the postcard he had been shown by Ivan Toscic. He regretted being less than honest with his friend. Their friendship was mutually useful. Bernard knew Ivan was a pork chop the minute he walked in the door. Among the chancers and grifters, Nolan knew Toscic was a decent cop. The kind he'd have made a friend of if they were in Ireland.

The most surprising people could pass through Nolan's and on at least one occasion even he had been recognised. The Irish ex-patriates, working as builders, engineers or civil servants on UN or NATO secondment, bought his cover: disillusioned, middle aged Irish Garda who had bought into a business opportunity - an Irish bar in a foreign city.

One night previous, a regular who had known him well from his days in Dublin asked him when he'd last seen Peter Cahill, because he swore he had caught a glimpse of him in Sarajevo a couple of days before. He hadn't seen him in three years, he said, although it wouldn't have surprised him to run into the likes of Cahill in a town like Sarajevo.

Peter 'Pedro' Cahill and he were old friends who had risen through the ranks together until Pedro had joined the Special Branch and their paths had parted.

Militia, mercenaries, black marketeers, informers and arms dealers used Nolan's as a meeting point. Rick's American Café had nothing on this place, thought Nolan.

He could see how Ivan struggled with the changes, the uncertainty and the chaos. Although he put his head down and got on with it in whatever way he'd been taught, there was a righteous streak in him that kept him human and hurting. Ivan was a man with a mop, sopping up the garbage, trying to stay clean.

The Irish pub in the postcard was well known to Nolan. His old mate, Peter Cahill, was a regular. The owner had a policy of employing refugees. They might be illegal but they were cheap and, for the most part, reliable.

Coogan's was a city centre pub, roaring with life, tourists and street trade by day. By night it housed rockers and regulars, some straight, some dodgy. The music was loud and the walls were sweaty. Like many city pubs it balanced the lowlife with the highbrows and the barroom philosophers. Coogan's had a curious selection of each. It was a self styled 'cosmopolitan' pub.

The Irish Government had for a long time turned a blind eye to the employment of refugees and asylum seekers but as their numbers grew their situation had to be regulated. Growing prosperity meant increased employment. Many Irish people who had emigrated to England, the European mainland and even America, returned to take up skilled jobs, leaving massive gaps in the service sector.

Employers filled the gaps with illegals. Their numbers swelled because of continuing conflict in central Europe and the Balkans during the latter half of the '90s and their desire to get as far away from the conflict threw them into the hands of international criminal gangs.

The Governments of the European Union changed their rules and criteria to limit the flow in human traffic and throw up impenetrable curtains of bureaucracy and red tape to keep them out. In Ireland, like anywhere else, those that got in could find work where they could when they were needed.

The postcard Ivan Toscic had, raised some interesting questions. He had gone to meet a contact the night before but she failed to turn up. Irina had a brother in Dublin and his name was Tito. She told him she wanted him to meet her brother. Now Irina was missing and there was a dead body called Tito on a slab in the morgue - with a postcard from Dublin in his pocket. Irina was scared when she called. She said her brother was in trouble and she wanted help. He went to their meeting place and stood there for an hour in the pouring rain. She didn't show. No wonder he was in a foul humour when he got back to the bar. Then in walked Ivan. Nolan didn't believe in coincidence.

The following afternoon, Nolan decided he'd have to make some enquiries of his own. There was one Irishman in particular, the only one he never met in his own pub. Every fortnight Nolan would take an afternoon off and head up town in his battered old Mercedes saloon. As he pulled away from the path, he didn't notice Ivan Toscic's car arriving.

Toscic spotted Nolan's car depart. He was still smarting from Chief Inspector Loe's admonishments. His Irish friend, he suspected, wasn't one of the run of the mill strangers scavenging around in the Sarajevo cesspit. The foreign garbage men Inspector Loe hated because they made his life a misery and his job a joke. 'We're just shovelling shit for these bastards,' Loe would say. He decided to follow. But it was going to be a trickier job than he thought. Nolan travelled just three blocks before turning down an alley and parking. He rummaged around in the back seat, collected something, got out, locked his car, looked around and checked the street before walking away up the alley, a white plastic bag under his arm.

Nolan was deep in thought as he trudged along purposefully. Toscic stalked the Irishman's roundabout trek through a warren of rubble strewn laneways. The route he took bore no obvious pattern or destination. He ducked, dived and scrambled. Nolan was a cautious man and hard to follow.

Bernard Nolan knew he had a tail. He turned, twisted, doubled back. He lost the tail in the shadowed ruins of a bombed out church. He turned a corner, dived through a gaping hole where there was once a window and stepped into a shattered confession box. Whoever followed walked on by.

Nolan's contact was a man named Bradshaw, Mickey Bradshaw, a scumbag lowlife and Nolan's best inside track to the underworld of post war Sarajevo.

Mickey was born and reared in Ballyfermot, a deprived west Dublin suburb where life was valued by the strength of the monkey on your back. He never knew his father, a merchant seaman from west Africa but dad left his mark. Mickey had the half caste look of Vietnamese children abandoned by their American GI fathers.

Growing up where he did and looking like he did, made

him tough, resourceful and vicious. He had two choices in life, crime or the army. After trying the first, he enlisted before his mistakes caught up with him. In the Curragh camp he learned to drill and march, polish and shine and fire any gun they gave him.

They taught him how to drive cars, jeeps and trucks and then he learned how to strip and rebuild an engine, any engine. He earned corporal stripes and did his time in the Lebanon as a transport jockey, working engines and goods. In the Lebanon he built contacts in the local bars and supplied Irish army units on UN duty with hashish, the local 'red Leb.'

He was short and lean. People in Mickey's neighbourhood who took a shot at bullying him learned their lesson once. Then they never repeated it. But he was always a square peg trying to fit into a round hole. He never made the football team but he was the first to have a tattoo. It was green and white with a shamrock over a football flanked by two diagonal green lines and underneath were the four letters, 'S.R.F.C.'

In Sarajevo he perfected his black market skills, working first as a transport jockey for the UN on secondment from the Irish army and then, discharged, as a contract freelance for SFOR, the UN peacekeeping force. He could access military and civilian supplies, bonded warehouses, food stores and even weapons. His unit moved anything and everything. He sold everything and traded in anything.

'Nolan, ye big bollix, what can I do ye for?' Bradshaw shouted, skipping from the cab of a big transport truck as he spotted the Irishman enter the depot. Mickey's bluster didn't impress Nolan as he watched his shifty eyes skipping around the yard, like a rat seeking a bolthole. Bradshaw licked his lower lip.

The sky was dull and overcast. It was a dry day but the downpours of the previous week hung like an invisible mist in the air. The yard was pitted with rain filled potholes. There was no love lost between the big Irish cop and the ex squaddie. He proved his use in the past but he was a loose wheel and Nolan knew he could never turn his back on him.

Nolan nabbed Bradshaw in his first drug bust but let him off in exchange for his services as an informant. The second time he was caught with a truckload of stolen blankets and medical supplies. He was trading the truck and its contents for a half a ton of hashish and four kilos of raw opium.

Mickey Bradshaw cursed his luck that Nolan was the copper to pinch him not once, but twice and in two far flung corners of Europe. He hated his nemesis with a vengeance and that last pinch left him in mortal fear of the Albanians.

Nolan nabbed Mickey with the truck and set up a sting to catch the Albanians. Bradshaw kept his freedom and his job. Nolan gained a vital contact. He found out where UN supplies were going, established a link with the Albanian gang and through them, discovered the Turkish source of the opium.

'I ran into a friend of yours last night,' Nolan answered, 'Inspector Toscic. He was asking after you, wondering what you were up to these days.'

Mickey hid his fear behind bravado. 'That bleedin' wanker…he couldn't catch a cold in a blizzard. What did he want, anyway?'

'Oh, he wasn't giving away much but he's investigating a murder. He asked me were you still in town 'cos he wanted to ask you some questions,' Nolan answered, studying Bradshaw.

'Jaysus, what the fuck would I know about any murder? I don't know anything…what did you tell him? Why's he asking for me?' Nolan could see Bradshaw's façade was crumbling. Beads of sweat were lining his upper lip, despite the gathering evening chill.

Nolan pushed the boat out a little further. 'Ah, he was talking about that young fella they found in an alley with a bullet in his head….and a postcard in his pocket.'

'A postcard…what's that about? A postcard? I don't know anything about that…had he no passport or id? Life is fucking cheap in this town, as you well know.' Mickey turned his back on Nolan and slunk off around the front of the transport.

'Do you know what was funniest about the whole thing?' Nolan asked, following behind.

Mickey was scouring the yard ahead as he darted a glance over his shoulder at the advancing Nolan, 'no, wha?'

The picture on the postcard was a bar in Dublin. Coogan's. One of your old haunts, I believe? And guess who it was from? Nolan paused to deliver his coup de grace. Bradshaw stood like a rabbit in the headlights, 'The Pigeon.'

Mickey bolted. He was too late. Nolan was an arm's length away. He caught him on the run and floored him with a fist between the shoulders. Smash. Mickey fell like a loose sack of potatoes.

'Fuck ye,' Mickey squealed as Nolan laid a size ten on his neck, 'what'd ye do that for?'

'Why'd you run?' Nolan asked, leaning over Bradshaw to frisk him, 'You wouldn't run away from a friendly chat if you weren't dropping a shite in your trousers, Mickey.'

Nolan yanked him roughly to his feet and tossed him against a stack of wooden flats, 'You used to drink in Coogan's, Mickey, with a whole bunch of scumbags that never seen a parade ground and one of them, if memory serves me, was a lowlife they called Joe Connolly or The Pigeon. There wouldn't be any connection now, would there? 'cos when I saw the postcard, I thought, 'nah, it must be just a coincidence…but there's no such thing as coincidence where you're concerned, ye little piece of rat shit, Mickey. You have thirty seconds to spill before I rip your head off and shite down your neck.'

Bradshaw knew exactly who Nolan was talking about. One story popped into his head. The only thing Connolly ever showed any love for were the two Staffordshire bull terriers that, years ago, he kept by his side. He had no family that anyone knew of but those dogs - Romulus and Remus, he called them - were his children. Connolly once had a business rival hung from a ceiling naked with his hands and feet tied so his testicles dangled four feet above the floor. He had taken exception to remarks he had made about the dogs so he had the man's balls soaked in gravy and encouraged the dogs to feast on them. The 'dog and ball' incident, as it became known, was different. Connolly had nothing to gain by his attack on his rival but his enemy lost everything for insulting his dogs.

He got the name The Pigeon when he tried to use carrier pigeons to courier information for a drug gang. When the Dublin police began making raids and swoops on the gang's international deliveries the gang's boss figured their cover had been blown by cell phone scans. Connolly came up with a plan to carry a pigeon with him whenever he travelled. He sent the drop point, time and date home with the pigeon. The scam never worked. The pigeon got lost. The name stuck.

Mickey Bradshaw shivered like his soul just left him for safer ground.

He wished he was somewhere else.

He wished his life was different.

Bernard Nolan played a long shot. Mickey Bradshaw jumped and caught it.

'I know fucking nothing about any dead guy. I know nothing about any bleedin' pigeon. Or Paddy the fuckin' Pigeon. I haven't seen or heard of that scumbag since I left Dublin... I don't have anythin' to do with him...why are you fuckin' pickin' on me?' He was shrill. He was in a funk of terror.

'Fair enough, Mickey, I'll take your word for it but the same scumbag Pigeon mightn't when he hears the Bosnians have been asking you questions. What do you know about the stiff in the alley, the dead punk with the postcard?' Nolan hissed threateningly.

'I've let you play your scumbag games over here so long as you're of use to me. You're shite has to go somewhere and there aren't enough Irish squaddies to keep you in silk stockings and little boys or whatever you get up to. So if there's a chance of fuckin' Pigeon I'll toss you to the dogs. Or the cats, for that matter. Now sing, ye little prick,' Nolan roared as his uppercutting fist crunched and snapped one of Mickey's ribs. Bradshaw sank to his knees in a puddle of mud and oil clutching his chest and retching puke and blood. 'Jesus, Mr Nolan,' he spluttered and croaked, 'I'll be a dead man if I tell you anything.'

'You're a fuckin' dead man in ten seconds, ye dirtbag, if you don't start talking,' Nolan drew back for the kind of roundhouse kick that would put a ball in any net when

Mickey raised his hand and squealed.

'No, Jesus, stop, no more, please…leave me alone, ye bollix…all I know is yer man with the postcard is an Albanian or somethin' He done the dirt on the Pigeon and The Pigeon's boys' paid him back. That's all I know. That's all I've heard. Ye don't ask questions about these boys if ye know what's good for ye… His own people done him. They're a vicious mob of fuckers who'd slit ye for looking sideways at them…'

Nolan picked him up again. Mickey flinched and ducked when Nolan fixed his collar and brushed his cheek with a tissue.

'What's the connection between The Pigeon and the Albanians? What have you been doing for them?'

For a moment Bradshaw thought of lying. One look in Nolan's eyes gave him a chill. He blurted: 'They give me the cargo and I provide the trucks. They'd take your eyes out for staring at them.'

'They fucked that Albanian, somethin' about his sister, an' he useta work for them. He claimed he was going to blow the whistle on them all so they put his lights out.'

'Where does Pigeon come into it? What does he do and how does he get paid? What does he give in return?' He shook Bradshaw who fell limp in his arms. His head lolled as a trail of puke and bloody drool streamed from the side of his mouth. He'd get nothing more out of him. He dropped him in the muck and walked away.

TITO'S DEAD

'What? You're joking. Tito, who worked here in the pub, the one with the pigeon?' Sergio's voice rose as he spoke, the incredulous note had a shrill timbre. His question was directed at Viktor, his kitchen porter, a Bosnian and a former drinking buddy of Tito's. Viktor shuffled uneasily, embarrassed by the attention. Everyone was listening now; first with idle interest and now, real curiosity with Sergio's growing agitation.

Viktor's eyes were downcast as though, by not meeting anyone else's gaze, they might not notice him. 'Tito's dead,' he mumbled again to his boss, the Italian restauranteur.

'He's what? What the fuck are you saying?', Sergio blurted, slamming his wine glass down so hard on the bar, the stem snapped, sending glass splinters and wine all over the bar. Now Viktor had everyone's attention, unwanted or not.

'TITO'S DEAD,' he repeated and much louder than he

intended, 'he was shot dead in an alley in Sarajevo.'

A solemn silence fell on the assembly of regulars in that curve of the bar the locals called 'cowboys' corner.

'Jaysus, he was some boyo,' Brando, the cellarman said, breaking the silence. 'There was always something dodgy about him,' another remarked. 'Fuck heem,' Sergio barked, 'we're better off without heem, he was no fuckin' good.'

Someone probed Viktor for more details, asking, 'when did this happen?'

'He was found three days ago. It was in the newspaper,' Viktor volunteered, producing a clipping from a Bosnian newspaper, 'it says the killing had something to do with a black market smuggling operation.'

'How do they know that?' Garvan Deare, the journalist asked, 'that sounds like pure speculation. Besides, there's more than one Tito in Bosnia, you can be sure of that. What makes you so sure it's our Tito?'

'Eets in the headline,' Viktor replied, holding the newspaper clipping aloft and translating, 'PIGEON POSTCARD MURDER CLUE.'

The silence returned, set to 'stunned'.

'Jaysus, that's your postcard, Garvan,' Brando joked, trying to lighten the mood, 'they'll be coming looking for you.' No-one laughed. Deare felt a chill, like a cold hand, touch his neck. It was the same uneasy feeling he got on Tito's last night. The young Albanian was here one night and then gone, like he disappeared off the face of the earth. Something about Tito disturbed Deare that night and left him with an uncomfortable feeling he couldn't explain.

What started as a well meaning joke among friends, he thought, has turned into a nightmare. He cursed the day he'd written the postcard.

Deare wasn't the only one among them with a feeling of uneasiness about Tito and the postcard. Peter Cahill made a mental note to make enquiries about the murder reported in the Bosnian newspaper and the so-called 'pigeon postcard' clue.

Deare drained his drink and put on his coat. He wasn't in the mood for company. Tito's final words to him that night in the bar, the last night he'd been seen by any of them alive, echoed in his head, haunting him, 'I will never forget you and if I ever go away, you must never forget me.'

There was one incident when a bunch of heavy set Albanians arrived and inquired about him. They asked a couple of Bosnian lounge staff where Tito was. There was a scuffle and voices were raised but the heavies slouched off when faced with Brendan, the bar's soft spoken bouncer and a karate fourth Dan.

The news of Tito's death was seized upon like a hot tip for the Derby by the pub's denizens. In the absence of a pending big race or football match, the absent Albanian was the talk of the pub.

TITO

Tito was like any other refugee whose numbers had swollen in this city. He was unlike them too. He spoke several languages with ease. He was Albanian though he spoke Italian with perfection. He could converse with ease and facility in English, French and German and his Spanish went much further than 'dos cervesas, por favor.' If there was a language problem to be solved, Tito was your man. His services were engaged to negotiate between the growing population of workers from Croatia, Bosnia, Yugoslavia, Albania and Rumania and their Irish employers.

His own compatriots appeared to have mixed feelings about him. In his presence they were deferential, perhaps because of his education but maybe, someone once speculated, they feared him too. Every Friday they'd all assemble in the bar to open their little brown pay envelopes. Tito earned more than the rest of them. Which wasn't much. But he dressed in expensive shirts, a black leather sports jacket and tight blue jeans. He wore it like a uniform. Although consulted with a deference at odds with his youth, he was scoffed at too, quietly and behind his back, for being too fly.

Despite his advantages and cheery, cheeky demeanour, Tito never made a public show of his power. He smiled and laughed. He worked hard. He had an eye for the women, was handsome in the dark skinned, brown eyed, auburn haired fashion of his Romany forebears. 'Look at her,' he would say, gesturing with his chin at a girl in a yellow teeshirt, 'do you think I can make love to her?'

For the locals he was more approachable than the run of the mill refugee. He worked with the Irish workers and shared their drinks and their jokes. On an occasional day off he might linger for a while in the bar to read his newspaper, drink a pint and chat and joke with whoever was in the bar at the time. But most of the time, like the other refugees, he would turn up for work on time, do his job and leave. The Irish never really saw them except when they were working. No one paid their homes a visit or met them for a coffee or a movie.

You never knew where you stood with Tito. He would question you at length about your own job and even broach topics of discussion like the refugee situation that others rarely mentioned. He spoke about himself sparingly and when he did open up you could never be sure he was telling you the truth.

One quiet evening in the bar as Garvan Deare sat reading his evening newspaper before eating his dinner and then embarking on another evening of story trawling through the bars and nightclubs of Dublin, Tito told him this much;

'I left home when I was 15. My family live in Tigrana. That is in Albania but you know this. I was the fifth in a family of six. I had four brothers and one sister. My father was a civil servant, a very powerful man who preferred to hide in his books and my mother, a teacher.'

Their circumstances, as much as you could glean were far from poor. His reasons for leaving remained obscure although he did allude to boredom and a desire for adventure. He never spoke about politics but then, none of the other lads did either.

Tito was the youngest of his brothers by three years. His sister Irina was four years younger than him. Although she had usurped his pampered position, his relationship with her was closer than with his other siblings. It appeared as though it was the sibling rivalry he endured as well as parental indifference that drove him from home. He was always restless and, according to his brothers - he told Deare - reckless.

Occasionally, as he sat in the bar on a Thursday afternoon waiting with everyone else for their pay packets, Tito's humour would change from the breezy sparkle that had seen him through years of hard knocks and strife, to a morose and brooding sulk. He would drink more than his customary pint of Guinness and snarl and snipe at his co-workers, foreign and Irish or he would shun their company and in a show of defiant bravado, lavish charm on the nearest pretty female customer.

Once or twice, if the numbers at the bar were few, he would open up and allow a brief yet too oblique glimpse at his past. There was an overbearing father, a protective but timid mother and brothers whose high academic achievements paved the way for their younger sibling's wandering.

There was a woman too, an older woman, according to Tito. But there was no way of telling how much of Tito's tales were fiction and how much were truth. He was certainly very young but experienced and intelligent. He had ability in a conventional way but he was also street smart and cunning. He could be volatile and moody although he was well thought of by most. His travels, he confided to Deare, had brought him to a succession of European capitals, menial service industry McJobs and in and out of love and trouble in equal doses. He had honed his wits in a hostile world. There was talk of a Croatian girlfriend who had fled with her family to Dublin from a holding camp outside London. Tito, some people who claimed to know him said, was by then working and living in Islington. He packed in his job, they claimed and followed her.

His friends, apart from those he worked with, rarely visited him in the bar. When they did they appeared grim and possessed of a greater self assurance than their compatriots. Despite his secrecy, Tito loved the mischief he could cause and played up to the legend. It was only on very rare occasions people got a glimmer of light through the fog.

Tito's mood swings became more frequent. He brushed the boss up the wrong way by his arrogance and at times, even when in a bright humour, his acerbic tongue let him down. One day he locked himself in the staff toilet and didn't come out for his entire shift.

Once, in an unguarded moment, he told Deare how the trail of dubious identity papers in his wake had begun to catch up on him. He claimed he wanted to stay in Ireland, to be with the mother of his child but first he had to prove he was eligible for refugee status. This was proving more difficult than Tito, used to blagging his way through anything with cunning, lies and false papers, had anticipated.

Talk in the bar had it that Tito's girlfriend was in the advanced stage of a pregnancy. There was speculation that this was why she and her family, Christians of the Orthodox Church persuasion, had fled London. Tito, an avowed atheist by his own protestations, was from a family of Muslims.

The girl, who was housed by the Social Welfare in a budget hostel in the Liberties area of Dublin, refused to see Tito. This, at least, was known for sure. Tito had said as much himself one day when he turned up late to pick up his wages. He had just come from a public confrontation with her at the hostel where she lived. It was confirmed by Viktor, the Bosnian who lived in the same building as Tito's ex-girlfriend, but his version was far more graphic.

'He went mad,' Viktor recounted later to everyone on 'cowboys corner', the part of the bar unofficially reserved for regulars, ' he shouted and banged on the door. He wouldn't go away when they asked him. Then they said they would get the police. But he stayed and kicked the door.'

Everyone in the bar that evening, Irish and foreign, listened intently. 'He is bloody mad, bloody foreigner,' Sergio announced with great indignation and without any hint of irony. His extreme views, like his food, were well known if not as highly regarded.

Brando, the bar's oldest employee and cellarman, stood up for Tito whom he considered a friend. 'That's not fair, now, you don't know the whole story,' he said. Brando took Tito under his wing and Tito, in return taught him Slavic slang phrases he could use to trade curses with the bejewelled Romany beggars who patrolled the streets of Dublin.

Molly, a mother of four from the Liberties with a flower stall on the corner, felt strongly for the boy too, she announced. Her sons and daughters, two strapping pairs of each and their father, Bert, a man aged before his time, gawped in awe of her. 'The young fella's missing his family and he wants to be there when his child is born. It's understandin' he needs, not the back of her hand,' she tutted noisily.

'That fucking pigeon,' Peter Cahill remarked, 'What the fuck was that about?'

'The pigeon might have been everything Tito was about,' Deare answered.

COONEY'S

'If pigeons could talk what would they say? Suppose a pigeon, a close friend of yours, decided to send you a postcard, what would he write? You're going to say that pigeons don't write. They don't converse in the English language if, indeed, all their billing and cooing is a language at all. They don't have fingers to hold a pen and if they dipped their claws in ink all you'd get is a spidery scrawl of pigeon steps.' Lunchtime in Coogan's and the dissolute barber with the soul of an artist and the liver of a drunk, was holding forth on the subject of pigeons.

People listened, distractedly. It wasn't background static. It was bartime banter, like Spring weather, thought Sean Mac, the barman on duty, blowing hot and wet.

'And if I were to reply in my most facetious fashion,' continued the barber, ' decimating your irrefutable logic with a stream of undeniable nonsense, delivered dripping in sarcasm and irony, I'd say, 'what about pigeon English?' You didn't think of that, did you?'

His audience expanded by an influx of football tourists anxious for a lunchtime feed in beery surroundings, Gallagher turned to address the company full on, 'I'd be fooling no-one but myself and creating a nuisance into the bargain. What would it serve me except the smug satisfaction of creating a stir and a wind up?'

In Coogan's as in every other pub like it every day of the week, the world's problems are cogitated and solved by a bunch of ne'er do wells, supping pints.

Coogan's was a street pub, full of passing trade and a motley collection of beer guzzling regulars. Some worked the streets like the news vendor. He had four stands on the main street and nothing moved without him knowing it. There were the flower sellers, three generations of them who spoke with the nasal argot of their inner city origins and arrived to work in S class Mercedes. There were the hawkers and buskers, colourful and thirsty , idly strumming and humming when they weren't playing or selling.

Workers from local offices and businesses vied for tables to wile away their half hour lunch breaks and the sales girls and hairdressers stayed an hour on Thursday as they opened their wage packets. There were local businessmen like Sergio, the Roman restaurateur, who played the horses all day as he sipped ruby clarets.

There was Queenie, as he was known by night, who had no name by day, or at least none that anyone knew. He worked as a drag queen in a local club under the name of 'The Queen of Heba' and when he wasn't in drag he was a quiet, neatly dressed mouse of a man. He arrived in the bar every night, an hour before his show, and drank two Snowballs in one of those highball glasses. It was only when he returned each night in full drag after his show that anyone ever addressed him and then, only as Queenie. Loud and flamboyant as his alter-ego wasn't, he'd down a large Cognac while he waited for his taxi to pick him up and bring him home.

Brando the cellarman was a fixture, perched, Sphinxlike, at the end of the bar where it curved. There were a couple of policemen like big Peter Cahill, a radiologist from a local clinic, the man from the music business and a journalist, Garvan Deare.

Few cared about their occupations but revelled in each other's company.

There were colourful characters like the whippet thin Dubliner with pointed features and a pencil thin, white moustache who worked one of the Grafton St news stands. His daily pint drinking routine was the stuff of legend.

He was a twitchy, nervous person, bald headed with a steely grey tonsure of hair that he kept shaved tight around his temples, lending him a vaguely Medieval demeanour. His ice blue eyes were beady and darting and his nose was long and thin and pointed. His upper lip was disguised by the thin, white Zapata style moustache that only accentuated his full lower red lip.

He didn't care a whit about those around him. Instead he fired darting glances at the pouring pint like an anxious parent checking the progress of his child through a medical test. For those who watched there were tell tale signals in his moves. If he rose, occasionally and almost imperceptibly, on his toes and peered with a narrow squint down the length of his thin, aquiline nose, then his pint was nearing the end of its cycle.

He never looked at the barman who delivered the beer but kept his gaze fixed intently on the pint. Once it arrived he would rearrange the beer mat below it like a woman fussing with the furniture before the arrival of a priest or a doctor. He would tilt his head sideways to see the pint's settling progress from a different angle. Before lifting the pint he'd stretch out his right hand, shooting the cuffs before licking his forefinger and thumb, not to hold the pint but to gently caress the glass, an essential ritual. Satisfied, he would tilt his head one more time, lick his lips, inhale and raise the glass, sinking his upper lip and moustache into the creamy cushion of beer froth while his other hand, resting on the counter, made a concentrated, silent twitching motion. Tilting his head backwards slowly to ease the passage of the stout down the silky path of his welcoming gullet, Adam's apple bobbing like a child splashing in a puddle, he'd drain the glass. After that the bar could breathe again. There was always someone like him or, as the case was this day, the drunken barber to provide diversion.

Despite the barber's ruminations providing some light relief, there was a pervading air of despondency about that day. Tito, the Albanian lounge boy, was in a deep trough of despair and his mood was spreading like a dark cloud over the rest of the company. He was lamenting the loss of a pigeon.

Perhaps, some thought and, as the barber suggested, Tito could speak to the pigeon. In one moment of personal amusement he named the wounded pigeon, Paddy. 'Yes, Pa-dee, that's what your name is, Pa-dee,' he pronounced with deliberation and chuckled to his private joke as he cooed soothingly to the bird and stroked its head. They spent days in each other's company as Tito nursed him back to health.

As the story went, Paddy was a local pigeon. Anyone could tell that from his general demeanour. He was scrawny and mottled. He had a shifty look about him and never seemed at ease when he was still. But he could strut with the best of them and was a regular on the steps of the pub when the chef tossed out some scraps in the morning. It was down the same lane beside the pub where Tito had first made his acquaintance. Poor Paddy had taken a tumble or had possibly been in a rumble with a scavenging crow.

Paddy's wing was broken and he lay on the ground amid the debris of fallen autumn leaves, discarded Tayto bags and used condoms. Flightless, he was a sitting target for every predator, winged or not. He would scrabble and peck but his days, if that's how he counted time, were numbered. Tito kneeled and spoke to him. He made pigeon sounds. He cooed and billed and murmured softly. Paddy squinted at him ferociously, scrabbling frantically if Tito moved. He kept his beak wide open but never made a sound. Tito took him in and nursed him back to health.

Half the pub turned out for Paddy's departure. It was like an American wake and the denizens of Coogan's were seeing off a member of the family. Pigeon stories abounded. Paddy flew away. He blinked when he first came into the sunlight. Tito lifted him gently to his face, speaking softly to the bird. When he unwrapped the cloth and let him go there was a flurry of feathers as Paddy struggled to keep himself aloft, testing his wings for faults and strength. Satisfied, he flew to the top of the nearest building, a municipal edifice opposite the pub. There, he paused, perching on the paint peeling gutter, staring down at Tito below. Then he flapped his wings and flew away.

Tito, his neck straining, slumped. Everyone in the bar at the time watched the drama unfold through the side window. When Tito came back to the bar everyone was in their seats. Not a word was said.

GLOOM

For two days a palpable gloom descended on the pub.
Regulars began to find excuses to go elsewhere and the
crowd at lunch was smaller than usual. On the second day
only Brando and Sergio stood at cowboys' corner.

'Whattahella is the matter with everyone?' Sergio asked
no-one in particular, 'issa likea funeral in here.' Brando
stared into his cider, his fifth of the day. It was five pm.

'It's Tito,' Brando barked hoarsely as he lit another
Sweet Afton, untipped, 'he's depressed about de burd.'

'He's berd?' Sergio scoffed aloud, 'they're likea rabbits,
justa leeving and breeding. He's a better off withouta her
from what I hear and he'll soona find another to takea her
place.'

'No, Jaysus, I meant his burd, Paddy…' interrupted
Brando.

'He's a queer as well? That's all we need,' continued
Sergio.

'Paddy the pigeon, ye fuckin' eedgit, the burd with the
broken wing he saved,' corrected Brando.

Sergio had missed the bird saga while on a visit to his
own homeland. Ordinarily, ignorance never stopped him

from expressing his own forthright opinion on everything from sport to abortion but a bird loving Albanian left him speechless.

Brando filled him in as best he could, relating the story of the hapless pigeon rescued, harboured and nursed to health by the volatile Tito. Sergio scoffed derisively at the tale of the departed pigeon. But it was clear even to him the pub had assumed the pallor of unspoken grief and loss. Something needed to be done.

That's where Garvan Deare came into the story. The pub was his haven of escape from the rigours of a life crowded by the empty clink of wine glasses and launch reception prattle; by the self important demands of half drunk editors and the indulgent paranoia of the B, C and D list celebrities he was paid to stalk. In this pub of human refugees he was just another face with a pint.

Everyone knew what he did for a living and no-one cared. Deare's real motivation was to get quietly drunk although this was a motivation, like all quiet drunks, he would have not attributed to himself. Truth was, he was a lonely figure, only recently separated from his wife and children, drawn to the barroom camaraderie of fellow drinkers.

That evening as Deare took up his customary perch at the bar on cowboys' corner, Brando and Pedro Cahill began their approach. 'Tito's good buddy has gone, he's flown the coop,' Brando began. There was a pause for the customary acknowledgement.

Brando was a past master at the non-sequitor and Deare, momentarily preoccupied, stared back at Brando, confused.

'The pigeon's gone,' big Peter Cahill prompted.

'I know that,' Deare said, giving the pair of them a look

that said, 'I was here' and asked, 'what the fuck?' 'He has more than the bird to worry about,' he volunteered. Sergio, standing on Brando's other side, looked up from his Racing Post, confused.

'We need to do something and you're the man for the job,' Brando growled, 'we want you to write him a letter.'

'What…?'

'From Paddy…the pigeon,' he continued, ignoring his question, 'he'd feel better if he knew the pigeon was safe and happy…'

'What…?'

'He might snap out of this depression if he got a letter from the pigeon,' he continued, 'and we thought (his hand swept the company, two waiters, three kitchen porters, a university lecturer, a newspaper vendor, two policemen and a Roman restaurateur) you're the very man for the job.'

'You want me to write him a letter from a pigeon?,' Garvan Deare spluttered, 'Are you taking the piss?'

'No, no…if he got a letter from Paddy it might cheer him up. He has enough troubles but he's been very down since the bird left.' Sergio's confusion deepened.

The company watched with interest and anticipation. Pedro Cahill, a keen punter, remarked how he'd scored well on a young novice called 'postcardfromapigeon' running at Gowran Park only a month before. Sergio nodded knowingly. At least Pedro was speaking his language.

Deare thought about it. 'Let me think about it,' he said and returned to his evening paper and freshly poured pint. Sergio asked to see the racing pages. There was an evening meeting in Clonmel and he fancied a leisurely beer fuelled flutter. There was a murmur of agreement and the talk turned to horses.

Deare's mind pondered the bird conundrum. It was a nice diversion from the 'Deare Diary,' his column in the local evening rag. There might even be a story in it, he thought. Paddy the pigeon was gone, of that there was no doubt. His departure had left behind a downcast Albanian and a depressed pub. Sergio left to make the bookies before the 6.30 race.

An idea occurred to Garvan Deare. The situation was patently absurd but so, without saying as much, was anything that was said or happened in the pub. That was its charm and they were all willing contributors.

One other occasional visitor to Coogan's took more than a passing interest in the 'Paddy the Pigeon' issue. He was a natural loner, despite his permanent shadow, a boyish youth in black who rarely spoke.

The stranger drank a pint of Guinness, read a newspaper and answered calls on his cell phone. His shadow stood nearby and never drank. The staff were deferential and polite. There was none of the customary badinage.

This visitor's skin had the pallor of cold porridge, made all the more stark by the shock of lank, greasy black hair that fell over his face in a half fringe. He had brows that were thick and bushy and overhung his eyes, dark as coals. By contrast the nose was thin and delicate, ending in a tip laced with veins and dotted with blackheads.

Peter 'Pedro' Cahill was the only one to pay him any heed. From his vantage point at the corner of the long bar, he watched the stranger intently.

THE POSTCARD

Tito's life was crammed with absurdities. He left home to seek his own identity outside the restrictions of family. Now he was unable to identify himself to the authorities so they could process his asylum request and this thwarted his desire to start a family. Tito was everyone he ever wanted to be and no-one to anyone else, least of all his ex-girlfriend. His depression was like a virus affecting everyone around him as though his problems breached the pub's surreal defences. Something had to be done.

Garvan Deare thought of the Pigeon House, a red painted, decommissioned lighthouse and watchtower that stands as a sentinel in Dublin bay for passing sea traffic. He was unsure why they called it the Pigeon House but it appeared to be the logical sanctuary for Paddy. First he thought to get a postcard of the Dublin port landmark and then dismissed the idea as patronising and obvious. A postcard of Coogan's would do. It would save him a walk in the rain too.

'Dear Tito,' he wrote, 'How's it going? I'm back with me mates down the Pigeon House and I have you to thank for it. The lads here are great crack and the wing has come on so much, the pain has gone. I'll never forget your kindness to me nor the taste of that bleedin' sock. Take care of yourself, I must fly. All my love, Paddy the Pigeon.'

He was unsure if the facetiousness of the final sentence might shatter the carefully constructed veneer of absurdity but Brando was very pleased with his effort and told him, stashing it carefully in the pocket of his jacket, he would pass it on to Tito when he saw him.

The following day Tito was a new man. He strutted and preened about the pub, joking and laughing in a Babel of languages. To everyone who would listen he showed the postcard, brandishing it with pride and a hint of whimsy. The night ended with Tito propped half against the bar and half draped around Deare, each as drunk as the other. As the evening progressed and as these things go when drink and sentiment are mixed, there were tears in their beer and a plaintive note in the songs they sang.

Brandishing the pigeon postcard, he would read it in bleary silence as though locked within its banal sentiment he found a secret to which only he could relate or understand.

Conferring alone at one time, Tito tilted towards his Irish friend and whispered, 'I will never forget you and if I ever go away, you must never forget me.'

That was the last anyone saw of Tito in Coogan's. He'd been deported, some said. He followed the girl back to London, others asserted.

INSPECTOR AND SERGEANT

Toscic couldn't understand how the big Irishman gave him the slip. He decided to confront him later in the bar. First he had to get back to the office where another email had arrived from Superintendent Tommy O'Brien of the Garda Siochana in Dublin.

O'Brien's email was brief but courteous. He asked Ivan to call him in Dublin at his convenience. The email said there was information they could exchange. He didn't want to communicate in any further detail with him until they spoke.

'Are you Superintendent Tommy O'Brien?'

'I might be, who am I speaking to?'

'I am sorry…Inspector Ivan Toscic, Sarajevo Metropolitan police…'

'Ah Ivan, er, Inspector Toscic…do you mind if I call you Ivan? My name is Tommy. I'm glad you called, I was expecting your call. I want to talk to you about The Pigeon.'

'The Pigeon?' interjected Toscic.

Ignoring him, O'Brien continued, 'but first I want to talk to you about Nolan.'

'Nolan,' spluttered Ivan, 'Bernard Nolan?'

'There must an echo on this fucking phone,' barked the voice on the other end, 'no offence or disrespect Inspector, but will you shut up and listen?'

'Yes, sir'

'Tommy, son.'

O'Brien told Toscic he had already spoken to his superior, Chief Inspector Loe and had brought him up to speed regarding an Interpol operation centred in Sarajevo and stretching through to Dublin.

The object of this operation, he told a mesmerised Toscic, was immaterial for the moment as far as he was concerned but Garda Inspector Bernard Nolan had requested his involvement in the investigation. Chief Inspector Loe, he said, had agreed reluctantly and at 1600 hours, Sarajevo time, he, Ivan Toscic, was to attend a briefing meeting in the office of Chief Inspector Loe that would be addressed by Inspector Nolan and another member of his staff, did he understand?

'Errrr, yes…yes, of course, sir, er, Tommy,' Toscic spluttered.

'Your Pigeon postcard has caused quite a stir,' O'Brien said, 'word has leaked out and the rats are running for cover. We have a chance to cut off their boltholes but we have to find them first. Nolan will explain all of this to you. You will co-operate with him and for the time being you will also answer to him and Sergeant Farrell even though you're the same rank as the Inspector and outrank her. Is that clear?'

'Her, sir?'

'Her?'

'Sergeant Farrell?'

'Oh, Garda Sergeant Orla Farrell. She works with

Nolan.'

The phone clicked. Superintendent Tommy O'Brien had hung up.

Inspector Ivan Toscic realised he had been standing to attention throughout the conversation. The Irish policeman, though friendly, spoke with an air of commanding authority. Now Ivan slumped into his office desk chair.

His mind was racing.

'TOSCIC… TOSCIC….MY OFFICE, NOW'

The tone in Chief Inspector Loe's voice cleared his head. Grabbing a notebook, Toscic leaped from his desk and bolted for his boss's office.

The Chief Inspector was pacing his office.

'Shut the door, Toscic.'

'Sit down,' he barked.

'It appears the pigeon shit has hit the fan and you've dropped us right in the eye of the shit storm,' he began, continuing to pace.

'Chief Inspector…'

A firm hand in the air cautioned silence. The Chief Inspector continued. 'I've spent the morning fielding calls from the Minister of the Interior, the Chief of Police, Interpol and now this Superintendent Tommy O'Brien of the Dublin police. This stiff Tito DeLillo was up to his neck in illegal activities and his boss is an international crime boss called the fucking Pigeon.

'As if that weren't enough,' he ranted on, 'we've got to listen to and co-operate with this Inspector Nolan who is due to arrive here with his partner within the hour. I must put you under their command, apparently at this Nolan's request who, it also appears, is well known to you … Toscic, TOSCIC…are you listening to me?

'Yes sir.'

'You have a career ahead of you, Ivan. I don't want to think it's behind you. When this is over you will still have to work here. Remember that. Have whatever files and reports you have on this case prepared for the meeting with these two Interpol people here in my office at 1600 hours. That's all. Get out.'

'Sir.'

THE BALKAN ROUTE

Bernard Nolan was uncomfortable with the way events were unfolding. But experience told him there was no plan; best to play the cards you were dealt. He had wanted to bring Ivan Toscic into the frame for some time. He had broached the subject with his superiors in Dublin before. Tommy O'Brien had no objection in principle, being a cop with years of investigative experience, but he cautioned secrecy.

'Apart from anything else,' O'Brien pointed out, 'Bosnian officials, whether they're politicians, civil servants or policemen, who were not lining their pockets are scarce as hen's teeth. They don't get paid a lot and they live in a society where public office is a support system for their extended families.'

O'Brien was right. Throughout the imperial history of the Balkans, power had always been concentrated in ethnic structures that were cemented by bonds of common language, religion and blood ties. Toscic's routine investigation of Tito DeLillo's death had changed all that. When Ivan turned up the postcard from the Pigeon he had unwittingly turned up the first concrete evidence to link the Dublin criminal with the Albanian and Kosovan gangs. For three years Interpol had followed false leads and chased their own tails up cul de sacs. By bringing Toscic into the investigation, O'Brien reasoned, they could at least contain the spread of this information.

Nolan was addressing remarks to Loe and Toscic in the offices of the Chief Inspector in Sarajevo Metropolitan police headquarters. Garda Sergeant Orla Farrell was also present. The atmosphere was tense and formal.

He continued, 'Officially, there are 12,000 refugees and immigrants in Ireland. Unofficially, the real tally could be double that figure. More than 50% of them are from European Balkan regions. The illegal ones were smuggled in and are living in fear of the gangs that transported them.

'But it's not just about smuggling anymore. It's about trafficking and it exists on a hierarchical structure of three or four levels. The smugglers at the bottom level provide local information, safe houses and transport and their bosses are the local godfathers who control the flow of cargo in their own areas and liase with smugglers in other areas. They, in turn, get their business through whoever organises the cargo from its country of origin. Then there's a top level, the brains behind the entire operation. It could be one individual or it could be, as we suspect, an alliance across Europe…'

Ivan Toscic found his mind wandering. One half of him was absorbing the information his friend - now a stranger - was imparting.

He stole surreptitious glances at Orla and struggled to focus his attention on the matter at hand instead of the flashes of lustful abandon with Orla. Christ, he thought, if I had a sharp object I should stab myself with it.

'An operation is underway right now and within it, somehow, lies the seeds of its own destruction. The Pigeon lead, found by Inspector Toscic, could deliver to us the card that could collapse their entire house. Tito DeLillo was shot because he had threatened to play that card himself. We suspect he has handed that card to someone else. We suspect that may be someone in Dublin.

'As you know, Ivan, I have worked here in Sarajevo for close on three years and Sergeant Farrell, this past six months. To my regret, we have little to show for our efforts.

'Trying to stop the flow of illegals through the Balkan states is like trying to stop a sieve leaking with your finger. There's 1,600 kilometres of border around Bosnia, most of it unpatrollable, remote country. One thousand kilometres of that border is with Croatia and the rest with Serbia and Montenegro. Rivers separate more than forty per cent of Bosnia Herzogovina from Croatia and Yugoslavia. Between all these countries there are more than 400 border crossings but only fifty two of those are registered entry points, for the most part manned by underpaid and badly trained border guards who consider the income made from smugglers a perk of their office.'

'These routes have been the trade links for heroin from the Golden Triangle of Afghanistan, Pakistan and Iran through Turkey and from there through the Balkan states for the best part of fifty years... Oh, we've built up a useful profile of some of the gangs operating here and there's a data bank of contacts, official and unofficial, gathered, but little or no results.'

'This Tito character appears to have been an operator and we must learn more about him. We will concentrate our efforts in Dublin where Inspector Toscic should prove useful…'

Ivan's reveries ended abruptly with mention of his name. He looked from Nolan to Loe and back. His eyes never made contact with Orla's.

'We want you to come to Dublin with us. As a Bosnian you might be better able to assimilate yourself. Ivan, will you come over to Dublin to help us nail these bastards?'

'Bloody right he will,' Chief Inspector Loe blurted in the gap between Nolan's concluding remark and Toscic's agape jaw, 'Toscic, pack your bags. Any questions? No, right. My secretary has a cash advance in an envelope for you, Inspector…from now on this operation, according to my instructions, will be run on a top secret, need to know only basis. No-one outside this room and Nolan's boss in Dublin knows where you are …now, get out of here.'

As Nolan thanked the Chief Inspector for his time and co-operation and the three retreated from his office into the corridor beyond, he turned to Toscic and said, 'I suppose a jar is out of the question? I could murder a pint!'

The tension broken, Toscic smiled at the enigma standing before him.

'Yes, yes, why not?' Ivan stuttered, 'I could 'murder' a beer myself. Will you join us, er, Sergeant Farrell?

'Smiling, she replied, 'sure, I don't mind if I do, Inspector, and I'm buying the first round.'

IDENTITY

In the car, Nolan reflected on how the sudden turn of events was sending him back to a city he once called home. Dublin was Nolan's home but he'd made a life out of pretending and he wondered now was it home for him anymore? When he took the job in Bosnia, he was leaving a life behind him, a life, in his darker moments, he felt had left him.

It wasn't the job, he told himself. There had been trouble. He had never been a politician and, though he knew there were moves expected of him as he rose up the promotion ladder, he hadn't budged. No amount of street work, arrests and undercover operations would gain him the extra bar on his uniform. He had known this and God knows, his allies had advised and warned him. But still he made no move.

His friends, who had interpreted his reluctance as old fashioned, held a grudging admiration for what they thought were his old school ways. Nolan knew better. He hadn't wanted promotion because he wasn't right for it. He had burned himself out in the Dublin underground. He was too well known. Many thought Tommy O'Brien had got the job by out manoeuvring Nolan in the 'Phoenix Park Two Step' - the political brown nosing dance up the ladder - but that was bullshit. Tommy and he had known each other in the early days.

O'Brien had been an up and coming detective Garda in Store St, the inner city barracks where Nolan was first posted after training. Nolan had arrived there with Peter Cahill, both of them wet behind the ears. They had worked with O'Brien on jobs and he had, in turn, looked out for them as he rose through the ranks. Nolan had risen with him.

Tommy was methodical when Nolan worked on impulse and hunches. Tommy was by-the-book, Nolan was Action Man. They made a great team.

If Tommy had outflanked him and got the desk job Nolan didn't begrudge it to him. Many suspected O'Brien had been behind Nolan's move abroad and in some ways, he was. Nolan had personal reasons too that he struggled not to brood on.

'But it was my own choice,' Nolan thought, 'in the end, it was the logical choice to go and do what I do best … somewhere else.'

'Here, this'll do,' Nolan heard Ivan tell his driver, indicating a quiet café bar just five blocks from police headquarters. He rarely gave in to introspection and now he shook himself, blinked his eyes, as though he was waking up from a deep sleep. The bar was nondescript and anonymous, perfect for their purpose.

Nolan noted how conversation between Orla Farrell and Ivan Toscic had become more animated and friendly on the short drive between police HQ and the bar. Toscic was a strange fish, he thought, a friendly, quiet lad but something about him didn't quite add up. He couldn't help himself smiling at the irony of his suspicions; is it only people with something to hide, suspect others of hiding something, too?

Orla Farrell was a very professional young cop, he knew, and unswervingly ambitious. If she doesn't spend much longer in this mission, he thought, she had the potential to make the top ranks, even the first female Garda Commissioner if she stays focussed. This Bosnian experience would look good on her CV so long as she doesn't drag it out.

Ivan reached the bar first, firing off a set of curt instructions to the morose bartender who stood with one foot propped on an unseen beer crate, leaning with an ear cocked to a small transistor playing at low volume. He wore the waiter's costume of creased black trousers, white shirt and a short, wine stained apron. A waiter's friend corkscrew poked from a pocket of the apron beside a pen and dog eared docket book. He was short and swarthy and sported a thick moustache that hung over his upper lip and with his sunken, darkened eyes anchored by undulating rings of flesh and the prominent blackheads and nasal hairs that suggested the phrase, hangdog. His eyes betrayed no reaction although his thick lower lip detached itself from the upper to reveal a thin row of yellowed teeth. He swept the dishcloth hanging from his right shoulder down as he turned to attend to Ivan's request but otherwise displayed no emotion or acknowledgement of their presence.

'I have ordered a bottle of wine for us,' Ivan said, smiling, 'their beer selection is pitiful and this occasion calls for something special…'

Bernard Nolan began to demur. He had no problem with drinking wine – many of the local wines were as exceptional as they were cheap – but he had calls to make before the morning's journey to Dublin and, in any case, he didn't relish the prospect of playing gooseberry between Ivan and Orla.

They settled in a table in the corner of the room while the waiter busied himself around them, straightening the table cloth with one hand, holding the unopened wine bottle and three glasses in the other. Satisfied, he placed each glass on the table with a deft flick of his wrist then with his free hand, swept the corkscrew from his apron and exposed the cork with two swift tugs while turning the bottle in his other. With the same deft ease he unscrewed the cork, using the corkscrew's lever to yank the cork free. Then he stepped back and with one hand tucked behind his back, poured three glasses in swift succession.

Nolan, Toscic and Orla Farrell concentrated on his actions, mesmerised by his practised dexterity. The waiter's hangdog expression never changed until the door burst open and Toscic's uniformed police driver bustled over to their table. Nolan couldn't help notice the sudden flash of anger and surprise on the waiter's previously expressionless face. It was like someone had coughed during a Shakespearian soliloquy, a great performance had been ruined.

The driver paid no attention to anyone but Ivan. Nolan watched closely for some tell tale sign of what caused the commotion. Toscic's expression gave little away. He listened intently then stood up and smiling at his company, said, 'please excuse me…there is something I must attend to…I'm sorry. We will meet again tomorrow…'

'I hope it's nothing serious, Inspector?' Nolan asked.

'A policeman's lot, Bernard, I remain on duty and a body has been fished from the river…my attendance will be routine but necessary, you understand?'

'Fair enough, Ivan, we'll have to get back to the bar in any case…er, maybe we'll catch you later?'

Ivan Toscic smiled and nodded without indicating any intention to answer Nolan's question and with a rueful glance at Orla Farrell, he smiled, nodded and left.

COMPLICATIONS

Ivan Toscic's mind was not on the investigation of another body fished from the river. It was a common occurrence. He'd investigated the deaths of countless 'floaters'. Some were the victims of internecine conflicts between rival groups; militia or mafia; some were simply suicides, desperate victims of the war and circumstance. The trick was to get everything done as quickly as possible. Gather body and evidence in as short a period of time as was possible, a classic 'put the lid on it' operation. It suited Toscic.

Ivan knew of Nolan's status before his phone call with Superintendent Tommy O'Brien from Dublin. The source would have caused considerable embarrassment for all concerned and might have resulted in his own death.

His thoughts were disturbed by the voice of his driver. 'It looks as though the body has been fished out, Inspector, they are waiting for your examination.'

Toscic surveyed the scene. An ambulance, two police cars, an armoured truck of SFOR observers and one militia vehicle, its occupants of indeterminate allegiance, parked in the shadows, a short distance away. The victim's body, stretched on the dockside, was covered by a heavy rubber tarpaulin . The usual huddle of officials stood around, waiting, a cloud of smoke from their breath. All he needed now was the rain.

He pushed a tentative hand out the car door, palm turned upwards. No rain tonight but another dead body to look at. A patrol officer, Nikola Grahovac, approached with his helmet tucked under his arm and his notebook held out in front of him.

'Sir,' Nikola began formally, 'I responded to a report we received at headquarters…'

'A report? From whom?' Ivan Toscic snapped back as he pushed his way past the eager young police officer towards the corpse. Ivan could see the victim was a youngish man of average height and build. He was a foreigner, too, a black man or, at least, of African extraction, he thought, judging by his skin pallor. He had taken a bad beating. His lips were ripped and shrivelled. Most of his teeth had been smashed. The eyes were wide open as though caught in a flashlight. Ivan couldn't shrug off the thought that he knew him from somewhere. There was a thin straight line of a slightly denser colour around his neck and some scratching and bruising directly over the carotid artery. This body was dead before it ever hit the water, Ivan thought.

'It was an anonymous phone call. The caller said nothing but 'there is a body in the Bosna…"

Ivan Toscic didn't acknowledge what Grahovac had said though he'd heard. His mind was crammed with the nagging notion that the body on the pier belonged to someone he knew. He sought the medical examiner who hadn't arrived yet. No-one looked pleased. Everyone would have to wait their turn, like scavengers at a feast.

Ivan suspected it was murder and knew he was in for a long night.

Happily, as he spoke to the ambulance men, the medical examiner arrived.   As the M.E. made his preliminary examination, Toscic withdrew to his car. He had only opened the door and sat down when the M.E., whom he hadn't recognised, approached.

Ivan got out of the car and didn't fail to notice the smile on the doctor's face. 'Inspector Toscic?' he asked, his smile broadening, 'this man has been murdered. Strangled to be precise. And with a garrot. He certainly didn't drown.'

There was a smugness about him that made Toscic dislike him as soon as he spoke.

' Time of death?' Toscic asked, curtly.

The Inspector's disdain was obvious. The young doctor's smile disappeared and, dropping his eyes and frowning in concentration, he answered. 'Sometime this evening. Perhaps in the past three hours. I will know better when I check his internal organs but right now there is only superficial submersion damage, very little bloating and the discolouration has been caused as much by the means of his death as by floating in the river. By the way, he received a severe beating too although that probably happened earlier. Maybe this morning or last night.'

His report complete, he turned as abruptly as he had appeared, threw his medical bag in his car and drove off.

Ivan Toscic found himself smiling in his wake. The doctor knew everyone wanted to get away and he held centre court. Ivan Toscic signalled to patrol officer Nikola Grahovac to approach.

'Grahovac, since you have had the misfortune to get here first you will also be the last one here…here is my signature on your corpse report. You can tell the ambulance to take the body down to the police morgue, the M.E. has more work to do and I'll expect a preliminary post mortem first thing in the morning. Before you do that, make sure the forensic and scene of crime people have everything they need… run prints through the usual channels etc etc.'

Ivan paused, staring at nothing in particular and thought.

'I suppose you didn't find an identity card on the victim…?' he asked.

'No, sir, nothing…apart from an oily rag…and the tattoo on his lower arm.'

What tattoo?'

BRADSHAW

Bernard Nolan never had thoughts of romantic entanglement with his pretty young sergeant so when they arrived they took him by surprise. Almost as soon as the thought appeared, Nolan banished it. He wasn't lucky with women. His marriage collapsed, spectacularly. He was working undercover on a job for two weeks and living in a flat in Rathmines. When the job ended sooner than expected he arrived home to find his wife with his best friend. He walked away and never looked back. There had been one night stands, and drunken fumbles but never a hint of romance. He set a lock on his feelings and forgot the combination.

Though he was lonely and he knew it, he hated feeling sorry for himself. Sometimes he thought, there's no harm in an occasional wallow. No, fuck that, stop feeling sorry for yourself, get out and make a move, take control again, of yourself…

'Inspector…Inspector….Bernard'

Orla Farrell was rubbing his knee and shaking his shoulder. Sergeant Orla Farrell.

'Wha?…sorry, Serg…er, Orla. Jesus, my head's away

with it…look, Orla, call me Bernard, will ye?…ye should be used to it by now…'

'I know sir…Bernard…it was just being in that police station brought something back to me…it's not like I don't know I'm on the job all the time but now and then you catch yourself wondering what the fuck is it all about?'

Bernard Nolan hadn't been asleep and neither of them was drunk. In the half hour since Toscic's departure, they'd nursed their drinks. Orla Farrell had echoed his own thoughts.

'I met a man today, Orla, and I gave him a good hiding. I've known him a long time and though he's a villain I wouldn't wish him any harm because life, I always felt, had dumped a lot of shit on him already…'

Orla Farrell reached across, picked up the wine bottle and filled their glasses while he spoke.

'Jesus, why am I talking like this?' Nolan said, 'maybe, like you said, it was the surroundings of a police station? It was like putting on an old suit, feelings of nostalgia that don't quite fit the shape…or is it the other way about?' Nolan tapped his bulging waist, a girth that had expanded even during Orla's time in Sarajevo.

'You were saying about this fella ye met?' Orla asked.

'Yeah, Mickey, Mickey Bradshaw…he's a Dubliner, but even there he never fitted in and fitting in is all he ever wanted to do. I asked Mickey about the Pigeon, Joe Connolly. Mickey worked for him in the past. I thought he might have heard something…'

'And did he?'

'Well, y'see, that's the thing. He was scared when I mentioned Connolly but there was something else that frightened the living daylights out of him. He never said but I got that feeling. There was something else…'

Dermott Hayes

TATTOO

Inspector Ivan Toscic was tired and bedraggled as he climbed from a police squad car at Sarajevo airport the following morning. He had been home long enough to throw some clothes into a small, battered suitcase.

After Officer Nikola Grahovac mentioned the tattoo on the floater's arm, Ivan tore a strip off him for not mentioning it before.

'Wait,' he shouted, waving at the paramedics who were shutting the ambulance door after packing up the body for delivery to the morgue, leaving the unfortunate Grahovac standing alone and forlorn, 'I need to see the corpse again.'

The paramedic, already annoyed at having to do the work of the coroner and deliver the body, walked away from the rear doors of the ambulance to the front of the vehicle, shaking his head in frustration. Toscic ignored him and opened the doors himself. The floater's corpse lay in a black zippered body bag on the stretcher. Toscic jumped up and opened the bag, gasping as the waft of river detritus and damp decay hit his face. He pulled back the torn and sodden sleeve of the corpse's shirt to reveal the tattoo, a crudely drawn, shamrock and a green football with the letters 'S.R.F.C.'underneath. Toscic knew where he'd seen the man before.

As soon as he got back to the office he trawled through his notes on Nolan's bar and under an observation marked 'persons of interest?', he ran his finger down a short list of names and stopped at 'Mickey Bradshaw.' A short while later, after he'd checked Bradshaw's own file, he found what he was looking for; the description of Bradshaw listed one tattoo he carried, a shamrock and a green football with the letters, S.R.F.C.

This revelation prompted further enquiries and before he knew it, the night had gone, he hadn't slept and he had one hour to make it home to pack and then make his flight to Dublin.

'Rough night?' Orla Farrell asked him, giving his bedraggled and unshaven appearance an amused once over. Toscic felt himself blush and patted his hands down on his shirt and the creases in his trousers as though it might straighten him out. He saw an opportunity to raise the issue of Bradshaw with Bernard Nolan.

'Yes,' he said, and directing his gaze at the big Irishman, added, 'my floater turned out to be someone I believe you know.'

'Oh?' Nolan asked,

'He was an Irishman, Mickey Bradshaw. A former soldier.'

Toscic knew Nolan knew Bradshaw on the beat in Dublin and Bradshaw had dropped into Nolan's on odd occasions. Nolan's reaction was guarded.

'What makes you think it was him?'

'The tattoo…the shamrock and the football and the letters, SRFC. I looked it up. It stands for Shamrock

Rovers Football Club, doesn't it?' Toscic studied Nolan's reaction. There was a brief flicker of recognition and it occurred to Ivan that maybe their relationship had been based on a little more than nostalgia.

'I paid him a visit yesterday after you produced the letter from The Pigeon,' Nolan told him, 'I recognised the pub in the postcard and remembered Mickey used to drink there with a fellow called Connolly, a nasty piece of work. He's the one they call The Pigeon in Dublin. I wondered if there was any connection.'

'And is there?' Ivan asked, realising the visit Nolan spoke about was most likely the time he'd tried to follow him but had lost him in the bombed out ruins of a church.

'There is. Mickey was always a scumbag but small potatoes. He was supplying the Pigeon's gangs with the transport vehicles they needed in exchange for whatever he could trade on the black market. He got very scared when I mentioned your stiff and the postcard but I talked him into giving me some information.'

'You 'talked' him into it?' Toscic asked, remembering the state of the dead Irishman.

He held Nolan's inscrutable gaze for a moment before the Irishman turned his head away and looked at the passing traffic. He'd seen the Irishman operate at close quarters. He knew he was an imposing, even intimidating figure but he never figured him for someone who could beat a man senseless, strangle him and dump him in a river. He stared at Nolan's reddening neck but the Irishman ignored him. Their conversation was over.

On the flight home, Nolan thought of Mickey Bradshaw who died as he was born, an outcast. Nolan knew the state he'd left him in would draw attention. It may have signed his death warrant. His 'enthusiasm', he knew, had been prompted by the prospect of the first break in a case that seemed impenetrable only a fortnight before.

The cost, unfortunately, was mounting. Bradshaw and Tito were not the only victims, he suspected, of the gang's rush to cover its tracks. He hadn't seen hide nor hair of one of his most valuable contacts in a couple of days. Irina was a young Albanian dancer he befriended since she began drinking occasionally in his bar. Smart and quick witted, she was a good source of information about the gang's operations in Sarajevo. Then she disappeared.

Nolan needed to sleep but he couldn't blank out the raw fear in Irina's voice the last night he spoke to her. She called the pub and asked him to meet her. Then she never turned up. He thought of Peter Cahill, I must look Pedro up when I get to Dublin, he thought. Then he wondered what Cahill had been doing in Sarajevo?'

As he gazed out over the softly undulating blanket of clouds on the horizon to the west he knew his weariness was more than physical. He was losing his taste for the hunt and that worried him. But the last thing I'll do, he thought, is see that bastard, Connolly, the Pigeon , in Hell.

CONNOLLY

No-one paid any attention to the group gathering in a room at the back of a Dublin snooker hall near Bolton street. They were a motley crew of lowlifes who wouldn't draw a second glance in that part of the inner city.

If anyone had been paying attention they might have noticed what a cosmopolitan crew they were. There were a couple of slick suited swarthy men, lean and hard looking. Some of them looked like the ordinary habitues of the local pubs only their clothes had designer labels and were sharp fitting. A handful of others looked like they'd just stepped off a tramp ship from some unidentified foreign port.

As they filed into the room and took up positions around the large table in the centre, another door at the far corner opened. A short, stocky but boyish looking man stepped through the door quickly, surveying the surroundings and everyone else in the room. There was a chilly stillness about this man that broached no questions. He was sharply dressed in black. Although short, even in elevated Cuban heeled leather boots, his muscles rippled through his black silk sweater and three quarter length leather jacket.

This was Gerry Fields, otherwise known as 'Pretty Heels', although not by anyone who had ever addressed him thus to his face. Heels was The Pigeon's occasional driver, when Bill and Ben, his bodyguards weren't around. The rest of the time he took care of Connolly's more unsavoury tasks. Wherever The Pigeon went, he followed. On his occasional days of leisure, Heels, a vicious bare fist killer, liked to bugger reluctant young boys.

The murmur in the room subsided. Heels, inscrutable in the gloom of the ill lit room in his customary coal black shades, turned back to the doorway behind him and made a barely perceptible gesture. The door opened further and there was a shift in the room as everyone strained forward and sat upright. Joe Connolly struck fear into the most cold hearted psychos. This was Paddy the Pigeon.

In contrast to his henchmen, Connolly's appearance was unremarkable. He eschewed the designer threads that set the others apart. He wore no jewelry.

But Connolly had a presence. It wasn't in the pale, oaten complexion or the lank, greasy black hair, the thick, bushy eyebrows or the thin, vein laced and blackhead dotted nose. It was all in the eyes or, rather what was not. They were the eyes of a carrion feeder.

A muffled flurry of seat shifting, coughing and throat clearing accompanied his arrival. Heels pulled a seat from the table for his boss and took a pace backwards to stand behind his left shoulder. Connolly sat.

'There could be trouble ahead,' he growled though the grimace on his face indicated this was his idea of a joke. It passed clear over the heads of the assembled hoods apart from Heels who snickered dutifully.

'That bollix Tito thought he'd stitch me up but we

cancelled his membership. It seems it doesn't end there, though. Word has got back to me from the late Mickey Bradshaw that an Irish pork chop has been asking questions about me…in Sarajevo of all places. Mickey was known to many of you and it may come as a surprise to learn of his sudden departure. He always loved a singsong, did Mickey, so you'll be glad to know his passing was not without some pain.

'Tito didn't talk much. He never did and I must say, I regret his loss. He worked well while he was with us but it appears he had 'issues.' According to the boys here,' indicating with his right hand the group of three Albanian roughnecks in black leather jackets and denim jeans, 'Tito turned up in Sarajevo looking for his little sister, Irina, who, he claimed, had become a party member, so to speak. The boys tried to reason with him and told him they knew nothing about his sister but Tito would have none of it and started shouting the odds. He told the boys in the club he had made a list of our European contacts, drop off points, strip joints, dealers and operators and he was going to turn it all over to the pigs if we didn't produce the sister. The boys here took exception to that and shot him.'

'Now there are people who would congratulate them for doing us this service,' he continued, 'they killed a weed that would have tried the patience of a gardening monk. But my mate, Horvar, there,' indicating one of the three, 'believes they acted too rashly and leads me to believe they've put our entire operation in harm's way, so to speak, because of their abrupt and frankly, stupid action.'

As he said this there was a perceptible shuffle of seats in the room as the gap between Horvar and his two compatriots on one side and the slickly dressed Italians on the other widened.

'Y'see, we knew Tito was in Sarajevo. We knew what he was after and we knew he was too late because his sister had already had her contract terminated, so to speak. Everything was under control.'

'Now some people might argue you did the right thing by nipping the danger in the bud but while I'm no gardener, I believe you better pull the root out if you don't want it to come back to sting you again .'

'So, boys. That's how it is…'

The two Albanians squirmed as Horvar moved away from them and though they had difficulty understanding all of Pigeon's spiel, they caught the horror of his drift. Pale and shaken, they made ineffectual attempts to grab concealed weapons but no chance. Two of Heels' boys stepped from the gloom, cut throat blades agleam and in parallel swift movements like co-ordination swimmers, reached from behind. In deft sweeping motions, they slit both throats cleanly from ear to ear. Soundlessly, they tilted the Albanians' chairs back and dragged them from the room for disposal.

Connolly had everyone's full attention. 'Anyway, as I was saying,' he continued, 'we think someone in Dublin has this so called list and we have to find them.'

Tito had been identified by the postcard in his pocket signed 'Paddy the Pigeon', Connolly told them and it came from Coogan's pub, a pub where Tito had worked and where Connolly himself occasionally enjoyed a quiet pint.

'The point is,' he concluded, 'we have to find out who were Tito's friends in that pub, who did he talk to, was there anyone he confided in, like the guy who wrote that fuckin' postcard? That fuckin' journalist, Deare? I reckon if we find him, we'll find our answer and put all this shite behind us. I want this dealt with, pronto. Now fuck off and do it.'

HOMECOMING

Ivan Toscic got the middle seat in the row beside Nolan while Orla Farrell got the window. It was the Bosnian cop's first chance to have a conversation with her. Once more, he was speechless. He had a different reason this time. He had spent the night watching Mickey Bradshaw's tortured body being fished from the river. As the Boeing Airbus completed its climb and levelled out for its flight to Dublin, Ivan Toscic, exhausted, fell into a deep sleep.

'Your man's out for the count,' Orla Farrell said to Nolan, nodding at the sleeping Ivan.

'He's taken a great fancy to you, I hope you can handle it,' Nolan replied.

'Inspector, I'm surprised at you…what would you be thinking?'

Nolan grinned. He liked Farrell's cheek. She was mischievous, yet a cop of the finest calibre - the 26 year old had more investigative experience than detectives ten years her senior. At 20 she graduated top of her class from Templemore, the Garda training centre, had a year of uniformed duty under her belt and was well on her way to graduating from Dublin City University with a degree in criminology.

That was when she had her first encounter with Nolan. A legend in the Irish police force, Nolan got results but demanded high standards. He commanded equal respect among the rank and file and the top brass. His investigations were painstaking and exhaustive. His lack of political ambition endeared him to the brass as much as his policing abilities. He was a cop's cop.

Since she was a child sitting on the knee of her father, Tom Farrell, a station desk sergeant all his working life, Orla had always wanted to be a cop. An only child, she lived and breathed police her entire life. When her mother died suddenly at the age of 36, Orla was just 10 but her father raised her on his own and with the assistance of a network of helpful relatives. By the time she was a budding young woman of 15 and studying for her Leaving Certificate, she was looking after her father, cleaning his shirts, polishing his belt and boots and pressing his uniform. She applied for the Guards before she sat her Leaving Certificate and when she achieved five higher level A grades and two Bs in those final exams she could have qualified to train for any profession. At her interview for her Garda application the Superintendent conducting it was sceptical about why she wanted to join the police. 'With these qualifications you could be a doctor or a lawyer,' he said.

'I could be a good policewoman too,' she replied resolutely. And something in her demeanour made him stamp his approval on her application.

She was a beat cop in one of Dublin's toughest precincts when she met Bernard Nolan; Detective Sergeant Nolan then, in charge of a small division of undercover specialists known as 'The Mockies', a name given to them with grudging respect by the criminal drug gangs they infiltrated and busted.

Orla Farrell applied for a transfer to Nolan's handpicked band. Late one night, a big, skinheaded, lumbering yob with a single gold earring, jailhouse tats and clothes so filthy they could have walked in on their own, stomped into the station. Full of attitude and menace, he pressed his weight on the bell at the front desk and kept it there until the glass hatch slid open.

'I wanna see Foley,' he demanded loudly. His ice blue, slightly bloodshot eyes stripped her bare. Orla Farrell, on desk duty for the late shift that night, knew her man immediately but gave no hint. 'What is your business?' she asked.

'I wanna see Foley,' he growled, leaning once more on the buzzer. 'And I want to know what your name is?' Orla replied evenly, 'then I want to know who this Foley is you want to see and why you want to see him?'

'Jaysus, youse fucking cops are a bunch o…'

'Sir, if you continue in that tone you'll spend the night in a cell and I'll find an army of Foleys to talk to you. Now, will you tell me your name…'

'Sir? Sir? Who d'you think y'r talking to, ye…'

'Ok, Garda Farrell, I'll deal with this,' Detective Inspector John Foley interrupted from behind her and opening the door to the public area he motioned for the man to step inside, 'you're lucky you turned up,' he said to him, 'we were about to come out and lift you.'

The big man, grinning, stepped inside. As the door closed behind he winked at Garda Farrell who said, 'I'm very pleased to meet you, DS Nolan, I've heard a lot about you.'

He threw his head back and laughed as he walked

ahead of DI Foley into an interview room.

The following day Orla Farrell was told she was to report for duty in Harcourt Square, to a special unit under the command of Detective Inspector Bernard Nolan. He greeted her himself. He had the same presence as that singular encounter in the barracks' station. But something else, something indefinable, made the transformation profound. It was as though she had met two entirely different people.

'Welcome, Orla, to our merry band. John Foley has only good things to say about you as have all your officers to date. You'll make a great cop, they all say, great potential.'

Orla was unsure if she was being tested or mocked. 'Congratulations on your own promotion, Inspector, you're well on the way yourself.' She bit her tongue as she blurted out the last sentence.

'That's the spirit,' he chuckled, 'shrinking violets are fuck all use to us here.'

For the following two years Nolan took a personal interest in her training as an undercover policewoman, throwing her into situations where she posed as a homeless crack addict, a strung out hooker, even a bank robber, and on one occasion, a five month operation as a coke dealer in a smart city nightclub.

During those two years with Nolan's 'mockies' she sat her sergeant's exam and passed, aged 25. She remained with the squad after Nolan left to work in Bosnia. His departure was abrupt and unexplained. When word filtered back that he quit to run a bar in Sarajevo, the shock reverberated through the squad he helped shape.

Nolan's methods, although effective, were frowned upon by some in Harcourt Square. It was said he was creating an elitist, exclusive force within a force and many of the old guard remembered how the Special Branch had achieved that through political favouritism. At the same time there were others who championed Nolan for his results.

Nolan, by contrast, enjoyed equal measures of admiration and opprobrium throughout the ranks. There was little known about the big Dubliner outside the job. He was dedicated and hardworking but no-one knew much of the man.

He was said to have gone too deep into cover while investigating a particularly brutal pimp. When the pimp got busted and his setup shattered, there were allegations of misbehaviour directed at Nolan by some of the pimp's women. The allegations were unfounded, according to an internal investigation but the whiff of wrongdoing stuck with Nolan to the delight of his detractors. So when he left abruptly there were few to sing his praise in public as though by so doing they might get their own one way ticket to the Balkans. 'There's no smoke without fire,' the bitter barrack room sages whispered, 'his going was too abrupt. The only question is, did he jump or was he pushed?'

Two years later Detective Sergeant Orla Farrell was surprised to learn she was being packed off for some 'volunteer' overseas experience with Interpol. She was even more surprised to learn her posting was Sarajevo. But her surprise was nothing to the shock she got when she was brought to a secret briefing in SFOR HQ and in walked Inspector Bernard Nolan.

'Orla, how're you doing? It's great to see you. How are things in Dublin?,' he asked as though his two year absence had been a routine vacation.

Two years since she had seen the man who had shaped

her career and in that time, he changed dramatically. The tall, fit and handsome Bernard Nolan of old was replaced by a man of the same height, yes, but there the similarity ended. Standing before her, was a behemoth of flesh and cheeks. His trousers sagged dismally below a bulbous belly bursting from the seams of his shirt. The eyebrow of a belly button poked from between the buttons.

There was a change in his face, too. Gone were the high, arched cheekbones replaced by unhealthy swelling and unshaven, fleshy wattles. Only the eyes were the same, sparkling with intelligence and wit.

Appearances aside, it was business as usual. Nolan quickly appraised her of his role in Sarajevo and the need for total secrecy. He stacked file upon file on a desk in a tiny office and left her to study them. Then he told her whatever she had done before was a rehearsal for the job ahead.

'We need Oscar winning performances here, Orla. You'll be an Irish barmaid in an Irish bar in Sarajevo and I'm your boss. Don't ask questions, don't give anything away. Just listen and learn.'

And that's all she had done for the past six months. Nolan rarely mentioned their operation or discussed its progress or lack of it. She was told nothing of his investigations but occasionally reported whatever she had heard across the bar as though it were casual barroom banter. They behaved just as they seemed, an Irish barmaid working for an Irish bar owner in an Irish bar in Sarajevo.

Sometimes she felt stifled by the frustration. She was used to results. In Nolan's she was a barmaid, not a cop, she thought. Sarajevo was an oppressive place. Once a beautiful city, it was now a shell without a soul. In Dublin, as a mockie, she felt like a cop. Here, as a barmaid in Sarajevo, she didn't even feel like a spy.

Out of loyalty to Nolan she never mentioned the unofficial approach Tommy O'Brien had made to her before she left Dublin. It never came up she told herself. Superintendent O'Brien had taken her aside at her last briefing in Dublin and brought her for a coffee on Harcourt St. He told her he was delighted she was going to get some experience abroad. It would do her career no end of good, he told her. Then he said he wanted her to keep an eye out for him while she was there. He'd said this with a conspiratorial wink, which, at the time, made her shudder. She hadn't given it much thought since. It was hard to imagine O'Brien hitting on her and he'd never appeared in Bosnia. So it never arose. It was only after she met Bernard Nolan when she realised the Super had asked her to spy on her own Inspector.

She was grateful to Nolan for the attention he paid her. She knew she owed a huge debt for her rapid advance in the Gardai to the big, gruff cop. But Sarajevo was a bust, a detour in her career path and, until four days ago, a cul de sac.

One thing she had learned from Nolan was there was always a purpose in what he did. She just hadn't learned his capacity for patience. He taught her the purpose of 'plod,' the slow, deliberative work of investigation. When the best plod work was done, a good cop could act decisively.

'There's no use shooting in the dark,' he had drummed into them, 'you'll only shoot each other.'

The other night she had caught snatches of Ivan's conversation with Nolan; the dead man, the postcard, the pigeon but it meant nothing to her. She admired Nolan's casual technique that bordered on mocking indifference, as though he were playing with the young Bosnian policeman.

Sometimes Orla felt a twinge of apprehension about her boss. There was nothing she could put her finger on, just a nagging question mark. Had some of the old spark gone? She wondered. He was always offhand as though he could never approach anything straight on.

But knowing Nolan, she knew this was far from any game. She felt sympathy for Toscic. She was aware of the Inspector's interest. She could feel his eyes on her when he came in the bar and she found his fumbling shyness around her endearing. She played up to his infatuation, playing the coquettish colleen, all smiles and sidelong glances. As Nolan toyed with and teased information from the inspector, she joined in the dance.

She felt happy Toscic was part of their investigation and on his way to Dublin with them. It was only fair and he would be useful, she believed. The people whose trail they were on were vicious; Ivan Toscic could help them get inside the immigrant gangs in Dublin.

But she felt apprehensive about his involvement and fearful they had dropped him in something for which he lacked the training that was second nature to Nolan and herself. She felt protective towards him. Ivan is young and idealistic, she thought, 'bright eyed and hopeful,' as someone had once described her. Yet the cop in her made her equally suspicious of Toscic and his big doe eyes.

Christ, she thought, stop that Orla, get a grip on yourself, girl. He's a cop like you. We're after lowlifes and they smell the same no matter what language they speak.

And as she pondered these thoughts that both disturbed and delighted, Inspector Ivan Toscic stirred beside her as the flight attendant announced it was time for passengers to put their seats in an upright position and fasten their seatbelts.

Ivan Toscic got his first sight of Ireland out the window to his left as the jet made its descent. There was a bright sun shining on the curved sweep of a golden, sandy beach below them. Ireland was green, people always said, but he was struck by its luminosity. The plane banked around a tiny island beside a fishing port and began its descent.

TOMMY

Bernard Nolan was thrilled to be back in Dublin and could hardly contain himself through the arrival formalities.

'Ivan, me boy, we're going to give you some welcome to Dublin tonight. The first thing we have to do is dump this stuff then we're off for a pint. A real pint, mind, 'cos there's nothing on earth like a pint of stout in a good Dublin boozer.'

Nolan's enthusiasm was infectious. Since he first caught a glimpse of Ireland, Ivan Toscic was straining to get out and sample it. Ireland, for him, was a country full of Nolans and Farrells; big, life loving men with lyrical wit and self deprecating intelligence and beautiful, strong minded, big hearted women, full of guile.

Sometimes, he thought, you got what you looked for in people. Trust your instinct, he told himself. If you believed in them and gave your trust you would get their best character. It made him think of his mother, like a breeze in the desert, in the distant past.

But none of that was true. At least not true to the exclusion of all other possibilities. Nothing, he knew, was ever what it seemed. Few people knew very much about him, least of all his employers in Sarajevo. Everyone led a double life.

He was apprehensive. The gangs they sought were ruthless. The lead they were following was tenuous. They knew little of Tito De Lillo; was it even his real name? Why had he fled from Dublin to Sarajevo? Why had he turned on the people he had worked for? All roads apparently led to Coogan's.

A casually dressed Detective Superintendent Tommy O'Brien in jeans and shirt, greeted Nolan, Farrell and Toscic in the Arrivals' lounge. 'Welcome home, Bernard, you've been badly missed. Do you still remember the language or will I translate?' O'Brien was lean and angular and he spoke from the side of his mouth.

'Fuck off, Tommy…how's it going? Jaysus, I never thought I'd say it but it's great to see you…here, let me introduce Inspector Ivan Toscic, one of Bosnia's finest… they grow them young and bold over there…and of course, you know Orla Farrell?'

Smiling and nodding, O'Brien said 'Sure, I know Orla well,…Inspector…you're very welcome to Ireland. I'm sorry you couldn't have had better company but you have to take what's going these days.'

'He's some bollix and that's your first taste of Ireland, Ivan'

Ivan Toscic glanced in bewilderment from one to the other. He could never imagine himself addressing his superior in such an offhand manner. There was much to learn about Dublin. He knew the banter they were engaged in was what Bernard Nolan often referred to as 'slagging' or 'taking the piss.'

'Right, follow me. I have a car waiting to take you to

town. I'll brief you in the car but we're not going to headquarters. We'll keep your presence in Dublin quiet as possible for the moment. Things have been gathering pace here and I need to bring you up to date. Have you all your luggage now? We'll have your stuff dropped off at your hotel, Ivan. I've booked you into Blooms. It's right in the city centre and it's named after our patron saint, Leopold.'

As they drove from the airport Nolan wondered why Tommy O'Brien felt the need for secrecy.

'What's been going on, Tommy?' he asked.

O'Brien explained, 'Pigeon had a summit conference the other day in a snooker hall down off Bolton St. It was the United Nations of Criminal Hoods, representatives of every gang he has something to do with from all over Europe including three boyos from Sarajevo. Interpol has identified one of them as an Albanian called Horvar and if you think Pigeon is a nasty piece of work, this Horvar and he are cut from the same cloth.

We had surveillance on the place and managed to mugshot half of them. Horvar arrived with two others but he left alone. The other two weren't seen leaving. Something has made them very jumpy or else there's a big operation going down. We don't know and we have to find out. The only thing we know is they want whoever wrote the postcard found in Sarajevo.'

'That must be our first priority then. We better find him before they do,' said Nolan pensively then he asked, 'why all the secrecy?'

'I don't want this operation compromised. We don't know what we're looking for but it's big enough to gather all those big shot scumbags in Dublin.

'A senior Dutch Government Minister was compromised last week when he was caught in a lapdancing club run by Pigeon's mob. No harm in him being in a lapdancing club but the same place was busted as a cover for prostitution, drugs and, we suspect, human trafficking. When they pulled in this Minister he coughed up the names of at least half a dozen senior officials including a police chief and a couple of judges who were providing protection for this organisation.'

He continued, 'and as if that weren't enough no sooner had he started shooting his mouth off than the mob started shooting. They shot him dead outside his office in broad daylight. It has scared the living daylights out of more than the Dutch. Word has come down to crack this gang before the whole thing gets out of hand. And if they could penetrate to the top levels in one Government you may be sure they're doing it everywhere else. This is an unholy alliance of Irish and British hoods, Russian and Albanian mafia and the Italian Cosa Nostra and any other band of scumbags in between. It's like a global corporate crime organisation. We think they're making a pitch to control everything and our boy, The Pigeon is in the thick of it. It's only a matter of time before the Yanks get involved or the Columbians. We have to hammer them now and if this postcard has anything to do with it then we must be first on the spot.'

Nolan wasn't satisfied. O'Brien was hiding something. 'That doesn't answer the question exactly though, does it?'

'Ok. One of our touts believes the two Albanians who arrived with Horvar were whacked at that meeting last week. The two boyos were Albanians too. They are suspected of having shot your Tito. They were also in the frame for disposing of Mickey Bradshaw in Sarajevo. Bradshaw was whacked because he was known to have talked to an Irish cop in Sarajevo. Yourself. If their contacts are as good as we suspect the only way they got that information was from Dublin.

'Aside from protecting you we don't want this operation compromised before we can nail the fuckers. Neither of you can go home,' he said, indicating Orla and Nolan, 'Sergeant Farrell, is in Blooms. You're in the Gresham, Bernard. We know you'll be twigged as soon as you show your face but at least this way we might keep the element of surprise for a short while. Any questions? There's a car in the Gresham's car park for you, Bernard. The keys are in an envelope at the desk.'

O'Brien's car pulled up outside the Gresham Hotel on Dublin's main thoroughfare, O'Connell St. Nolan got out as the boot popped. He collected his bag and leaned in the window of the car. 'I'll pick you two up in half an hour,' he said, 'we're going for that pint.'

TOSCIC

Ivan Toscic was glad of the respite, however brief. After they had checked in he went straight to his room without addressing Sergeant Farrell.

Despite his age – he was 34 although people often thought he looked at least ten years younger – his job and where he came from, he wasn't used to this kind of clandestine policing. He was unsure how he might help or what assistance he could be in Dublin to Bernard Nolan and his superiors. But he had another task at hand. He threw his bag on the hotel room's spacious double bed with its beige wool coverlet and starch crisp, white cotton sheets. He paused long enough to relieve himself in the en suite bathroom, wash his hands and run a wet hand through his mop of black curls before he was out the door again. In the lobby he asked the receptionist for change, handing her a five Euro note from the money he had exchanged in the airport bank. She smiled at him and he found himself smiling back. That sideways, long look with half shut eyes was pure Orla Farrell.

'Is your name Orla?' he asked her.

'No,' she said, 'it's Deirdre,' she replied, pointing at her tag and smiling, amused.

'Oh, I'm sorry…I didn't…er…'

'Never mind, Mr Toscic,' she said, 'sure, it'll take you a while to get used to Irish names…is this your first visit to Ireland?'

Embarrassment more than caution made Ivan stop. 'Thank you,' he said, 'which one do I use for a local call?' Ivan proffered his open palm full of coins and Deirdre leaned closer and ran her finger around the flat of his hand before she picked the coin he needed.

A prickly heat surged to the tip of his ears as he felt himself blush and Deirdre, the 20p coin held aloft, smiled at him coquettishly.

He thanked her and left. He had no intention of using the hotel phones.

DEARE

Garvan Deare woke in a sweat. The sheets he lay in were soaked. He sat up, rubbing his eyes and shaking his head. He thought of taking his own temperature but dismissed the thought. This was no 'man 'flu' or a panacea for the blue funk he knew was the root of his fever. He couldn't identify the cause of his fear. He had a restless night and his mind was gripped with a vice like, mortal torment of sudden death.

He shrugged off the wet sheets and, rubbing his eyes, stumbled across the hall to his bathroom. The shower door was open and he reached inside and turned it on. The hot, rushing stream spat out a fog of steam. He lifted the toilet seat and pissed, blinking and unblinking his eyes as though a new reality would manifest itself. No such luck, he thought, stepping into the intense heat wishing it might wash his dreams away.

He couldn't get Tito out of his mind. That night, in the bar, he thought, what? less than ten days ago? I might have been the last person to speak to him, at least, in the pub. Now he's dead. Fuck. He knew now the source of his nightmares but he dismissed the thought before it awoke

109

the torment again.

'Get your shit together,' he said to himself, aloud as he toweled himself with abrasive vigour. He dressed, then checked his fridge for essentials. He lifted the carton of milk and shook it, deciding he should go to the shops and restock. Do something, he thought, but stand around and think.

He gathered his phone, keys and iPod, fidgeting with the earphones. Then he grabbed a bag and headed out the door, selecting 'shuffle', as the heavy front door of his apartment building shut behind him. Rosie Flores was singing, 'This Ol' Honky Tonk.' He smiled ruefully at the unintended irony in the song's lyrics, a plaintive lament for the empty solitude of a night in a bar.

Tito loved the plaintive, maudlin sound of cry in your beer, country music. Deare decided he had to get Tito out of his mind, for his own sanity. He grabbed a basket and surveyed the colourful display of fruit and vegetables before choosing essentials like a bunch of onions, garlic, tomatoes, peppers, chillis and assorted fruits like apples, pears and satsumas. He hadn't made a list so he worked on memory. The trouble was he couldn't shrug the Albanian from his thoughts. He paid for his goods, adding bread, milk and coffee to his basket but when the shopkeeper, a familiar figure with whom he enjoyed a daily banter, engaged him, his response was perfunctory, even curt.

He felt dizzy and began to think it might be his diabetes that was making him feel physically sluggish but mentally disorientated. He headed home but the short, flat walk felt like he was climbing a steep hill.

When he got home, he fixed some breakfast, absently and while an egg boiled on the cooker, he took out his diabetic kit, a glucometer to check his blood sugar level and then the two pen needles of insulin. That ritual completed, he poured a cup of coffee and cut and buttered a slice of bread. He took his egg from the saucepan and set it out on the kitchen table with his coffee and bread. Then he sat down and thought he hadn't thought of Tito because he was busy doing things and, at the same time, realised the Albanian was back in his head. He had two bites of the bread and patted the crown of the egg with a spoon. But that was it, he had neither appetite nor interest in eating. He dropped the spoon with a clink on the plate and standing, took a gulp from his mug of coffee, before grabbing his coat from the back of the chair and headed out the door.

Deare knew he was taking a risk not eating properly. He didn't usually have any problem cleaning his plate but right now, eating was the last thing on his mind. And the first thing, too, because he'd learned his lessons the hard way.

Diabetes, or 'the sugar sickness', as it was once known, was a nasty and insidious illness. Eat the right food, exercise regularly and stay away from the sweet stuff and you could survive. But only if you kept a regular check on your blood sugar level and then injected the appropriate doses of insulin. It was a precarious balancing act and unnatural, too.

He kept his drinking to a minimum, he told himself, by never lingering at receptions. He was careful with his diet, too. In his darker moments he thought his fastidious attention to nutrition a load of old bollocks; the damage his drinking inflicted on him far outweighed the benefits of his fire brigade approach to healthy eating.

There was no time to dwell on it, he thought and

gathered his things to head for town. He was in luck as a bus arrived just as he arrived at the stop. In eight minutes he alighted on St Stephen's Green, bought a paper in the corner shop and headed off with a jaunty step, down Grafton St. It was one of those 'brisk' Autumn days when the sky was a vivid blue, the clouds were wisps and the air was neither just cold or sharp, it was crisp.

Coogan's was coming alive with the lunchtime rush. He found a stool at the bar beside the pub's entertainment manager and cellarman, Brando. They exchanged the usual pleasantries - 'how's it goin'?', 'there's the man', 'Story?', 'any crack?' None of them were ever answered, specifically, because, if there was something specific to address, it would be done in good time, once the proprieties were dispensed. Deare flung his coat around the back of his seat, tucking his coat and scarf on the shelf below the counter. He sat down and spread out his newspaper, lifting it as Sean Mac, the barman, wiped the counter top with a wet cloth. 'What'll I get ye?' he asked.

'A pint of Carlsberg,' says Deare, forgetting his earlier resolutions of abstinence.

'That was dropped in for ye last night, Sean Mac said as he tossed a plain brown package on the counter before placing a beer mat and cold pint of lager in front of him, 'are ye havin' something to eat? I'll order it now before crowds get in.'

'Bangers 'n' Mash, Sean, easy on the gravy, heat the beans and tell the chef to shove the mushy peas where the sun don't shine. It was a daily ritual, this time delivered by more rote than rhyme.

Deare picked up the envelope, tentatively squeezing and prodding, feeling its width for content. He tilted it to his ear and shook it, gently. Then he put it down and raised his pint with his right hand. Closing his eyes, he drank and let the cold beer ease the tension he felt but refused to acknowledge.

'How's that beer, Garvan?' Brando asked, 'is it alright? I had trouble with the coolers this morning.' Brando was always on the case. A former soldier, he took pride in his turnout and arrived to work every morning at 7am to supervise the collection of empty barrels and the arrival of their replacements. Before the pub opened for business, Brando's job was to get everything in order. He met suppliers and ordered fresh stock, cleaning products and glasses and even special bar snacks for particular customers. By noon, his work done, he took up his position at the bar and drank pints of flat cider for the rest of the day until 6.30pm, when he headed home for a night of television and a chicken curry takeaway from his local Chinese.

Deare swallowed, smiled and tilting his glass towards Brando, uttered, 'Grand.' He unhooked the leather pouch attached to his belt and produced a glucometer test strip. He pierced the skin of the forefinger on his right hand with the spring loaded Microlet and squeezed a drop of blood from the puncture. He took the tiny test strip and allowed the red bubble of blood to soak into the strip, before sliding it into the glucometer. The small machine beeped and began the 20 second countdown to reveal his condition.

When the countdown ended and the figures on the lit up screen showed his blood sugar level was a comfortable 5.2, he produced a pen style needle from the inside pocket of his jacket and without taking his eyes from the newspaper pages laid out in front of him, deftly stabbed himself in the upper thigh, through the trousers of his dark suit. Sean Mac placed cutlery wrapped in a paper napkin in front of him. In the same movement he slid salt and pepper along the bar with a cruet of sauces in sachets.

Cuisine in Coogan's was simple and traditional. Fish 'n' chips and shepherd's pie were popular. The portions were generous and the prices reasonable. By 1.30pm every day it was heaving; the cowboys' corner regulars took up position, ordered their drinks and began their boisterous dissection of the local gossip, sports results and the day's racing card. Some of the staff from the hotel next door dropped in at the end of their early morning, graveyard shift. Between the banter and the blarney there was always a nugget of gossip to start Deare's day. Gerry, the night porter, and two of the cleaners were good and regular contacts. In the bar, they ignored him, apart from the usual pleasantries. On quieter moments, they met below the stairs and, for a folded twenty, kept him up to date on celebrity guests, and, with luck, their late night indiscretions.

A buzzer went behind the counter and Sean pulled open the dumbwaiter with one hand while he flicked off a beer tap, topping Deare's fresh pint of lager. A steaming plate of three jumbo sausages, three mounds of mashed potato smothered in a thick brown gravy, was plonked in front of him with his fresh pint. In one slick movement Sean Mac whipped Deare's empty glass away, smiling and winking. Deare's sausages were surrounded by a moat of cold baked beans and a mound of snot green, mushy peas. Deare sighed but didn't complain. He followed his customary ritual and chose a plastic sachet of brown sauce. He bit the plastic in the corner and squeezed out the sauce in a tiny pool on the edge of his plate.

Sergio arrived at the same time as his food. They

nodded to each other. The genial Roman's eyes flitted about the company seeking a vulnerable point for an injection of playful humour. 'I see all the cowboys have-a hitched up-a their horses to the trough already,' he laughed, 'does anyone want a drink?'

'Keep your money,' Garvan interrupted, 'this is mine, Sean…give him a…what do you want, Sergio?'

'No, no, I'll get it. I was first. Look, I have it here,' he said, waving a wad of crumpled notes.

'Give him a glass of ale,' Deare ordered, reaching his own fiver further than the frowning Roman's, 'I just got one, Sergio, so it's still my round.'

'Thank you, Garvan,' said Sergio, then turning his attention to the rest of the company, said, 'well, whatsa news?' while gesturing to Sean Mac to get him a small plate of bread. Before Deare knew it, the genial Roman was cutting himself a piece of sausage and wrapping it in a slice of fresh bread.

'You're some bollix,' Deare joked. It was a familiar routine.

'I heard you got a letter from Tito,' Sergio whispered as an aside to him.

Deare almost stabbed himself with the loaded fork.

'Jesus, where, the fuck, did you hear that?' Deare spluttered.

'The letter, the letter that arrived for you last night. It was handed in here. There was no postmark but Viktor, my kp, said it was from Kosova. We all figured it must be from the mad Albanian,' said Sergio, 'the dead Albanian, if you believe halfa these fuckers.'

Deare looked down at his plate of sausages. He dropped his knife and pushed the plate away. He thought, with no small degree of irony, how little you could get away with in this town.

'I just got it and haven't opened it yet. Look, I better fuck off to work. I'll talk to you later,' said Deare and with that he drained his second pint of lager, threw some money on the counter, gathered his briefcase and newspapers. Then he was gone.

Outside, in the sleepy brightness of a mid-Autumn day, the street florists' display of carnations and roses burst with a clarity of colour. Their combined bouquet exuded a pungency that made him think of an orchestra tuning up.

His customary casual stroll to the office, took in Grafton St's bustle of pedestrian commerce; the tang of Wicklow St's restaurants through Temple Bar's cram of tourists and street hustlers and over the Halfpenny bridge into the city's northside Liffey street, a gateway to another culture; two cities co-existing but divided by a river.

Almost every day Deare made this walk, greeting and buttonholing people along the way. It gave him time to mull over what he had and what the day, ahead, might have in store for him. Today he might have been walking down a blank office corridor for all the attention he paid.

The afternoon passed in a blur. He flicked through the post at his desk in the newspaper. After filing his invites, brochures and letters and picked out the most likely prospects, he made a few calls to follow up on story leads he had stored like a squirrel's winter feed. Then he wandered downstairs for a quick discussion with the editor about what he would be working on that night.

He felt like a sleepwalker, present but disconnected, his mind obsessing on the package in his bag and the seed planted by Sergio that this was a communication from Tito. Deare called a taxi and headed home.

He tossed the envelope on the kitchen table. He kept his eyes on it as he filled the kettle at the sink overlooking the Dodder river, running by the back of his apartment building. He caught the watchful movement of a fox in the undergrowth on the opposite bank. The fox crouched and glared at a parade of ducks sailing down the shallow river, just beyond his reach. As he set the kettle down, Deare pulled a chair out and sat at the table. He picked up the envelope and looked at it again. His name was misspelt, he noted. There was an 'i' in Garvan instead of an 'a'. He made tea, sat down and looked once more at the envelope. He picked it up and, with a sharp intake of breath, prised it open. The note inside was written in the same neat handwriting. A padded bundle fell from the bag.

HEELS

Gerry Heels tipped a small sachet of sugar into his tea. Brando paid no heed. He hadn't recognised the voice and only wondered fleetingly who the man was when he sat down in the stool beside him and ordered tea. The rest of the bar was empty.

In the afternoon slump in Coogan's, the morning shift was making preparations to leave. A lounge porter swept the floor of food, cigarette butts and discarded napkins. A barman wiped down the counter with a wet cloth while another restocked the counters of mixers, bottled beers and soft drinks.

Only Brando, in his usual seat at the end of the counter, sat motionless. This was his time of leisure after a morning of backbreaking labour, shifting barrels and sorting stock. A pint of flat cider sat in front of him. Another sat waiting ready for him under the counter, covered by a beer mat. As he sat at the corner of the bar, the world came to Brando and this was his world. He knew all its citizens and they knew him. Those who were close would greet him warmly and ask about his well being. He greeted those few as family, told them jokes and snippets of local gossip. The rest of the time he sat, sphinxlike, cider to hand, a cigarette burning in the ashtray.

Brando had the stature of a jockey and was consulted on major race days by customers mistaking his ruddy complexion and size for signs of a man who'd spent his life aboard a racehorse instead of a barstool. He knew a few jockeys and trainers who drank in the bar. But Brando relied on his friends, the Coogan's' cowboys, for his tips and they were as hopeless as he was and only occasionally, as lucky. Brando was an old school gentleman, his life dictated by loyalties built on rules of etiquette and good manners. Three generations of his family had served in the Irish armed forces, as non-commissioned officers with distinction in every UN peacekeeping detail since the Congo. He was dedicated to his job and loyal to a fault. He commanded respect among the staff, the suppliers and the customers.

He was the eyes and ears of the owners too. A trusted retainer, he first approached them on his discharge from the army. Arriving into the pub on a Saturday morning in full parade uniform he handed over his severance cheque to the current owner's father and asked him to supply him with drink until it ran out. Ten days, a case of Malibu and white lemonade later, they offered him a job and he'd been there since. If he had another name besides Brando only the owners and himself knew what it was. He'd always been fond of the Hollywood actor and did impressions of him as Don Vito Corleone in The Godfather or as Terry Malloy, the prince of palookaville in On the Waterfront.

Heels never drank alcohol. He hated it. His father was a hard man who drank. His father thought he got harder when he got drunker. One night he tested this theory on Gerry when the youngster got between him and his wife after a hard night in the local. Gerry proved to him the flaws in his theory.

Though small, Gerry was strong and had attended all of the martial arts classes he could from the age of eight. So when his father came home that night reeking with drink and aching for a bust up he was greeted by a 16 year old Gerry who was not going to take it any more.

The beating was so bad his father lost the use of his right arm and all his teeth. He lay in a hospital bed for three weeks recovering from the trauma and bruising.

Gerry's mother gave Gerry her last £20 note and sent him off to her sister in Cork. 'Don't come back, son, 'til I send you a letter.' Gerry took the £20 note and moved into a derelict house in the next street. Every night he sat on a wall in an alley to the rear of his mother's house and watched. When his father was discharged from hospital Gerry followed him home. His father felt the terrifying uncertainty of a shadow he couldn't see. The old man never went home.

Brando and Gerry grew up in the same rough and tumble inner city neighbourhood. It was a hard spot where growing up was something you learned to do quickly.

Heels became a criminal by default. Without any tangible skill to earn a living he became a protector, enforcer, debt collector and occasional bouncer. He bore no personal malice towards those who were on the receiving end of his ministrations although he did take professional pride in his ability and reputation.

He took on three enemies of The Pigeon singlehandedly one night as they tried to gain entrance to a Parnell St bar in which Connolly had a financial interest. They had been shortchanged their share of a heist by the Pigeon and they were intent on revenge. They didn't reckon on Gerry Heels.

First they tried to push past but discovered the five and a half foot tall man in their way was planted deep in the ground and had the texture of granite. One took a swipe which Heels easily dodged with a deft leftward sway and followed through with a sharp finger punch to the kidneys.

Another tried a head butt but crashed to the floor when his own head met with Heels'. The third was reaching for a concealed weapon when Heels grabbed his wrist and swung him about as though they were jiving. The sucking crack that followed this macabre pirouette was the sound of his assailant's arm popping from its shoulder socket. Connolly was impressed and offered him a job.

Neither Brando or Heels had progressed beyond their fifteenth birthday in formal education. Both had been dedicated to their mothers. In Brando's case, he assumed control of the family home after the death of his mother, his father having lost his senses through grief.

Brando hated most sports and would only watch motor racing on the pub's TV. They both loved Grand Prix racing and world champion, Michael Schumacher and the Ferrari F1 team were their only heroes. Brando wore his devotion on his sleeve; he owned a selection of bright red Ferrari F1 bomber jackets that Heels thought was the coolest, short of his own matt black ensemble.

'D'ye reckon Schuey'll take a fourth championship this year?' was his opening gambit.

'No question,' replied Brando ordinarily monosyllabic but always willing to expound at length on his favourite subject, 'he's the best driver in the world and he's in the best car. There's no beating him.'

Heels suggested the German ace was getting a run for his money this year from Brazilian driver Juan Pablo Montoya for BMW McLaren and the latest flying Finn on the circuit, Kimi Raikonnen, Mercedes and Barrichello, Schumacher's Ferrari teammate, wasn't good enough this season to provide protective support.

Brando took a long swig on his cider and slowly lit another Rothmans as he considered his answer. 'Their cars are improving but they're no match for Schumacher,' he announced dismissively, ignoring the question on Barrichello as he found himself in agreement.

He knew Gerry Heels, by reputation and by sight but they had never spoken. He occasionally came into Coogan's with his boss, Joe Connolly. Brando had grown up around the city's gangsters all his life and he was neither in awe nor fear of them.

'Yeah, but has Schumacher slowed down or is he losing his edge since he broke his leg in Canada?' rejoined Heels.

'No way, no way,' Brando proclaimed, draining his pint.

'D'ye want another one of those?' Heels asked, nodding to the barman before Brando could answer. Brando accepted the pint with good grace and continued, 'the point is there isn't a driver alive who can match Schumacher on the circuit today and the only way they'll beat him is by changing the rules.'

'Well, they're doing that already,' Heels replied, 'with the way they've changed the qualifying…'

'He'll win again this year no matter what they try to do,' Brando declared, 'your name's Gerry Heels, isn't it? My ma knew yours.'

'Yeah, that's right…they used go to Bingo down in Foley St together…'

'Thanks for the pint. I owe you one,' said Brando, 'you don't usually come in here on your own?'

'No, the boss isn't with me. I just fancied a cup of tea and some quiet.'

They both sat in silence for a minute before a couple of Rumanians from a nearby restaurant came in and got themselves a drink. Both said 'hello' to Brando.

'There's not as many as those fellas working here these days,' observed Heels.

'They come and go,' Brando replied, 'we have a few working in the kitchen and a couple of Chinese students.'

'Yeah, there were more in the past. There was a fella called Tito here a year ago, remember him? He was a laugh.'

Brando's shutters went down as quickly as they'd gone up. He thought of the package that had arrived for Garvan Deare and wondered if it had anything to do with Tito. He made a mental note to call him later.

'There's so many through here I can't keep up. Excuse me,' Brando said rising. The conversation was over. He turned and headed out the side door leaving Heels to finish his tea alone.

DEARE HUNTING

Bernard Nolan pulled the silver Mondeo out of the car park at the rear of the Gresham Hotel and swung onto Cathal Brugha St before heading up O'Connell St and across the bridge to turn right on College Green at the end of D'Olier St.

The city had changed in the three years of his absence. A towering, silver monument stood where Nelson's Pillar had been before the IRA blew it up. He wondered at the irony of a city with a drug problem erecting a sculpture that looked like a syringe. To such locals 'the spire' was known as 'the spike.' At least it's monumental, thought Nolan.

He phoned Farrell before he left his hotel and told her to get Toscic. He pulled into the recess reserved for tour buses. They were waiting in the hotel foyer and spotted him pull in.

There had been little chat between Orla and Ivan. She had showered and changed. She called Ivan Toscic's room to tell him Inspector Nolan was on his way but there was no answer. She made her way to the foyer and arrived just as Toscic walked in through the front door. There was no time to ask him where he'd been; she could see Nolan pull in to the bus bay. Why did Toscic look so furtive and sheepish? she thought.

Ivan thought Orla Farrell looked stunning with her hair tied up, dressed in a slim russet trouser suit and a simple white blouse that set off, in his mind, the emerald green colour of her eyes and her creamy Irish complexion. They jumped into the car and Bernard swung out again, continuing through College Green before turning left into Trinity St.

He was enjoying driving in Dublin again. He knew the streets of this city as well as any city taxi driver. From Trinity St, he turned right at the Trocadero and straight up South William St before hanging right behind the St Stephen's Green centre and then another right down Digges Lane and circled back across Stephen St in to Drury St before swinging into the municipal car park. At least the streets still run in the same direction, he thought.

They'd have to walk to the bar across three streets and past at least five pubs and half a dozen restaurants where his face had been familiar in the past. At least this way he felt he had some control over his reintroduction to Dublin.

In the car he suggested they separate and Orla follow them at a safe distance to cover their back and watch for any unusual activity. When they reached Coogan's she was to sit on her own with an evening newspaper and act as though she's waiting for someone.

That way she could clock the interested parties.

Nolan hoped an old pal of his, 'Pedro' Cahill, would be in his usual haunt, studying race form between trips to the bookies on Chatham St. Peter was a Special Branch detective, one of the country's top murder investigators, a compulsive gambler who was hooked on the idea of leaving Ireland some day to retire to a modest casa somewhere on the Costa del Sol.

Pedro always joked about never feeling lonely on the Costa with half the hoods he'd put away in the past living in retirement villas in the south of Spain having left Ireland because it was too hot for them at home. He was an old school cop with a wicked sense of humour. He once straight facedly told a rookie on his first murder case, as they gazed at the body of a man with a knife so deeply imbedded in his back he was impaled to the wooden floor beneath him, that it was the clearest case of suicide he'd ever seen.

Nolan hadn't spoken to any of his former colleagues since leaving Dublin two and a half years before. He heard Cahill had moved somewhere to head up a new anti-terrorism squad but without direct contact, he was completely out of touch. Someone said they'd spotted him in Sarajevo but their paths hadn't crossed.

Ivan Toscic was holding up well, he noted. He slept soundly on the flight and now looked fresh and alert. He seemed eager to get on with the job and not the slightest bit daunted by the task ahead. Nolan had considered keeping him away from Coogan's as his presence there might spoil whatever role he could play later in infiltrating some of the foreign gang haunts. Instead he decided they'd breeze into the bar like a couple of old friends reunited.

Coogan's was familiar to Nolan and he to many of the denizens regardless of whether Pedro were there. Nonetheless he hoped he might run into him. The tea time rush was gathering steam in Coogan's when they slipped in through the side door. Tired shoppers and worn out shop assistants, street traders, office workers and students were piling in for their first of the day. The cowboys had begun to gather at the nearest corner of the long saloon bar. Nolan recognised two of them. One was Sergio, the Roman restaurateur, the other was Brando, the pub's legendary cellar man. Without introducing himself, Nolan stepped up to the bar and called for a couple of pints of Guinness for two thirsty travellers.

'This is the place for a thirsty man who hasn't tasted a decent pint of Guinness in three years,' he announced to no-one in particular. Out of the corner of his eye he could see Brando sit up to take a professional interest in the delivery.

'It takes a long time,' observed Ivan who was watching the barman closely.

'You can't rush a good pint,' Nolan pointed out. He'll pour three quarters of the pint, let it settle and then come back and top it up. And that won't be the end of it. He'll let that settle again and then the final touch will leave the creamy head of the pint standing just a shade over the lip of the glass. Watch this.'

By now Brando was on the edge of his seat paying as much attention as Ivan. There was pride at stake.

'Of course,' Nolan continued, 'the quality of the pint will depend on another couple of factors. The glass must be spotless and above all, dry. The pipes will have to be clean and even if there's stout in the pipes in a pub like this it shouldn't matter because, if you look around, there's plenty of it crossing the counter. Now the temperature of the stout is another issue and that's down to it being stored in the best conditions.'

Nolan finished his soliloquy as the two creamy pints were set in front of them. Brando waited in anticipation. Nolan let him wait. He stepped back, tilted his head and surveyed the pint of black liquid in front of him, its smooth, creamy head standing proud above the rim of the glass. But he wasn't finished yet. He reached out as though to lift the pint but touched the beer mat below it instead and slowly, gently revolved the pint taking in the full vista. He looked at Ivan, smiling and waiting in reverent admiration. He looked at Brando and winked. Brando narrowed his eyes and, embarrassed, raised them as though he was trying to spot some indeterminate object further down the bar.

Nolan could wait no longer. He lifted his pint to eye level, said a loud 'Slainte' closed his eyes and sank his puckered lips into the creamy froth and took a long draught.

Brando sat transfixed. Toscic's mouth fell open in anticipation.

Finally Nolan surfaced and smacking his froth moustachioed lips uttered a loud 'Aaaaaahhhhh! Pure heaven.'

Brando sat back in his stool and blinked a smug smile as Nolan raised the pint to his lips again, nudging Ivan, 'get it into you, I'll be ordering a second before you've even started.'

Ivan raised his glass and dived into his pint. Emulating Nolan, eyes closed, lips sunk deep in the froth, he sank half his pint in one swallow.

'Jaysus,' said Nolan, laughing, 'steady on.'

'Best pint in Dublin,' announced Brando, proudly.

'It's his first pint in Dublin,' said Bernard Nolan, 'I had to chose the spot carefully and I reckon I chose well. Do you not drink stout yourself?'

'No. I never touch the stuff,' said Brando, rubbing his stomach with a sour grimace like someone who'd just swallowed a lemon, 'it doesn't agree with me.'

'What's that your drinking? Lemonade?' asked Nolan pointing questioningly at the almost empty pint of cider in front of Brando.

Wounded, Brando said 'no, it's cider, draught cider.'

'Give him a pint of that stuff – I don't know how you drink it, though it's the only man on a hot summer's day – and two more pints of Guinness for myself and the virgin here.'

He ignored the look Toscic flashed him while Brando thanked him for the new pint.

'Do you like the Guinness?' Brando asked Ivan Toscic, 'is that your first taste of it?'

'No,' said Ivan, smiling, 'but it's the first I've ever had in Dublin. It's true that it's different here.'

'I don't mean to pry,' said Brando, prying, 'but where are you from?'

'Bosnia,' said Ivan, 'I'm just visiting.'

'That's what they all say,' joked Nolan, laughing. Brando's look was almost as sour as Toscic's.

'Don't mind your friend,' he said, 'are you working here?'

'No. really, I am only visiting…on a sort of working holiday,' he replied before Nolan swooped with the coup de grace in their carefully constructed routine.

'He's a journalist from Sarajevo here on a job,' the big Irishman said, 'I'm showing him the sights.'

Curiosity aroused, Brando inquired what was the story he was on?

Toscic produced the postcard of Coogan's, wrapped in its cellophane bag, the original postcard from the pigeon and placed it in front of Brando. 'I'm looking for the person who wrote this postcard.'

Sergio, who had been standing in the background talking in rapid Italian on his mobile phone leaned forward and blurted, 'that's Tito's postcard. Garvan Deare wrote it. Where did you get it?'

Brando flashed him a look that said his silence was urgently required, probably in another bar. Catching the look, Sergio glanced exaggeratedly at his watch, drained his beer and turned and left without another word. Brando picked up his cigarettes and quietly slid off his stool and out the same door as Sergio.

'Right,' said Nolan, bemused, 'at least we have a name. Drink up and let's get out of here.'

A couple of calls later they knew Deare was a columnist in a local evening paper and they had an address.

TITO'S LETTER

Deare stood in the dining room of his apartment. The low lying evening sun cast a bright yellow glow across the room through the floor to ceiling bay windows overlooking the river behind the house. The rush hour traffic roared by on the motorway in the distance and a chorus of cheers and screams bellowed from the rugby grounds on the other side of the river. He was oblivious.

His eyes were set on the brown parcel on the glass topped table in front of him. He was aware of its presence like it was a mean looking stranger in a bar, staring him down.

Tito's dead, he thought. Or maybe he isn't. There's only the newspaper story, translated by Viktor, to go on. The postcard? Pure coincidence, he thought. The potential news value of the package occurred to him, too. A letter from a murdered man must have some value. But if this was a letter from a murdered man then it was potential evidence. Maybe he should turn it in.

Deare knew he was procrastinating to avoid the inevitable. A package arrives in a pub, addressed to him. So, it's his. Everything else is purely speculation. So don't run ahead of yourself, he thought, just open the fucking package and get on with it. He ripped the brown, wrapping paper cover part to discover a small, grubby notebook surrounded by pages and pages of a handwritten letter. A perfunctory flick through the pages of the notebook indicated an address book or ledger of some sort, written in a language (or code?) he didn't recognize or understand. Each entry carried an adjoining set of figures in two columns.

He set aside the notebook and picked up the letter. The handwriting was the same as the writing on the brown wrapping paper. He began to read.

'Garvin my friend,

If you are reading this then I have gone and you may never see me again. You have been good friend to me so I must trust you with this information. My life was worth shit in Dublin.

I leave because my sister Irina's life was in danger and it is my fault.

All my life since I left my home in Albania I live to survive. Some of my story I tell you but there is much I have not tell you. There is much I could never tell you because if I told you, as you would say, I would have to kill you….'

Jesus, thought Deare, typical Tito, fucking drama queen, but as he read, he became more intrigued by Tito's story.

'I have always dreamed of a different life. But I never dreamed of how it would become. Freedom was not what I looked for. I wanted adventure. I wanted to get away. I thought I was living in Hell. I thought life was shit. Now I know true Hell and it is shit. …'

Deare was aware, as everyone else was, of the

overwhelming numbers of foreigners flooding the streets of Dublin and other Irish cities. Many of them were so called 'refugees' from the civil strife tearing their Balkan homes apart. How they got here was a disregarded mystery and their numbers, it was assumed without any official estimates, far exceeded any internationally agreed quotas. It was a fact of life, labour followed the money and right now, Ireland was a fat sow, ripe for the milking, even when we wallowed in our own mythology of a ferocious 'tiger.' Tito was just another one of those adventurers.

Of course, getting there was the first priority and the fact there were many obstacles, physical and legal, made it an endeavour and enterprise ripe for exploitation. The Balkan passes, once used by those who brought drugs from Turkey and Iran was now plied by trails of hopeful emigrants who were soon exploited by human traffickers who replaced the smugglers. Their human cargo had far more added value than their passage fee across a border. Traffickers used their cargo as the raw material to build new criminal empires. Tito was recruited when he made his first illegal border crossing from Kosovo to the Bosnian capital of Sarajevo. From there, he found a contact who offered to smuggle him to Italy aboard a tramp ship packed with hundreds of his compatriots, trading their life's savings for a crack at freedom.

In those days when Serbs, Bosnians, Croats and Kosovans were pitted against one another in wars more bitter than the horrific phrase 'ethnic cleansing' could ever convey, desperate refugees were piling across borders and floating their way across the sea in boats barely more seaworthy than a leaky tea chest. Crouching on the crowded deck of a cramped steam tramp, the choking smells of sweat, sickness and fear were redolent in the fetid, noonday air. He sought and found passage through a man he met in a bar. Everyone knew who to go to, there was no mystery about it. All you needed was the money or the gold. Tito had neither.

He found a job in a bar, the Bienvenue, cleaning tables, running errands. He slept on a tiny cot in a cupboard below the stairs. He woke at 7am and prepared the bar for its 8am opening. From then he worked, tending tables, washing up, running for stocks. The owner, Ernesto, a rough brute with a vicious tongue and a peculiarly effeminate grace in the way he carried his bulk, was gay.

' …this man kept prostitutes, men and women. They were from everywhere and were poor and most ignorant . Some of them worked with Ernesto hoping to work their freedom. Others, and there were more in this boat than in the other, had no choice. They worked the bar's tables by day and evening and their beds by night for the safety of their own families – they traded their own freedom, to pay the passage for their loved ones. And though many believed their sacrifice had achieved this aim, they feared the worst for their families. With good cause too. Many had never seen the deck of a boat or if they had, they'd been cut adrift on a crowded, leaking dinghy to fend for themselves. I saw all these things. Indeed, in my shame, I did many of them because as Ernesto employed me less for my working skills, he found more use for me as time when on because I made myself useful. I resisted at first but I was raped for my insolence and thrown in the filthy cellar. On my first night in that hole a cornered sewer rat attacked me. But it was I who was cornered so I killed the rat. That was my first step to survive. Ernesto took what innocence I had and to survive I turned the tables and became his seducer, more wanton than even he could imagine. I learned the languages of those who used the bar and soon became his bright eyed boy, his right hand. Hundreds were stripped of their clothes and money by Ernesto and his gang. Sometimes they were raped, sodomized and shot. We dumped their bodies. This was my youth, Garvin. It shames me to tell you this but I am proud too that I did survive…'

Jesus fuckin' Christ, Deare gasped to himself.

'…Although I never took another's life I was their last trusted soul. My smiling innocence was their own downfall as I led them to their deaths. But I could never despise myself because I stayed alive even with the taste of Ernesto in my mouth.

Ernesto; once, to me, an all powerful monster; was just a small wheel. His masters were the gangs who brought him his cargo. He was the go-between for them with the international criminal gangs – Roman, Calabrian, Rumanian, Russian, Ukrainian, Dutch, French, English, Moroccan, Algerian and yes, Irish. They supplied and traded drugs and guns for humans. Ernesto's 'Welcome Inn' was their trading house. Many times I think of Coogan's where people smiled and made me feel welcome. It was real and it became my home. It was where I wanted to be but back then, how was I to know these things?.

As the months went by many of the gangs got to know me and I, them. Although they laughed and traded with Ernesto, they despised him as much as the cargo he provided. He was distrusted for his cruelty. His pleasure was too obvious and for this, a weakness. Soon, many would defer to myself, entrusting me with their confidences and errands. When it became too obvious to

Ernesto he became jealous and raged at me but he dared not touch me, not in their sight, in any case. I became fearful and offered my services to my new allies, Albanians, with whom I had common links of family and home.

Their business interests spread to every capital city in Europe. I could speak Italian, French, Spanish, German and English as well as converse with Kosovan, Croat, Serb and Albanian. I could even hold my own in Russian. My education in Ernesto's amounted to a degree and I graduated with honours in the space of one year. I could become to them what I had become for Ernesto. This was my second step.

One gang, led by a bunch of Neapolitans operated a ferry service by tramp ship to Italy. These boats left almost every day from the main port, unheeded by the port authorities or customs, all privileged customers of Ernesto's. These same people traded information on incoming cargo ships, their holds bulging with international relief aid that were hijacked by Ernesto's shore land gangs. I was put aboard these ships to travel back and forth, posing as another refugee but spying for my new masters to find the traitors in their midst, who would turn over their boats and their cargo to the Italian authorities before they could be landed. In this way I betrayed two such spies in almost ten sea journeys. Their journey was cut short, mid sea and they were tossed to the sharks. Nine times I could smell freedom. Nine times I returned to Hell.

On my tenth journey when I was on the verge of jumping ship to test my swimming skills and take my chances inshore, my new masters declared they had a new role for me.

Deare's reading was interrupted by two sounds. First, his mobile phone, then the front doorbell, rang. Startled, Deare felt like a schoolboy caught with illicit reading material. Rising hurriedly from his dining room table, the chair he sat on fell with a crash. Ignoring it, he gathered the discarded pages of Tito's letter, scattered across the dining room table. The cell phone continued to play the theme of countless Hammer horror films while a heavy hand leaned on the front doorbell of the apartment.

'Jesus, fuck, bollocks,' he cursed as he struggled to find his mobile while he stuffed the jumbled pages of the letter into a file marked 'communication' in his bedside desk.

'Christ, alright already, keep your fucking knickers on… I'm coming,' he hissed through gritted teeth. As he opened the hallway door he could hear a couple of unfamiliar voices outside the door of the apartment building. He lived in a neo-Georgian building with six apartments, two per floor including the garden level basement.

Whether it was the shock of interruption or the content of Tito's letter, Deare felt an icy tremble that made his hand stop halfway to the front door latch. He retreated quietly back inside his apartment, silently revolving the latch to shut his hall door. No-one knew he was home, he thought. He wasn't expecting anyone. People ordinarily phone to find out if he was home.

'No,' he shook himself, 'I'm just being paranoid. That fucking letter has me jumping.'

Nonetheless he withdrew to his bedroom and lying flat on the bed, prised the heavy curtain material from the crack nearest the wall to catch a glimpse at his visitors; two men, one tall and heavyset, the other of average height, tanned and dark haired, foreign. He didn't recognise either and he had no desire to make their acquaintance.

The ringing stopped and the two men spoke to each other while they peered at the windows on either side of the hall door. Deare jumped back and held his breath. Had they seen him or the curtain move? He lay on his back and waited. His cell phone continued its ludicrous dirge and now in the silence it reverberated like an orchestra through the building. He cursed it but decided to let it ring out. Perhaps they couldn't hear it, he thought, remembering he had left it recharging in the kitchen at the rear of the apartment. The cell phone stopped and he released his breath slowly. Minutes passed as he listened for signs of life outside. He slid off the edge of his bed and ducking, stepped into the apartment hallway. Short of shutting the kitchen doorway behind him there was nowhere else in the flat where he could remain unseen from prying eyes at street level. He slid to the ground and waited. When five minutes had passed in silence he was startled when the phone rang again. He slowly leaped across the gap between the hall and kitchen door and pressed himself upright against the intervening wall before he grabbed the phone.

'Garvan,' came the gruff voice of a half sozzled Brando, 'There's a lot of interest in an old friend of yours today.'

Brando paused and Deare realised with dismay he was playing his usual conversation gambits and this was no time for them. 'Brando, don't talk in fucking riddles, what are you on about?'

'Jaysus, keep your hair on. Tito…remember Tito…'

'Yeah, yeah, I remember him…what about him?'

'D'ye know Gerry Heels? They call him Pretty Heels…'

'Who? Brando, what the fuck…?'

'Heels…he's a hood. He knows Buckets and all those

138

guys. He came in asking about Tito'

Christ, thought Deare. He didn't know Heels but he did know Buckets of Blood, to give him his full title. He was not the kind of person you'd invite around for tea with your mother.

'What was this Heels asking about?'

'Tito. But he wasn't the only one. A couple of old pals of Tito came by this evening asking if I knew him. I told them he hadn't been around for the best part of six months but they said they knew all about the postcard and wanted to speak to the guy who'd written it. I said I knew nothing about no postcard and then one of them produced the fucking thing from his pocket, wrapped in a plastic envelope. I thought they must have been cops but the small one, the foreign one, said they were journalists…'

Deare interrupted Brando's ramble impatiently. 'Brando, Brando, shut the fuck up a minute. Was the other one a big fucker as wide as he was tall and the small one dark and foreign looking?'

'What? …yeah…yeah, he had a foreign accent but the other one was Irish. I know him from somewhere. He's been in here before, years ago. I couldn't place him but I seen his face before. He didn't say much but he bought me a few pints and he could sink them himself, pints of Guinness they both drank.'

'Brando, Brando, listen, will ya? What did you tell them about me? Did you tell them where I lived?'

'They said they were looking for the fella who wrote the postcard.'

'Fuck, fuck, fuck…what did you say? did you tell them where I lived? They just turned up at my door.'

'They had the postcard, in a plastic bag. I told them

nothing.'

Deare's mind was racing…who were these strangers? How did they have a postcard that was found in the pocket of a dead body in Sarajevo? He caught the end of Brando's speech and froze..

'…Then Sergio walked in and saw the postcard and he said that's Garvan's postcard and asked them where they got it.'

'Oh Jesus, Brando…who the fuck were they? If they come in again asking about me don't tell them anything.'

Deare hung up. Brando's pissed, he thought. Ordinarily he was cagey but these two guys had got into him with a couple of pints. Who the fuck were they?

Deare knew he had to get back to work and he figured lingering in the apartment with a light on in the gathering dusk would only attract the attention of anyone else who decided to come snooping. Despite the dangers, he was compelled to read on. He unplugged his bedside lamp and plugged it in the hallway. He gathered up some cushions from the settee in the living room and tossed them on the hallway floor. Deare poured himself a large snifter of brandy, closed the doors leading from the bedroom and the living room, turned on the lamp and settled down on the cushions to continue his reading.

' …they set it up so I could work in Italy. They gave me new suit of clothes and shoes of Italian leather. Everything they gave me was neatly packaged in boxes and tissue paper: silk shirts and socks, crisp, cotton underwear and a black leather jacket of the lightest leather I have ever known. They gave me an envelope full of cash money and when they brought me ashore, it was in the speedboat used by my bosses and not the rotten hulled fishing boats they brought their cargo ashore in. I was a king.

Soon I was working in a bar in the docks of Bari. There was a warehouse next door with a container yard where the cargo was brought before they were released.

We took their money for carrying them across the sea. Then we took their money to get them a job and we took half their pay once they were working. They could live in the apartments we provided and we took rent. All of them were overcrowded but beggars could not be choosy, eh?

Women who travelled alone were put to work in the lap dancing clubs and the whorehouses, my bosses owned.

My job was to help get them settled. I translated the conditions and collected the rent and the wages. There was plenty of money and no trouble. The bosses paid off the local authorities.

It was easy to make myself useful. Most of the guys who worked for the bosses were idiots; militiamen who could only bully. I had the intelligence to be able to count my own fingers and talk without dribbling. so I was their bagman and translator.

The longer I was there, the more jobs they gave me. When we set up a new club I got to pick the women and set them up with lodgings. I paid them and kept them in line. We watered drinks and sold drugs to the women and the customers.

Soon the bosses told me they were moving me to another city. Things got big quick as more and more people scrambled out of the war regions. They paid in gold and dollars. And as the numbers increased, so did the tariff. The authorities seized more ships in order to satisfy the public noise of protest. We didn't mind. We had collected their money and if one or two ships got nabbed then twice as many got through.

The traffic switched from junk ships to high speed dinghies. Our couriers carried the best communication equipment so we monitor the border patrols. When push came to shove in a high speed chase, we dump the human cargo and left them to swim while our boats escaped. But we had to expand. More people wanted to go further and Italy was overflowing. It was in Amsterdam where I first met the Irishman they call The Pigeon. You will know him. He drinks in Coogan's …'

Now Deare was confused. There's a real person called The Pigeon? Someone would have known about him, he thought, scanning in his mind's eye, the regulars he knew in the popular city bar. Coogan's, though, is a big pub; he knew many of them to see but not all by name by a long shot. Who the fuck is he?

'Soon they were helping to transport the people and his network took over from us in Amsterdam to get their cargo to Britain and Ireland.'

Why me? Deare thought. Suddenly canapes and empty social chatter felt like the most appealing thing in the world. He had to get back to work. He thought about Tito's letter and the notebook and decided to take them, folded in a yellow Jiffi bag, and hide them in the caretaker's cupboard under the outside stairs of the building where he kept his bicycle locked up.

VIKTOR

Heels was certain Brando knew more than he was letting on. He froze when Heels mentioned Tito and since he hired and fired a lot of the staff in Coogan's it stood to reason he should have known him. The cider sozzled fucker couldn't be that stupid, he thought.

Another idea occurred to him while he sat in Coogan's. Half the Bosnians, Rumanians and Albanians in the neighbourhood were paying tribute to the Pigeon, though they didn't know where their money was going. None of them were legally in the country having taken advantage of the Pigeon express service in a container through Rosslare from a French port.

Every Thursday evening when they collected their wages they handed over half their money to one of The Pigeon's collectors. If they didn't, the Pigeon took their sister for payment or sent them home in a Government paid raid.

Heels put the word out among the collectors and before long they found Viktor, Tito's kitchen porter friend. Heels suggested they invite Viktor to a meeting in the snooker club.

Viktor knew who the two men approaching were when he stepped outside the Italian restaurant he had worked in for three years. A hardworking Bosnian, Viktor had been accepted as a refugee and had already acquired a work visa and was working his way towards his citizenship papers. He avoided the organised gangs and their strong arm bully tactics and kept his nose clean.

Viktor knew them because he'd always known them. He had spent his life fleeing the men in black. He turned and ran. Anticipating his move, two more approached from the opposite end of the alley in a small green saloon car. One of them stepped out of the passenger's side and opened the rear door for him. He got in without arguing. The other three climbed into the car and they sped away.

Sergio spotted his KP climbing into the car with the other three and wondered where the hell the porter was off to in the middle of his shift. 'Hey, Viktor! Where the fucka you going?' No-one heeded him. Unluckily for Viktor, Sergio wrote his departure off as yet another fickle defection by his footloose staff.

In the same back room of the snooker hall where Horvar's two Albanian companions were dispatched, Heels sat on the edge of the table as Viktor was led inside.

There was no sign of the earlier carnage. The room's bare concrete floor had been mopped and swept. The grey, plastic mould seats had been stuffed in a corner. One bare lightbulb lit the room. A faded and torn cinema poster advertising George Romero's Night of the Living Dead was the only hint of the building's previous incarnation.

Viktor stumbled as he was pushed into the centre of the room in front of Heels. The four thugs who had brought him took positions by the wall nearest the door. A single chair was pushed into the centre of the room behind Viktor. A hand grabbed his shoulder from behind and pressed him into the seat. Heels looked up and handed him a cell phone.

'Speak to your brother, Viktor.'

Viktor silently took the offered phone and raised it to his ear. Whoever was on the other end startled and alarmed him.

'Nicolae, Nic....?'

'Yes, Viktor, that's your younger brother Nicolae, isn't it? Works in a club in Liverpool as a toilet attendant. Hard working young man with prospects, by all accounts. Studying accountancy, isn't he?'

'What do you want with my brother? Who are you? What do you want with me?'

Without warning Heels turned around and swung the steel pointed tip of an elegant leather cowboy boot into Viktor's stomach. The KP made a whooshing noise like a deflating balloon.

'I never said you could ask questions. I never even said you could talk. If you're lucky I will say you and your brother can continue to breathe. I'm going to ask you a question and you will answer. If it is the answer I want to hear, I will be pleased. If it is not, your brother will lose a finger. I will continue to ask questions until your brother has no fingers or I have all the answers I need. Do you understand me, Viktor?...that's the first question'

'Yes,' Viktor answered, suddenly alert. Winded, he could feel the piercing pain and a blotch of bruising form on his midriff.

'Did you know Tito De Lillo?'

'Yes.'

'Good. You're catching on.'

145

'Do you know Paddy the Pigeon?'

'No…' Heels raised the phone to his ear.

'No…I mean, yes…it was just a joke they pulled on Tito…there was no harm in it.'

'You better explain yourself or your brother's about to lose his grip.'

Viktor blurted out the story.

'You must think I'm some kind of fucking eedgit…your brother's gonna have one less finger to count when he's doing his sums.' Heels barked an order into the phone. Viktor screamed and made to jump at him but was restrained by the same heavy hand that had pushed him into the seat in the first place.

Heels held the phone to Viktor's ear. The agonised scream of his brother Nicolae could be heard by everyone in the room. The driver of the car, standing nearest the door, giggled but stopped after a cold look from Heels.

'It's true about the postcard,' Viktor pleaded, 'the story was in the newspaper when they found Tito's body. That's how we all knew he was dead. I can show you…' He scrabbled for the wallet in his rear pocket but in his frenzy he dropped it. Heels' henchman kicked it away from him while another stepped forward and picked it up, emptying the contents onto the table. He picked out a faded, worn newspaper clipping.

Heels, who could barely read or write English, stared at it. 'What does it say?' he asked. The henchman passed it to another of the gang who could read Bosnian.

Translating, he said, 'PIGEON POSTCARD MURDER CLUE'…

Heels looked at Viktor. 'You're doing very well, Viktor…just a few more questions to go…'

'Who wrote the postcard?'

Viktor answered immediately. 'Garvan Deare, the journalist…he drinks in Coogan's…the others asked him to write it for Tito after his pigeon flew away.'

'And that's it? Is there anything else you want to tell me…before I pass judgement on you? This is the million dollar question, Viktor…you have no lives left but the one your in right now…you can't phone a friend or ask the audience and there is definitely no 50:50…think very hard…and very carefully….did Tito leave anything behind him?'

Viktor realised he had reached the end of the line. He knew his life had just run its course. He only hoped he could save his brother.

'TOO LATE, VIKTOR…' Heels' bellow woke him with a jolt.

'NO…NNNNNOOOO,' he screamed back, 'please, let my brother go…he doesn't know what this is about…he is of no use to you…I have told you everything…please let him go…'

'I don't think you've finished talking, Viktor but your brother's about to lose a hand,' Heels hissed.

'A package. Tito left a package. It was addressed to the journalist. He told me to give it to him if we heard anything about Tito or if he hadn't been in touch within six months of his departure from Dublin. I was about to give the package to Deare anyway when I saw the story in the newspaper. I left it in Coogan's for him last night. I don't know what was in it…I swear…I don't know anything more…please.'

Heels walked straight past the whimpering Viktor and out the door.

NO GAMES

'What the fuck is this about, Heels? I've more to be doin' than readin' the fuckin' newspapers,' he barked.

A copy of the Evening News lay spread out in front of Joe Connolly. He was staring at a picture of Garvan Deare and the Deare Diary. Heels had walked into his office and without explanation, slapped it down in front of him.

'This is the man, boss. He's the fucker what wrote the postcard to Tito...the fella who signed himself 'Paddy the Pigeon.''

Connolly was not impressed, 'Him? The gossip guy in the fuckin' Evenin' News? Somebody's pullin' yer fuckin' leg.'

'No, it was him. We axed a guy from the pizza parlour around the corner, a Bosnian. He knew Tito and he said himself and the reporter were buddies.'

Exasperated, Connolly replied 'That explains fuckin' nothin'.'

Heels then related to Connolly the story Viktor had told them; 'It was all a fuckin' joke.'

'Jesus Fuckin' Christ,' was all Connolly could say 'It

148

would be funny if it wasn't fuckin' tragic,' he said, 'ye spend half your fuckin' time trying to keep a lid on everything and the whole fuckin' thing blows up in yer face because of a fuckin' gossip. Jesus.'

'It gets worse,' said Heels, enjoying his moment at centre stage, a misjudgement.

'What the fuck d'ye mean? Don't play fuckin' games with me, Heels, give me the whole fuckin' story before I have your balls roasted for lunch…'

Heels gabbled, 'Tito left a package behind for Deare… he told the Bosnian to hand it over to Deare if he wasn't back in Ireland in six months or if they heard anything about him…so he brought it into *Coogan's* for Deare the other night after he read a story about Tito…'

Connolly was on the point of exploding. He felt, correctly, that Heels was enjoying his discomfort with this riddle talk…'What the fuck? Has Tito been giving interviews or somethin'?'

Heels knew the tone. It was time to spill. 'No, boss. The Bosnian had a cutting in his pocket from a newspaper.' Heels was rooting about in his hip pocket and produced the tattered article. He opened it gingerly and spread it out in front of Connolly.

'It says 'PIGEON POSTCARD MURDER CLUE', boss; it's about Tito.'

Connolly stood up abruptly, angrily crashing his chair on the ground behind him, 'I DIDN'T FUCKEN' THINK IT WAS ABOUT ME, YE FUCKEN MUPPET.'

He turned his back on Heels and paused to think. *There's something fucken rotten about all of this and I'm going to get to the bottom of it.* Heels watched the back of his boss's neck turn an angry red. Then Connolly turned and snarled,

'FIND THIS FUCKEN' DEARE GUY AND BRING HIM HERE. I WANT TO SEE THAT FUCKEN' PACKAGE.'

STALKING

Deare's apartment was in a smart district on the banks of the Dodder river. *He has to be renting*, thought Nolan, *you couldn't buy on this road on a journalist's wages.* Toscic and he were standing outside a mock Georgian apartment building. Wide steps lead up to the columned neo-Georgian door and the building's first floor. There were two floors above the garden and a garden level 'lower ground floor.'

'It looks like there are six apartments, two on each floor…I wonder which one is Deare's?'

Toscic climbed the stairs and began inspecting the doorbells to the left of the front door. There were four numbers but only one had a name on it and it wasn't 'Deare.' Nolan joined him.

'We'll have to ring all four to see what happens,' he said, pressing numbers five and six while he leaned back to check the upstairs windows for lights or signs of life. Nothing. He buzzed them again. Nothing.

Toscic tried the second row of numbers, three and four. He buzzed and buzzed. Nothing. Nolan had a go and kept his fat thumb pressed against the buzzer. Nothing. They both stood back and checked the windows again.

Nolan said, 'd'you hear that?' Toscic listened intently. They could hear the faint electronic buzz of what sounded like a cell phone ring. 'Someone's a fan of Hammer Horror films…probably a Transylvanian,' joked Nolan.

Toscic either ignored him or the joke went right over his head. Either way the macabre ringing continued uninterrupted. No-one answered the door.

'C'mon, let's try the two doors downstairs,' Nolan said as he turned to stroll back down in the stairs in the gathering twilight gloom of evening, 'if we don't get him here then we'll have to go around all his regular haunts and take pot luck. At least there'll be a few pints in it for us.'

After buzzing the downstairs apartments once they got one reply. A red haired girl emerged from the apartment to the right. She was bleary eyed and dishevelled. *She could be getting up after a rough night on the tiles but given the time of evening she had probably just fallen asleep after returning from work*, thought Nolan.

She's tall, he realised, as she stared at him at eye level through the gap between the door and the length of the door's security chain.

'What d'ye want?' she asked in a sharp Northern Irish accent.

'We were looking for Garvan Deare,' Nolan said, 'does he live here?'

Blinking, she squinted at them through one eye, taking in both of them in one single, sweeping glance. 'Never heard of him,' she said, 'now fuck off' and shut the door in their faces.

Toscic looked at Nolan, confused…'what was that about?' he said.

Nolan shrugged, 'c'mon, let's buy an evening paper. I have to see a man about a dog.'

Toscic stared at the hulking Irishman as he stalked out the garden pathway. *I don't understand these people*, he thought.

SANDY

Deare allowed half an hour to elapse before he ventured outdoors. He surveyed the garden and the street beyond its stone wall through a crack in his bedroom curtain window. He poked his nose out into the damp, night air and scurried down the front steps. At the bottom he turned right and took the last four steps to the basement in one bound. He fumbled in the dark in the archway under the flight of steps. Mr Murphy, the caretaker, had shown him where he hid the key for the below stairs storeroom so he could leave his bicycle there safely. As he reached his hand into the gap in the lintel above the door and felt around for the key, the hall light in the apartments behind went on, illuminating the entire area. He froze.

'Garvan…is that you? What the fuck are ye doin' there?'

Deare eased a sigh and the tension in his balls relaxed.

'Christ, Sandy, you put the heart and soul across me. I nearly fucking died there. Jesus.' He turned and steadied himself against the caretaker's storeroom door. Sandy Nelson stood in her doorway, looking gorgeous as always, he thought.

'Have you been in all evening?' she asked, ' I thought I

154

heard you moving about upstairs. What's goin' on? There were two fellas here looking for you ten minutes ago. One of them was foreign. He didn't say much. The other was a big fella, Dubliner and a cop if my sense of smell is anything to go by.'

Sandy Nelson had a nose when it came to detecting bullshit. She was well proportioned and just a shine short of brassy, a late twenty something Presbyterian from Ballymena. She worked as a hairdresser in Dublin and was one of a small but ever increasing band of her peers who found more common ground in newly thriving Dublin than they would at home in the still grim and rooted in history mood of Northern Ireland. 'Sure, there's more craic down here', Sandy once said, 'and you don't have to mind who you're talking to 'cos no-one gives a shite, anyway.'

Deare now secretly blessed that Northern Irish sense of awareness. Sandy could guess a person's background and inclinations within thirty seconds of contact.

Cops, Deare thought, what the fuck do they want?

'What did they ask you?'

'Wanted to know if you lived here and did I know you...I told them I'd never heard of you and then told them to fuck off. The big one was cute, though.'

'Look, Sandy, if they come back or you see anyone else around the building asking about me, would you give me a buzz on my mobile or send me a text?'

'No worries. No questions, either, although it sounds a tad dodgy. You haven't gone and written something nasty about The Corrs again, have you? Now if they were after me that would put the fear of God in me...'

'They're not, thankfully. Although the worst I might expect is they might sing through my letter box like the

155

CIA did to Noriega. Look, I'll be back later on and I'll explain it all to you but if you're not going out will you keep your eyes peeled for me?'

'No bother. I have your number and you can stop in for a nightcap if it's not too late when you get home.'

Deare found the elusive cupboard key, opened the door and disappeared into the gloom, groping for the light switch. He pretended to be fiddling with the lock of his bicycle while he waited for Sandy to close the door behind her. When he heard the door shut he looked around for a suitable place to hide Tito's letter and notebook, which he had rolled up inside its original brown envelope. He settled on a stack of empty flower pots, hiding the package curved around the inside of the biggest earthenware pot.

He turned off the light, closed the cupboard door and locked it, replacing the key in the gap above the lintel.

Caution was now an imperative. He puzzled why the police should be looking for him and who, in God's name, was the foreigner?

It was approaching 10pm. It was time to hit the town and get on with the Diary. Not for the first time the thought occurred there must be easier ways to earn a living.

He felt comforted by his brief encounter with Sandy Nelson. There's an Irish mammy in her, he thought, Northern Prod or not. The two had become firm friends since the Ballymena woman had moved in. She liked to party and went with him to club events some times. But most of their contact was in his apartment when Sandy would come up and have a cup of tea with him after he came home from his night prowls. She'd put on the kettle and make light of the late hour. They were lonely and took more comfort out of each other's company than they'd ever admit. Diarists led a blessed existence, ankle deep in free booze, swanky parties and celebrity company. Gossip oiled the wheels of society - you could say it was the heart of the city - letting everyone know the pecking order: let them make moral judgements about others. Everyone wanted to read it but distrusted and even despised those who wrote it. And those who wrote it, he knew, if they had any wit and self respect, had a deep sense of their own absurdity.

Unfortunately Deare's mind was not focussed on the job at hand. Wandering into the Horseshoe bar of the Shelbourne, he absentmindedly registered the usual suspects of divorcees, drunks, laggards, chancers, journalists, barristers, politicians, property developers, socialites, wannabe socialites, artists and poets. They were all there and on any other night of the week it would be like taking a stroll through an Aladdin's Cave of social gossip and scandal. Now he was distracted by Tito's letter and by what he felt about it. He struggled with an overwhelming feeling of shame at his covetous, sleazy thoughts on the matter.

Jesus, he thought, a man could spend a lifetime fumbling in a thousand greasy storylines, reporting scandals of a salacious or fraudulent nature and never find the opportunity to experience the thrill of a real story unfold in your lap.

He felt detached from his own job. He reported the foibles, the scandals, the obsessions and the attachments but he couldn't even pretend to care about the people society let float to the top. Americans, he read, had become so used to living in a society informed by cinema and television fiction it had begun to shape their own understanding of the real world. People obsessed with themselves looked for validation by seeking their name in the social pages.

How much had Brando told his two visitors? No harm to Brando, he thought, if push came to shove it was Brando I can rely on. But Brando didn't know what was going on. No more than himself. And deep down he doubted his own capacity to deal with a story of such enormity; his own shallow self might drown in its murky depths.

Coogan's was off his itinerary tonight. He toyed with the idea of calling in sick and dismissed it just as quickly. He felt compelled to go home to finish Tito's letter but realised those men might be watching his house. He knew that regardless of the predicament he must get home to finish the letter and find out what had compelled Tito to send it. First he had to fill the 'Diary' and besides, with all this worrying his throat was cut for the want of a drink and some congenial company. He shivered and turned from the Horseshoe bar where he had sat alone amongst all the casual bedlam. I might need some protection too, he thought.

SERGIO

Sergeant Orla Farrell sat alone in Coogan's, long after Nolan and Toscic left. She sat at the bar, close enough to hear and see everything that was going on but not close enough to get involved.

She had to admire Nolan's technique. Earlier, instead of wading in with his size 12s, asking questions, he had let Brando make the opening gambit. It was textbook stuff, if Nolan ever bothered to write the textbook. The quickest way to get to the truth was to tell the truth. Not all of it, he'd caution, but enough to keep the door open.

They had walked in like a pair of thirsty tourists and asked for pints. The whole rigmarole about the pouring of the pint was Nolan's way of appealing to his subject's interest and vanity. By the time he was finished it looked as though Brando was going to order a pint of Guinness himself.

Everything was going well until Toscic produced the postcard. The journalist on a job from Sarajevo gambit had worked like a dream, there was genuine curiosity and interest. The postcard, unfortunately, had the same effect as producing a Euro of rashers at a Bar mitzvah. Luckily, the Italian, who had spent half the time talking on his cell phone, didn't hear the first part of the conversation and blurted the name. He got a sharp look from Brando. Then the pair found urgent things to do elsewhere and left.

Brando and the Italian returned two hours after Nolan and Toscic left Coogan's. The rush hour crowd had dissipated too. There were just a handful of people sitting along the bar, one loud bunch of eight English women wearing identical teeshirts emblazoned 'Elsie's Last Stand' at a big corner table and a few couples. Coogan's was a typical Irish pub and like no other Irish pub at the same time.

Orla had only been in it on a couple of occasions before. The flags of every country in the European Union hung from its ceiling. There were street names from European capitals screwed into the walls and one huge glass cabinet filled with masthead cuttings from all over Europe, all dated January 1, 1973. Absently, Orla figured it had something to do with Ireland joining the European Economic Community as it was then known. The beer mats all bore the legend, 'Coogan's, the cosmopolitan pub.'

Her presence had not drawn attention. She had ordered a glass of Guinness and nursed it slowly through Nolan and Toscic's encounter with the wily Brando whom everyone seemed to know and the bar staff clearly deferred to him. Now she wondered if she should leave to phone Nolan or order another drink and check out what might happen next. Her dilemma was resolved as a fresh glass of stout landed on the counter in front of her. She looked at the barman inquiringly?

'Sergio bought it for you,' he said, whisking away the empty glass in front of her and indicating with a jerk of his head the grinning Italian at the end of the bar who was raising his own glass of ale in salute.

'Are you waiting for someone, bella?' Sergio leered, 'perhaps you would likea to join us?' She hadn't noticed the Italian's return. The invitation might have been easily shrugged off in other circumstances but now Orla spotted a chance to get in the inside.

'If you wouldn't mind,' she replied, 'I think I've been stood up. He said he was working late and I should wait for him but that was an hour ago since he was supposed to be here.'

'If he leaves a beautiful gerl waiting in a bar alone for this long you shoulda forget heem,' offered Sergio grinning. He pulled aside the stool next to Brando and invited her to sit. Orla lifted her drink and sat on the offered bar stool.

'Hello, my name is Orla,' she said, extending her hand to Brando whose eyes by now had shut to slits in his boozily florid face. Brando smiled and took her hand, 'my name's Brando and he's Sergio. Don't mind him, he's always like that.'

Sergio asked Orla if she worked in the neighbourhood. 'No,' she told him, 'I've been out of the country and I just came home yesterday. I'm only getting used to it again and trying to catch up with old friends.'

'This man you were meeting, he is an old friend?'

'Well, we used to work together but I haven't seen him in years. He's obviously not that anxious to see me.'

'Hee's a fool,' said Sergio.

There was an awkward silence. Sergio and Brando started a quiet conversation together. Orla pretended to search in her handbag for something while Sergio mumbled to Brando.

'Queer bloody things going on, Viktor fucked off today in a car with four other men. In tha meeddle of he's shift.'

'Viktor?,' Brando whispered, 'he was a friend of Tito's…'

Orla looked up and asked Brando and Sergio if she could buy them a drink?

'No, no, bella, put your money away…let me get this one,' offered Sergio but Orla had already put her ten Euro on the counter and was indicating to the barman to give them all the same again. She wanted to find out more.

'It sounds like you've been busy. I heard you mention Sarajevo earlier…that's where I was working. I'm a nurse,' she announced.

'Ah Jaysus,' interrupted Sergio, 'thees isa too much… No-one mentions Sarajevo for sixa months and now, all of a sudden, everyone'sa talking about it.'

Orla flashed a dazzling smile and an enquiring look. Brando recapped the story; dwelling on the drama of the murder in Sarajevo and its links to the bar.

'That's an amazing story,' said Orla, 'do you think it was the same fellow, this Tito?'

Brando gave her a patronising look and said, 'there can't be too many people in Sarajevo walking around with a postcard from a pigeon in their pockets. Especially if the postcard's from this pub.'

Then Brando spoke. 'Jaysus, I just thought, Sergio, suppose Viktor running off had something to do with this? Did he say anything to you?'

'No. I just saw heem getting into a car in the laneway witha four men and he didn't answer me when I called to heem. He was still wearing he's apron. It was not like heem…'

'Maybe I should phone Garvan and warn him. There's

something not right about all of this…first Pretty Heels comes in here asking about Tito, then those two 'journalists' and now Viktor disappears…sorry, Orla, we're talking riddles here, do you want another drink?'

'No, thanks,' Orla replied, her mind racing. Pretty Heels? She knew that name. It was Gerry Heels, a nasty piece of work and a known associate of The Pigeon. She had to get in touch with Nolan, 'ah, sure, alright, Brando, isn't it? Sure I'll have another one if ye're going to have one.'

'That'sa the spirit,' said Sergio.

'A bird never flew on one wing,' said Brando.

Orla stood up and excused herself, 'where's the ladies?' she asked. Brando pointed towards the stairs near the front door. She gathered her bag and picked her way through the bar that was slowly filling up again. When she got to the top of the stairs she ducked outside reaching for her cell phone in her handbag. She pressed the speed dial button for Bernard Nolan. It rang four times before Nolan answered.

'Orla. How's your first night back in Dublin?'

'Have you found Garvan Deare?' she asked, ignoring the conventions.

'No… no, he wasn't at this flat or if he was, he wasn't answering the front door. We're on our way back to town to start searching for him around his usual haunts. I rang his editor and left a message but he hasn't called back yet. What have you heard?'

Orla quickly explained Gerry Heels was searching for Deare too and then told Nolan about the suspicious disappearance of the kitchen porter. She said she might be able to get Deare's phone number but it would mean blowing her cover and she wondered if she should do that.

163

'I think you bloody well better. We don't want him falling into the hands of a lowlife like Heels,' Bernard Nolan said, adding, 'call me back as soon as you've heard anything.'

Orla Farrell returned to the bar. *It was funny*, she thought, *to hear Bernard Nolan say 'Heels,' and that can't be his real name, surely?* A fresh glass of Guinness sat in front of her. She thanked Brando who grunted. Sergio flashed his best leer.

Brando was preoccupied with his mobile phone. His head was bent, face flushed as he listened intently.

'He's not fuckin' answerin' or else he's in some noisy boozer and can't hear his dog,' he said, addressing Sergio.

'Send him a text,' Orla suggested, hoping it was Deare they were calling.

'That's a good idea,' agreed Brando, 'he's always texting people.'

Brando and Sergio exchanged a look. Neither of them had ever sent a text. Both were enthusiastic cell phone users but neither had ever used text and Sergio had only recently begun to read his messages.

'What will you say?' asked Sergio, subtly passing the baton to Brando.

''Jaysus, I don't know…will you not do it?'

'Not me,' said Sergio, 'I never usea text.'

Orla grabbed her chance. 'Look, do you want me to do it?' she said, picking up her own phone which she'd just put on the bar as she sat down, 'what do you want me to tell him?'

'Ehhhh…' Brando hesitated, 'ehhhh…'

'Tell him to call Sergio, urgently.'

'Ok, 'c-o-l   S-e-r-g   r-g-n-t-l-y,' there, what's the number?'

Brando called out Garvan's cell phone number. Orla keyed it in and pressed 'save', tapped in 'gd' for an ID then 'send'. Sergio and Brando watched intently but since they didn't use text she gambled they weren't paying too much attention. She sent 'gd's' number to Bernard Nolan.

PROWLING

Heels was confident he was closing in on Garvan Deare. He had a network of security contacts around the city.

Never mind he was barred from all of the upper crust clubs because of his own reputation. It didn't bother him. He had moved on from the club security game, he told himself.

Those muppets are only door jockeys, he thought, while dialling another number on his cell phone as he cruised the streets on the look out for Deare.

'Tony, how'r'ye…it's Gerry Fields, yeah. How udoin', hombre? Just driving around. Are ye busy? Nah, I suppose it's early yet. Listen I'm looking for someone…you might be able to help me out. Y'know yer man Garvan Deare, the journalist from the 'News? Yeah, that's him…look, I want to meet him. Would you give me a shout if you see him but don't tell him I'm looking for him? Spread it around if you get a chance…I'll look after ye…good luck.'

Tony Collins was a doorman of five years and had worked most of the major clubs and pubs. A former soldier, Tony left the army after an incident in the Lebanon involving a couple of kilos of Red Leb and a

166

seriously mashed corporal who stuck his nose in where it wasn't wanted. Although there were no witnesses and no evidence linking Tony they let him know he'd be doing parade drill in Bundoran with the FCA for the next four years while he worked out his time.

It was easy for a big lad like him to get into the security game. He got interested in Aikido in the army and kept up his studies when he left. The dojos and clubs were the natural recruiting ground for security staff. The good ones got the personal security jobs. The tough ones got the pubs, the handsome ones, the clubs. Heels and Tony had fought each other on many occasions when Heels was still in competition. Tony wanted to work for Heels – better pay, slick clothes, respect, fear – so he'd do anything to stay sweet with him. Well, as sweet as possible with someone like him. He gave Collins the creeps.

A few more calls and Heels felt he'd set his trap. Time to pay a visit to his own favourite spot.

He swung around Parnell Square and up into the back streets behind Dorset St where Albanian and Nigerian gangs had set up their own illegal shebeens among the warren of artisan dwellings, semi-derelict buildings and abandoned warehouses. This one was owned by Joe Connolly and he kept an office there, his personal headquarters and bolthole.

As he eased the black Mercedes into a parking space at the entrance to the alley he checked the street for suspicious cars. Satisfied, he turned off the engine and slipped out of the car, clicking on the remote alarm as he walked away. The place he was going to had no name - although to regulars it was referred to as 'Hurricane'. It was open 24/7 for a select clientele.

The bouncer on the door of the club, a Senegalese

mountain who had been an Olympic power lifter in his youth, greeted Heels with a friendly nod and a knowing leer. Heels ignored him. The building's gloom was not alleviated by the lurid red lighting lining the entrance corridor that illuminated the faded burgundy wallpaper and sticky threadbare carpet underfoot.

At the end of the corridor through a glass beaded curtain the club's main room was another dank space with red leatherette banquette seating and low tables. The only lighting at each table was a glowing electric lamp designed like an old fashioned hurricane oil lamp, hence the club's unofficial name.

'A slick, sallow skinned man in a crumpled tuxedo with plucked eyebrows and faintly rouged cheeks stepped up to greet him.

"eels, you are very welcome…your usual table?'

'I'm only staying a short while, Armand, is Ashley here?'

Armand clicked his fingers into the gloom and light from an unseen door burst through momentarily, 'Certainly, would you like to take a seat while we fetch ….?'

'No,' growled Heels, heading down the corridor behind whatever minion had been sent to prise Ashley's lips off someone else's cock, 'I'll do it.'

Armand, a half caste Algerian, shrugged inscrutably in his best Gallic fashion and returned to his station by the entrance.

HIDING IN PLAIN SIGHT

Garvan Deare understood the idea of 'hiding in plain sight' but it was no comfort to him as he sat in a corner of a tiny, family owned, city boozer. Although he was known there, it wasn't one of his usual haunts.

It was close enough to a couple of local hotels and celebrity haunts for him to catch friendly porters and bar staff, out for a quick pint and a sandwich. It was also a small pub and if you sat in the right place you could see everyone coming or going without fear of detection.

He positioned himself in a recess at the far end of the bar, well away from the main door. To his left, a stairs descended to the right, to the toilets. Further to the left, just over his left shoulder, was the little used side entrance into a laneway, his escape route, if required. Deare turned his phone onto silent while in the pub. He didn't want to be disturbed and he didn't want to draw attention.

He was waiting for the bar manager from a local hotel whose fondness for horse racing always left him short a few bob. For that reason and out of well established habit, they would meet once or twice a week and in exchange for a couple of entirely unattributable snippets of celebrity gossip. Deare would supplement Stephen's income with a score or two, depending on what was on offer. It was a mutually agreeable arrangement.

Stephen loved to see his stories in print. He had a chip on his shoulder about 'so-called celebrities', a product of a lifetime in service. He preferred to refer to them, witheringly, in his sing song West Donegal accent that started in a high register, dipped and then soared for the punchline, as 'Shit hit with a stick flies high.'

That night Deare was in luck. Stephen had a story about a politician who stood up as guest of honour at a fund raising dinner the night before and read the wrong speech. He talked for ten minutes on his salty exploits as a youthful caddy in a golf club but he was addressing the local Lions' club, wives and all. He had another story about a minor pop talent who got in a nasty punch up with a visiting English footballer after the well known Premier league player hit on his girlfriend in the hotel bar.

Bonanza, thought Deare as he left the pub by the alleyway exit. The drunk politician, with a little padding, would make a page lead and the other story would provide some colour and picture opportunities. At this rate he wouldn't even have to hit the clubs and might get home before midnight to finish the letter.

He had tried to contact Pedro Cahill whom he knew from the pub. He knew Peter was a cop and might be able to help him out. He also remembered it was Peter who had landed him in this shit, indirectly, at least: he came up with the idea of the postcard with Brando in the first place. Unfortunately, Peter wasn't answering his phone.

REMAINS OF OUL DACENCY

Nolan and Toscic walked in the door of the Horseshoe
bar when Nolan noticed he had a text message. He
paused and looked at the number on the screen. 'It's from
Sergeant Farrell,' he said. 'gd? Who could that be? Fuck,
it's Garvan Deare's number.'

They turned and walked out into the hotel's foyer.
Nolan dialled the number. It rang out. 'Damn. He must
have his phone turned off or he isn't answering.'

They walked back into the bar and sat down. Nolan
recognised some of the people standing in the historic
horseshoe shaped bar with its distinctive ceiling height
mirrors and ornate, ceramic engraved, wooden bar. There
were a handful of barristers and at least one defrocked
judge.

Nothing changes around here, thought Nolan. Here, the
'remains of oul' dacency,' assembled during the Spring
Show and the Horse Show or on their occasional visits to
their bespoke tailor. They drank their champagne and
sherry and after a bad day at the races, they'd give the
whiskey and brandy a lash. Beer and stout were kept for
rugby match days.

A well known English actor swayed on his bar stool as he held court over a tightly formed semi-circle of sycophants that included at least two underage Wicklow socialites. A brace of politicians and political journalists crowded another corner of the bar, their voices raised loudly in drunken debate.

Nolan caught the manager's eye and knew at a glance he'd been recognized. Immaculately turned out in tuxedos, the staff of the Horseshoe knew every customer by name, title and often reputation. They saw everything and answered nothing without courteous caution.

'Have ye seen Garvan Deare from the 'News?…I was supposed to meet him here for a drink but I got delayed and now I'm afraid I've missed him…'

'Ye have,' the manager, Colm said, wiping the unsoiled counter between them with a damp glass cloth and sweeping one drained glass out of sight,

'he was on his own and he's only gone an hour or so now. He didn't say where he was going…'

THE VELVET SLIPPER

Sensing Gerry Heels' mood, Armand instructed the earphone wearing goon in front of him seeking Ashley to simply point out the door, step aside and retreat.

Heels was not a man to be checked.

Bursting through the doorway with a 'whoop!', Heels had his flies open and was upon the unsuspecting Ashley who was naked, mouth full, hunched over a customer.

'Aaaarrrgggghhhh!' gurgled the pinioned Ashley.

'Jesus,' screamed the agonised punter who had just become the bite more than Ashley could chew.

He didn't get a chance to say any more as the back of Heels' hand smashed into his face, crushing his nose and dislocating his jaw with one jabbing move.

'FFUUUUUCK,' roared Heels, sated by his brief but explosive sex play. Then his phone rang. He didn't see himself as queer. He was just a straight guy with a strong sex drive who didn't mind where he put it so long as it was warm, wet, tight and with any luck, unwilling.

Without a glance at the whimpering Ashley, Heels climbed off, buttoned his flies and dug his cell phone from his jacket pocket.

'Yeah,' he barked.

'Gerry? It's Tony…you know your man you were lookin' for? He's just gone into The Velvet Slipper.'

'Is he with anyone?'

'No, he's on his own. One of the lads on the door rang me.'

'Right, thanks, I owe you one,' he said, walking briskly down the corridor past the bemused but unflappable Armand by the entrance.

Quietly, Armand released the breath he'd been holding since Heels first appeared. Ashley was accustomed to Heels' violent, impulsive behaviour. His unfortunate client wasn't. Now Armand would have to deal with the damage.

Heels had other fish to fry. His car alarm 'bleep – bleeped' as he crossed the street, the front and rear hazard lights winked in anticipation. Within seconds of opening his door, he pulled into the traffic and zoomed south to Capel street bridge.

The Velvet Slipper was a seedy dive off Parliament street on the other side of the river. Being new and so far unspoiled by the masses, it held the cachet of discovery. Just the sort of place you'd find Deare, thought Heels, full of poofs and posers.

Tony Collins nodded at Heels as he approached the door of The Velvet Slipper. 'He's sitting in the corner talking to a couple of people,' he whispered as Heels walked past him through the door.

The sweaty, blast of heat and noise hit him as he walked inside. In the gloom he could make out a few faces, tattooed and pierced, talking animatedly, chomping gum, sloshing colourful drinks in tall glasses, twitching jerkily to the pub's PA, set at a volume somewhere between 'my ears are bleeding' and 'I see a white light.' In another three months, he knew, the place would be forgotten and this crew will have flown to the next cool thing.

Each table was surrounded by a booth and a couple of small, white leatherette stools. The tables were white and underlit while a single blue candle floated in a glass of water on top. The bar was long and high and snaked around the corner to a wider seated area.

Heels made his way to the back, scanning the bar and the tables as he went, greeting some people and acknowledging others but never stopping to stray from his objective. As he squinted in the murk he could make out three figures at the last table, one man facing who was not Deare and a man and a woman with their backs to him, a seat on the stools.

'Garvan Deare, me oul' mate,' shouted Heels, leaning down to insinuate himself between the man and the woman and stretching an iron grip around to pin the man's left forearm and delay his reaction, 'I've been looking for you everywhere.'

He could see before he finished, he had the wrong person. But as the startled man blurted 'who the fuck…?' Heels interrupted his flow by grabbing his lapel and snapping, 'where is he?'

Heels meant business. One look into the black holes he called eyes and the man swallowed his protest. 'He's just gone out the back door. Ye just missed him. He got a text and he said he had to leave and he didn't say where he was going…'

Heels was up as abruptly as he'd arrived and snapping the rear fire exit handle, he was gone.

JUST BECAUSE YOU'RE PARANOID

What the hell could Sergio want at this hour of the night? Deare wondered as he hitched his collars against the night chill in the greasy lane behind the Velvet Slipper. It had rained that evening but now the air was drying, despite the cold. A faint mist of spice scented cooking oils hung in the air as kitchen heat met the chill autumn night. White cotton clad kitchen porters spilled out into the chilly gloom up and down the lane, to fill olive drab wheelie bins and steal a furtive puff.

Deare glanced at the text and frowned. Sergio doesn't use his text and why didn't his call sign come up on the phone?, he thought, the Roman, being of an age group that wears the badge of 'technophobe' with pride. So who the fuck, he wondered, would send a message from Sergio asking me to phone him? His brow was furrowed in thought as he considered his route and destination.

The awareness that paranoia was settling in like a cold, clammy rash occurred to him. Am I in the middle of this? I've done nothing to them. I wrote a postcard for a mate. It turns up in a dead man's pocket and suddenly every hood in Dublin is after me like this was some urban fox hunt. Tito was no standup citizen and he's involved in some shit, he thought, and this is out of my league. Beam me the fuck out of here, Scottie, not even lithium crystals will do the job here. He thought of phoning Sergio. But who would answer the phone? He called Sergio every second night of the week to meet him for a pint or a plate of pasta and a bottle of wine. Just because I'm paranoid, he thought, doesn't mean they're not out to get me. The cliché gave him no comfort.

His thoughts distracted him from his route as each foot tumbled in front of the other, as sure they knew where they were going as Deare was unsure and hesitating. But there was no room for doubt. There were things that had to be done. At least five good stories were needed for his daily column and he had those in the bag. He needed to get home to finish reading the letter because it held the key to this unfolding lunacy. He had to stay out of the way of Connolly, Heels and the two strangers before he did that. He had to go home. First, he had to phone Sergio.

'I'll text him,' he thought, 'he reads his text and at least I can use some sort of code he'd understand.' 'No,' he decided, 'I'll phone him because if a stranger answers I can hang up and if Sergio answers then I can ask him questions without giving myself away.' He felt good about this plan until he hit Sergio's speed dial number. Conversation with the colourful Roman was often bewildering, even to the long initiated. The phone rang once before Sergio's distinct voice answered; 'Pronto…'allo, who ees thees?'

'Sergio…it's Garvan. Don't say my name…who are you with?'

'Hey, my friend, you must be busy tonight. We haven't seen you but Coogan's is like a bus station and everyone wants to get on your bus.'

Garvan smiled. It was good to hear a friendly voice.

'Where are you and who are you with?' he asked.

"Ees jus' me and Brando, enjoying a digestif. Do you want to come and join us?'

Digestif, me arse, he thought. It was far from 'digestifs' Brando was reared.

'Is it just the two of ye?' he wanted to know, adding, 'where are yis?'

'Well, there's a beautiful young woman too. We don't know her but she was on her own so she joined us,' Deare had a mental image of Sergio moving in, his eyes boring holes through the outer garments of the girl he was talking about , 'she useta be a nurse in Sarajevo,' she says.

Do not pass 'Go,' Deare thought. Two parties of strangers from Sarajevo and a gang of Dublin hoodlums asking questions about Tito in the same bar in the space of 24 hours… rat soup on the boil. Think fast before it burns or spills.

'Can you go outside, Sergio, away from Brando and the woman you're talking to? I need to talk in private'

'Sure, sure, my friend,' he said and in the background, 'Brando, do you want another drink? I have to go outside to hear this call…get them another drink.'

The loud buzz of pub activity receded. Deare could sense the Grafton street night around Sergio now. 'What's up, my friend? You are very popular today.'

'Sergio, how come you text me a message…you don't use text?'

'No, ees true, but the gerl in the pub did it for us because we were trying to find you and you weren't answering your phone.'

'Ah, so she sent the text from her phone?'

'I suppose. I never noticed.'

'Who is this girl? Have you seen her before? What did she say about Sarajevo? She didn't mention Tito, did she? Jaysus, did she ask for me?'

'No, no…at least I don't think so. She was sitting at the bar on her own so we started talking to her in between trying to contact you so she suggested we text you. She's an Irish gerl, a nurse, dark and pretty, just your type.'

'What did ye want me for that was so urgent?' Deare asked.

'Well, there have been so many enquiries about Tito today we're thinking of starting an answering service… and to top all that, Viktor's gone missing.'

'Viktor? The kp from your place…Tito's mate? How do ye mean, he's gone missing?'

Sergio filled him on the day's events - 'everything's got a queer turn today,' he told him.

'It's not a good idea to get on the wrong side of that Heels. He'sa bad news.'

'You said a mouthful, mate. I don't like the sound of this girl in the pub either…too many things happening to be coincidence. I'm going to stay offside. I need to get the diary done and I need to get home. I'll call you or Brando later.' He hung up and noticed he'd missed three calls.

ALL ROADS LEAD TO...

Bernard Nolan was getting more than a little annoyed with Deare. ' Bastard won't answer his phone,' he thought, 'strange for a hack. Those fuckers live by their phones.'

'Do you think he's in trouble?' Toscic wondered.

'I don't know,' Nolan snapped, venting his frustration, 'That's the worst part of this. I hardly know why I'm calling him. And I bet he doesn't either. Or who we are.'

Being methodical was the only way to proceed in police work, Nolan knew but it was easier said than done.Things were moving like scenery on a Bullet train. Nolan decided a pub to pub trawl of inner city Dublin would be no use.

'Connolly and his crew are after Deare already. They'll be checking the same haunts. If he's aware of someone searching for him then he might have some notion of the danger he is in. He must go to ground. He's gone home.'

He resolved to stake out Deare's Donnybrook apartment on the basis that if he wasn't there already he'd certainly go there, sometime. Meanwhile they would check on Sgt Farrell. Maybe Deare has contacted his pals in Coogan's.

Orla Farrell focussed all her attention on the wandering

hands and eyes of Sergio. The Italian's's main interest were horses, women and food though not necessarily in that order. She suspected the call he received was from the elusive Mr Deare. Sergio had gone outside to finish the conversation on the pretext that the reception and noise in the pub were too much for him to hear. He made no reference to the call when he returned and Brando made no enquiry.

She wondered whether, in Deare's interest, it was now time to break cover and find out his whereabouts. She wished Nolan was there. Her phone rang as though on cue. Answering, she stood up and left the pub, in the same direction as Sergio, gesturing to the noise and her ear.

'Sgt Farrell, can you talk? Has Deare showed up?'

It was Nolan. 'He called his friend back but I don't know what was said and I don' t know where he is. He hasn't turned up here and I don't think I'm going to get anything out of his two pals unless I blow my cover…'

'What does your instinct tell you, sergeant? I'm inclined to think if he has called his friends then they've told him about today's comings and goings and that includes us. Time is running out and we must get to him before Connolly or Heels…'

'I think we should tell them…'

'I agree, sergeant, but wait until we get there. Our appearance might   convince Brando we mean business. Don't be fooled by the dopey image, those boyos can hear the grass grow. Hold tight, buy another round.'

Heels was beginning to doubt Deare existed. This will o' the wisp had slipped through his hands at least twice already. And Dublin can't be big enough to get lost forever. Or so he thought.

There were a handful of trendy spots in the city

favoured by Deare and the people he wrote about. He had already covered the most popular hotel and pub haunts like The Bailey, Cocoon and the Horseshoe Bar in the Shelbourne. He'd tried Café en Seine, Ron Black's and Samsara, a triumvirate of 'superpubs' standing alongside each other on Dawson St.

They were all stuffed to bursting point. The smell of booze and stale smoke was rivalled only by the intense fug of expensively perfumed body odour. Belly topped hairdressers, makeup artists and models vied for space amongst slick suited auctioneers, estate agents and accountants. The music was loud and the drinks, potent. But Heels could find neither hide nor hair of Deare since the tipoff from the bouncer at the Velvet Slipper.

I might, he thought, return to Coogan's to check in with his drinking buddies there. That was a possibility although Heels knew if he had been in contact, he'd surely have been warned that someone looking for him. The only other possibility was that he'd gone home.

At least there he knew he'd be safe and it wasn't just Deare he was looking for : it was the package he had got from Tito that day – the package that could hang them all. Yes, thought Heels, he'd go home. Now all he had to do was go and get him.

Garvan Deare instructed the taxi to pull up in Donnybrook village, giving him a five minute walk home. He had no intention of going straight to his own front door. The day's events made him cautious but he had an ace in the hole and her name was Sandy Nelson.

Sandy's cell phone must have been sitting beside her as she answered before the second ring.

'Sandy?' her television blared in the background. He could hear the theme tune of 'Friends.'

'Houl' yer turn,' Sandy snapped as the muffled scramble suggested she was rummaging for the remote and probably cursing the caller at the same time. Garvan knew she was an avid tv fan and her evening began with a bottle of Rioja, a tv dinner and Emmerdale.

'Who's that?' she asked.

'Sandy, it's Garvan…I need your help,' he blurted, 'I'm sorry for disturbing you. It's the American sitcom time of your evening but throw a blank one in your VCR and hit record, there is work to be done and dirty deeds afoot.'

Half a dozen loud heartbeats rumbled before there was any response.

'Jeeesus…Garvan? Well, I'm very well, thanks, how are you? Slow down a wee minute, take a deep breath and start at the beginning…what are ye talkin' about?'

'Look, I can't tell you the whole story on my mobile… I'm around in Donnybrook village but I need you to collect something for me and bring it here…and don't mention me to anyone…if they ask.'

'Who? Ask what? What do you want me to bring you? What the fuck is all this cloak and dagger about? …'

Garvan told her where Tito's package was hidden. He asked her to get it, conceal it in her handbag and then meet him in Ciss Madden's pub in five minutes. He told her that under no circumstances was she to talk to anyone, tell them where she was going and, above all, who she was meeting.

'Roger, boss, I'm on my way,' Sandy replied huskily and joking 'I will be wearing a grey raincoat, dark sunglasses and a Hermes silk scarf depicting scenes from Ascot but how will I recognise you? Garvan?... Garvan?'

He was gone.

NO KIDDING A KIDDER

Sandy Nelson wasn't easily spooked. She enjoyed a good ribbing too. But something about the tone of Deare's voice, what he said and the way he said it gave her cause to think. She had grown up aware. Her father was an RUC reservist and carried a Government issued pistol at all times.

They routinely checked the bottom of their car with a broken wing mirror tied to a broomstick and never answered the front door without using the intercom and cameras guarding the entrance of their modest semi-detached home in Ballymena. Growing up as a teenager she had travelled to Belfast or Portrush every weekend for the clubs and the craic. She, nor her friends, ever forgot the code of watchful behaviour ingrained in their lives, no matter how wasted they got.

She found it hard to relax when she came to Dublin first. Before the salon offered her a job as a colourist in their first Dublin branch she'd never been further south than Bangor. But there are people from home working in Dublin now, she thought, it mightn't be that bad and anything's better than this shite. So, though her first months were spent getting used to the buses, the price of food and the Dub-a-lin accent, she found a flatmate and they'd explored the city together.

Now she lived alone and was comfortable with her own company. She'd ventured out into the world of night classes, the singles' alternative to nightclubbing. She tried yoga and pilates but discarded them as fads. Then she discovered Krav Maga, an Israeli martial art that was more akin to street fighting. Sandy took to it like a duck to water. It was based on instinct, finding focus in fear and danger and using those to help you react effectively with force and aggression. After her first course she felt she had control of her new life. She found herself letting go of the old cautions as though she'd shed a skin.

She hadn't forgotten though. Sandy turned to the bay window of her basement apartment before she opened the door. She did it without thinking until she found herself reaching gingerly for the corner of the heavy ceiling to floor curtains that surrounded the half moon shaped alcove. Without pulling the curtain aside, she reached her hand along the wall near the door and switched off the living room light so the room was dimly lit by a standard reading lamp on a low coffee table near the fireplace.

The sound of an unexpected car engine, an unscheduled ring of the front doorbell, a car door shutting, strange voices in the street outside, all of these things awoke an instinct in her to be cautious and prepared for imminent danger.

It was that same instinct that seized her now. She eased the edge of curtain back a fraction and scanned the walled garden, the car park and the parked cars protected by the tall electronic gate. She could see nothing. She could hear voices or maybe one voice on a telephone. She couldn't risk opening the door or pulling back the curtain any further without drawing attention to herself.

There had been some comings and goings upstairs tonight what with Garvan arriving and going out again and then the two men who called downstairs to ask about him after he had left the last time. Then there was his phone call. Was he having her on? she thought, before dismissing the thought. There was something wrong.

Right, she told herself briskly, time to get your skates on, Miss Nelson.

Her first thought was to call Deare and ask him again did he know who was looking for him and why?. He was very vague on the issue the first time around. She dismissed the idea as she thought of it. This time he would just be evasive. Blood would flow from a stone sooner than Deare would talk, once his mind was made up, she figured. What she didn't need was half an hour of his evasive bullshit because sound enough as he might be for keeping his mouth shut, he couldn't tell a lie to save himself.

Sandy switched off the lamp. The light could not penetrate the thick curtain but she was glad she'd turned it off as she could hear the footsteps of a single person – leather soled – clack their way down the granite stone steps.

Holding her breath she crept to the facing wall and pressed herself tightly to it. The footsteps stopped outside her window, three low steps above the basement level. She imagined a foot poised in mid-air. She held her breath and struggled to stifle a giggle as she reminded herself of the shoes. It was a game she'd always played, listening to footsteps and imagining what they were wearing. It made them human, she thought. And they're probably boots,

Chelsea style.

Another footstep fell on the garden step. The tone is deeper, she noted, descending, waiting, listening, watching. She told herself to breathe slowly and evenly. The last two steps darted light and skipping. He's got his ear to the window, she thought.

The doorbell released a trickle, a dot of pee in her panties. Christ, she thought, close to giggling nervously, fuck you, Garvan Deare, for scaring the living pee out of me.

The doorbell rang again. She didn't move. She didn't breathe. She tried not to think. The figure outside was listening silently, she knew. This is my game, she thought.

After less than half a minute, thirty seconds, three thousand nanoseconds, the boots turned and their footfalls receded, ascending the garden steps slowly, silently. At the top of the steps they stopped and turned. Whoever it was waited and listened again in silence. She didn't move. She listened.

The crunch of gravel on the pathway to the car park galvanised her into action. She leapt across the darkened room and yanked the chord that would close the curtains at the rear of the house. The foot crunch got louder as the leather boots descended the steps to the rear and the pathway overlooking the Dodder river flowing ceaselessly below and past the house.

This time she pushed herself against the back wall of her living room to the right of the window. Now the entire apartment was in darkness apart from the thin sliver of moonlight and the cooling floodlights from the rugby ground behind that give the damp night air a ghostly shine. She felt him lean into the window, squinting for a gap in the curtain or a glimpse of movement through the uncovered kitchen window.

Fuck, Garvan Deare, she thought again, 'that could be one of my friends paying a visit,' dismissing the idea as soon as it formed – 'my friends would phone first to see if I was in.' 'And they wouldn't go creeping about the house, ringing doorbells and squinting in windows without a peep out of them..They'd call my name. I'll fucking murder that Deare boy, ten ways from Sunday when I get my hands on him.'

The gravel crunch settled into a grind as though Leather Boots was trying to twist his way underground through the loose gravel. She could feel the sash window rattle as the prowler bent his knees, took a grip on the top sash and tried to shake it loose. She kept all her windows shut through force of habit but if he had half a wit and a good penknife, she thought, he'll be in the window in a second.

She cast her eyes about the gloom of her living room for something heavy to protect herself. Nothing came to hand but a recent hard back edition of Larousse, the French cookbook she borrowed from Garvan and couldn't understand. But the book was heavier than a phone directory and sure to make an impression on any intruder, she thought, long enough to make a getaway. The window rattled again and there was a pause. She heard a cell phone ring, then a voice.

'Yeah, boss, no…no…there's no sign of him here. I'm round the back of his house to see if I can get inside to have a look around. He might have been here earlier and left it behind him. Anyway, it would be better to be here waiting for him…to give him a surprise, like…hehehe.'

Boots' voice was harsh with a shiver of cruelty. That's a welcome party Deare could do without, it occurred to

Sandy. The rattling resumed. She heard the snap of a switchblade and became aware of its scraping and probing in the gap between the sashes. She tiptoed across the room, leaning over the sofa to snatch her snowboard jacket, absentmindedly patting the pockets for her cigarettes and lighter.

She left the living room door ajar as she stepped into the hallway. The motion sensor light made her gasp as the hallway lit up, its glow, she knew, penetrating all the way to the back of the flat and the kitchen window. She could trace his crunching scramble along the river footpath then turning, curving up the six steps to the car park and around the house to her front door again.

Gripped by the tattoo of approaching footsteps Sandy failed to notice the shadow fall on her through the frosted glass panels of her own front hallway door. She heard the shrill ring of her doorbell though. Frantic, her mind racing, in that split second she realised it couldn't be 'Boots'. She peeked through the door's spy hole and saw the same big man she'd made for a policeman earlier. Fuck it, she thought, he's still the best option. She opened the door.

'You again,' she chirped shakily, relief palpable in the tone of her voice.

'Sorry to disturb you again, Miss Nelson,' Bernard Nolan said, flashing his most charming and disarming smile, 'we haven't caught up with your neighbour, Garvan Deare, yet and we were wondering if you've seen or heard from him yourself. We are very anxious to talk to him.'

'Look,' she began, at first defiant and bolshy. Then Nolan noticed a hint of anxiety cloud her face as she peered into the garden's darkness, beyond his left shoulder, 'why…why don't you come in for a minute? I was just getting ready to go out so maybe we can walk together to the corner.'

Nolan noticed the look. It spelt fear. Something had spooked this girl and very recently. That afternoon she was prepared to show them the door without ceremony. Now she was a rabbit caught in someone's headlights. Sandy stepped back inside her flat. Nolan paused, turning to Toscic who had stood behind him during this exchange, he indicated, with a nod to the garden and the car park that he wanted the space checked out. Then he turned and followed Sandy Nelson inside.

'Miss Nelson…'

'You're a cop, aren't ye?'

'Wha…where did…?'

'Don't bullshit me, mister, ye can't kid a kidder. I clocked you for 5-Oh as soon as I clapped eyes on ye…'

'I don't know where you got…'

'Right, if you're not a cop you can turn around and fuck off right now…and if you are, well, you can fuck off anyway…on principle.'

Sandy regretted what she said even as she said it. She flashed Nolan her most winning smile with just a soupcon of contrition.

'I'm sorry,' she said, 'I was just in a bit of a hurry and everything's up in a heap and along come you fellas three times in one day asking about my neighbour…'

'Three? This is only our second time here…has someone been here before us?'

Sandy appeared to ignore Nolan as she peered anxiously in the direction of the darkened pathway that lead around the house to the river wall. Nolan followed her gaze.

'Miss?…Sandy…was there someone here already?'

She liked the sound of her name in his voice. She liked the sound of him. And the look of him. 'Lord Jesus,' she thought, 'listen to me. I've just had the wits scared out of me by noises in the dark and I'm getting randy thoughts about a peeler. They never told me this about the Free State.'

'Hang on a wee minute, now. You're very good at asking questions…almost as good as you are at avoiding them… mister…are youse cops or not and what d'yez want wi' Garvan?'

Nolan turned and walked away from her, stepping slowly, crouching and silent, towards the side of the house and the garden pathway where Toscic had gone two minutes earlier.

'Fine…don't answer…', she pouted.

Sandy shut up as Nolan raised his left hand in the air to indicate hush. Her rebuke had been half hearted anyway. Nolan figured Toscic hadn't gone for a moonlit river walk and the path around the house should have taken less than a minute.

With the floodlights shut down from the rugby grounds across the river the back of the house is in pitch darkness, only the first two steps of the pathway were visible in the gloom of hedge and shrubbery.

Crouching low, Nolan eased his pistol from its shoulder holster and gently slid the safety into the fire zone. The absolute stillness in the air made the river's trickle sound like a torrent. He waited to let his eyes settle in the gloom, listening so the torrent sinks into the background hum and his ears could pick out other sounds.

He whispered 'Ivan?'

Ivan replied, 'shhhhh.'

Nolan realised the Inspector was crouched behind a

forest of shrubbery just three feet from him on the other side of the first step. Squinting in the gloom, they established eye contact. Toscic raised his left eyebrow and tilted it down the pathway into the darkness. Nolan motioned for him to stay put and quiet, using his flattened palm and the forefinger of his right hand held to his puckered lips. He eased himself backwards, crouching, holstered his pistol and returned to Sandy who was standing in the archway below the front stairs, her body slightly crouched, like theirs as though standing upright might be heard or noticed by whatever they were concealing themselves from. The problem was, thought Nolan, we don't know what it was. She does.

'Miss Nelson…'

'Sandy.'

'What the fuck is going on here? One minute you're telling us to fuck off and the next you want us to stay…is there someone hiding at the back of the house?'

'Look, five minutes before you two showed up someone rang my doorbell and I didn't answer. I don't if I'm not expecting anyone and no-one has called to say they're coming over…old habits die hard and fools die faster… anyway, I don't think he went away…I heard his footsteps around the side of the house to the river walk. Then he had a go at opening my window…'

'Did you call the police?'

Sandy smiled. 'There didn't seem much point with you two at the door…'

Nolan didn't respond so she continued, 'I was going to call them but I wanted to get out of the flat first…with him around the back I figured I'd have enough time to make a run for the road and then I could dial 999…and that's where you guys came in…'

'Do you have a torch?'

She ran in to fetch the RUC torch from the cupboard under the sink in the flat's tiny kitchenette. It was made of thick vulcanised rubber. She handed it to Nolan who took it wordlessly and turned away again. This time he didn't hesitate. As he reached the first step of the descent to the garden wall he turned on the torch's full beam and strode with purposeful determination down the path, the torch's beam sweeping the shadows. Toscic followed closely.

'Is there anyone there?' boomed Nolan as he reached the end of the garden path. He swept the space from the low river wall on the left to the back wall of the house on the right, satisfied himself the coast was clear, then quietly to the still crouching Toscic, 'what did you see around here?'

Looking sheepish, Toscic explained, 'when I got to the top of the steps I had this feeling there was someone waiting in the shadows at the bottom of the path so I decided to wait and listen…perhaps I might flush him out…,' his voice trailed off, aware of the flimsiness of his explanation.

'Jesus, I hope you're not going to say you're afraid of the dark too.'

Blushing, the police inspector decided prudence was the better part of valour but knew his inaction had left him open to ridicule. All he could do was grin and bear it. He had no intention of presenting a have a go hero image to Nolan. He had other things on his mind.

'There's something up. That girl was spooked and if I'm no judge of character, it would take something to spook her,' Nolan told him as they turned for the front door of the flat again, 'by the way, she keeps asking if we're '5 – Oh' but don't let on anything for the moment.'

'5 – Oh?' Toscic asked, 'I don't even know what '5 – Oh' means?'

'Cops', said Nolan.

Toscic blinked uncomprehendingly at his receding back.

'Here's your lamp back,' Nolan said to Sandy, handing her the torch, 'there was no-one there. You should call the police just to be safe.'

'I think I'm safe enough with you two around and anyway, I was on me way out.'

'Can we drop you somewhere?'

'You never answered my question…are youse cops and why do you want Garvan?'

'That's two questions. Which one should I answer?' The flash of anger in her eyes told him she was not amused.

'No, we're not cops,' he said, anticipating her reply, 'we're journalists. We know Garvan. We're just here for the night so we thought we'd look him up and hit the town together…there's no better man.'

'Look, fuck off. Did no-one ever tell you ye can't bullshit a bullshitter? Forget I asked you anything and if I do see Garvan I'll tell him to take long steps around you two.'

'That could be a mistake,' he hesitated, measuring in his own mind how much she could be trusted, 'my name is Nolan, Bernard Nolan and this is Ivan Toscic. I'm a stringer for PA and he works for a paper in Sarajevo…'

'And I'm the Pope in Rome… what the fuck does that have to do with Garvan?'

'Ivan here's researching a story. He's in Dublin for a night or two and I'm just back for a break so we thought we'd hook up with the old Deare for the night…that's all,' hc could see she was struggling to believe him.

'Yeah, well, whatever? He hasn't been home, I haven't

seen him and I have no plans to either.'

Nolan hesitated. He knew she was lying but he wanted to keep her onside without giving too much away.

'Look,' he said, 'if you see him tell him we're looking for him. It is in his own best interest to get in touch with us, that's all I can say…and sooner rather than later. Here's my phone number.' He handed her a scribbled note from his notebook.

'No business card? I thought you hacks had those things to throw around like confetti at a wedding…'

But Nolan had turned his back on her and motioned Toscic out of the garden to their vehicle parked outside.

CLOAK AND DAGGER

Sandy watched their figures retreat through the garden gate before she closed her hall door. She turned off the hallway light and stepped inside her darkened living room. She waited ten minutes in the darkness, peering through a sliver of a gap between curtain and window, watching for movement in her garden and beyond.

When she was satisfied her intruders had all left, she rummaged in her closet for the grey raincoat and the Hermes scarf she promised Garvan she'd be wearing. Grinning, she chose a pair of green tinted Gucci shades from a sideboard and stuffed them in her pocket.

She left through her front door again, pausing long enough to reach inside and turn off the outside hall light triggered by her movement. In the darkness she groped around for the housekeeper's key and inside the pitch dark shed, fumbled about for Deare's package, hidden, as he described it, in a flower pot.

Like most things about Garvan Deare, she thought, his instructions lacked substance or detail. '*There's more flower pots in here than the Chelsea Flower Show.*'

Sandy wasn't sure if she should risk phoning Deare or

just go on rummaging in the dark and risk drawing unnecessary attention to herself. Not for the first time she asked herself, '*What, in God's name am I doing?*

There's Garvan, coming over all cloak and dagger, even scared when I spoke to him on the phone. There's only one thing for it, she thought, *get the package, bring it to Deare and get to the bottom of whatever he's got me involved in.*

Sometimes I'd like to ring his neck, she thought, *or make him a bowl of chicken soup.*' Sandy was aware of her mixed feelings for her neighbour. Garvan had been a good friend to her since she arrived in Dublin but there had never been any hint of attraction.

She knew she was anxious for him but now she suspected her concern meant more than she was prepared to admit. It took at least five minutes of rummaging about in the darkened shed before she found what Deare had been asking for, a brown manilla envelope stuffed between two earthenware pots.'*Garvan, ye'd be lost without me.*'

Anxious to get going she stuffed the package under her jacket and beneath the elbow of her left arm, locked the shed door and replaced the key in its hiding place.

WET FEET

Gerry Heels wasn't happy to wade across a river in pitch darkness. His brand new **R.M. Williams'** boots, 'a high quality, hand stitched, all leather comfort experience,' as the salesman described them, were sodden and ruined. To top that he ripped a gash in the knee of his designer jeans as he clambered up the steep bank of wet clay on the other side. He wasn't sure why he'd had a go at the window of that basement flat.

The night had been frustrating and he was losing patience with his quarry, Mr Deare. His short fuse was ignited when the hall light came on. Whoever was in the flat had been listening to him. They'd heard him ring the doorbell and ignored it. *They must have something to hide.* The sound of voices had stopped him in his tracks. He crouched beside a thick clump of leafy shrubs against the metre high river wall. He soon found the drop on the other side was closer to three metres.

In the gloom he hadn't a clue who was there and believing in living to fight another day, he froze, motionless, as one of the men scoured the garden pathway. Then he slipped silently over the garden wall into the river when the coast was clear.

LONG SHOT

Nolan and Toscic stepped through the gateway, onto Anglesea Road. The night was dark, the rush hour traffic long gone and, save for one old man and his dog, shuffling familiarly from one lamp post to another, there wasn't a soul on the street.

Bernard Nolan didn't utter a word until they got to the hired car, parked less than 50 metres from the front of Deare's apartment.

'She was lying. She knows where he is. That girl wouldn't spook too easily and something spooked her. Did you see anyone 'round the back of the house?'

'Not a soul but it was very dark, very silent…apart from the river, of course. It looks like a nice place to live…'

'Never mind that…I don't like it. We have to find Deare because the longer he's floating around the less our chances are of finding him before …wait a minute (whispered hoarsely) get in the car…'

Toscic ducked his head instinctively and tugged at the yielding door handle on the passenger side. He slipped inside the car and closed his door as gingerly as Nolan had closed his.

'Look…that's yer woman, Sandy. She said she was going out…I wonder where she's going? It's a long shot but if you're drawn even in the dying minutes of an All Ireland final, a long shot can be your best bet…let's follow her.'

'OK,' said Toscic, restless and preoccupied, wondering, again, what the hell Nolan was talking about. He exited the car as quietly as he'd got into it. Nolan's door stayed shut. Ivan bent down and peered through the window, inquiringly.

'Are you not coming?'

'I am but I'll follow in the car. If she gets on a bus or grabs a cab, we'll need the wheels. Besides, it's easier for one man to follow her than two.'

Nodding, Ivan turned and slouched off in the same direction Sandy had taken. It occurred to Nolan he was looking at a different person. 'He's an odd fish,' he thought, fondly, 'one minute he's wet behind the ears, the next minute he'd scare the living daylights out of you.'

It occurred to him he didn't know much about his Bosnian friend. He had always taken him at face value. There was a strong bond of friendship between the two since that first night they had met in Nolan's bar. He missed those days. Working in Sarajevo had been a mind opening experience. The bar had become his life because he felt he had left nothing behind in Dublin and landed in the Balkans like Prospero in The Tempest.

'Ivan's like me, maybe,' he pondered, 'pretending to be someone else as though his real self or the life he was leading might be so depressing or disappointing, there'd be little reason to get out of bed in the morning.

Ivan came to Nolan's to investigate him. The Irishman was under no illusion about that but they had forged a friendship based on mutual respect, he figured. But what does Ivan know about me? he wondered, for as green as the young cop might like to appear, Bernard suspected there was more to him that met the eye.

The loud ring of his cell phone jerked him back to attention. He looked at the glowing screen. It was Toscic.

'She has turned right at the bridge and is heading towards a village…'

'Donnybrook.'

'What? I don't understand…'

'The village? It's called Donnybrook…stay with her. If she goes into any of the pubs down there don't follow her in. Stay outside, out of sight and call me back.'

Nolan dropped the phone before Toscic could reply. He started the car engine, checked his rear view mirror and pulled out.

Ivan Toscic watched the car drive away. Time to make that call, he thought.

CISS MADDEN'S

Garvan Deare's anxiety had not diminished since he sat in the corner of Ciss Madden's. The pub was a dingy annex to the much larger Kiely's bar. It came straight from the country shebeen style with pictures of old sporting heroes, cardboard ads for Sweet Afton and a swing bar over the gas fuelled 'open' fireplace.

That night, Madden's was stuffed. There was a big football match on, a European championship game and it appeared Manchester United were in with a chance of taking the title.

Deare wished he'd paid more attention to the football banter in Coogan's as sitting there in the middle of these pundits made him stand out like a foxhunter at an anti-bloodsports rally.

Donnybrook remained a village and strangers were noted. His was a familiar face but not on football nights. But most significant of all to Deare was the Garda barracks across the street, one of the biggest in the area. Off duty detectives and Gardai liked to enjoy a pint in Ciss Madden's and Deare wasn't sure if he should be relieved or more anxious than he was. At least the pub's smoky and overcrowded, he thought. He sipped his pint, casting surreptitious glances at the pub clock behind the bar.

'The only time I've seen you look that anxious, Garvan, is when you've a hot date or a hot story on the way, can I get you another pint while you're waiting?'

Colm Murray, Ciss Madden's manager, startled Deare from his jumbled reveries.

'Ehh…yeah, yeah, why not? Here, Colm, have you seen Sandy come in here in the past twenty minutes? I don't want to miss her in the crowd…'

'Oh,' said Colm, smirking knowingly, 'it's like that, is it? Playing a home game tonight, are ye?'

'No, no…I just told her I'd meet her here for a pint but I wasn't sure if I'd missed her, the place is so stuffed…' he improvised.

'I haven't seen her so far tonight but sure, why don't you give her a call? She could be in here and 'The Ould Orange Flute' is always a dead giveaway in a pub like this…'

Sandy loved to provoke and poke fun although Garvan thought her choice of ringtone sailed too close to the wind. Better than yours, Sandy always rejoined, that sounds like a vampire's wedding.

An idea occurs to him. I'll text her, he thought, and get her to hand the package to Colm.

'Will you do me a favour?' he whispered, as Colm put the fresh pint on the beermat in front of him. Colm rested his elbows on the bar and leaned in to Deare as he told him his plan.

Gerry Heels hated being wet. He took the utmost care to traverse the river without a sound. He knew someone had come around the house and waited silently in the darkness for him to make his move. He heard the first person's companion join him, heard their hushed, whispered confab and then decided to make himself scarce. This proved harder than he thought.

There was a three meter drop to the river but he was unsure of how deep it was in the darkness. Undeterred, he eased himself over the wall, forcing his body into the contours of the night, moving slowly and with caution. He was strong enough to lower himself into the water and splash as silently as his cushioning knee bends would allow.

His timing was immaculate. The glow of a torch hit his fingertips on the wall just seconds before he released his grip and dropped into the cold chill of the flowing river beneath. Crouching, he held his breath as a voice directly above asked 'Is there anyone there?' Something about the voice rang familiar in Heels' mind.

He waited five minutes, crouched and soaking in the fast moving but mercifully low river, then waded gingerly to the opposite side. From there he groped blindly in the undergrowth to reach the bank and made his way to a gaping gap in the wire fence of the sports club on the other side.

Happily for him, there were people playing floodlit tennis; the lights helped steer him back to firm ground again.

OULD ORANGE FLUTE

Sandy was whistling The Ould Orange Flute before she realised her phone was ringing. By the time she dug it out of her handbag she had missed the call. Then a text message appeared. It was from Garvan.

'Nter K's,
Giv pkg 2 Colm.
Sit at bar n hav a pt.
Leev thru CM's.
meet me in Mad's.'

This boy is really laying it on, she thought, as she opened the door to Kiely's and felt the full on waft of a rugby night in Donnybrook; beer, smoke, puke, peanuts, crisps and testosterone. She slipped the sunglasses into her handbag and battled her way to the bar where she could see Colm had spotted her before she, him.

'How're ye, Sandy?,' Colm said, planting a vodka and Red Bull in front of her, 'have ye something for me?'

Sandy produced the thick envelope from the inside pocket of her jacket and put it on the bar without a glance. At the same time she struggled to get her wallet free of her handbag.

'It's ok,' Colm said, winking and in the same movement, picking up the envelope, 'that's paid for already.'

She didn't know whether to make any further comment but decided against it. *Garvan's paranoia has me jumping now*, she thought, *wait'll I get my hands on him*

She stopped herself peering furtively at the faces in the bar. It was match night and all the usual suspects were there; the young, off duty policemen with their blue ties discarded, shirts unbuttoned; rugby players from the club next door, their training ended; rugby groupies, with green padded bodywarmers and their sunglasses tucked into their hair, discussing men and shoes.

Her phone beeped again, another message.

'Njoy ur pt.
Tanx 4 pkg.
W8 10 mins,
leev thru CM's,
up lane n cros
at Mads.
C u soon.'

TRACKING HEELS

Ivan Toscic hung back as he trailed Sandy. It was a quiet night and a clear, cloudless sky spread out above him. No breeze ruffled the silence, broken only by the occasional bus and the kids chatting noisily as they wrenched open their bags of chips from the local chipper.

He noticed she walked with a purpose in her stride. Only when she arrived at the door of Kiely's bar did her pace change. She paused long enough to scan the street ahead and behind her, long enough, too, for Toscic to duck into the gateway of the rugby club. When he was sure the coast was clear again he rang Nolan who told him to wait where he was while he parked the car.

Miss Nelson, he told Nolan, has been in the bar for the past five minutes. Nolan had decided its time to confront her. He had already called Sergeant Farrell from the car. Deare had failed to materialise in *Coogan's* so she had begun a trawl of the local nightspots.

'It's a hard job…' she quipped.

'Yeah,' he laughed, 'those are the breaks…are you sure you'll be alright on your own now, Sergeant, you don't want me to send young Toscic around to hold your hand?

He'd be good cover for you…'

'I can handle myself,' she replied, abruptly, regretting her anger immediately, 'yeah, maybe, whatever? I suppose he needs to learn his way about…'

Nolan, amused at her confusion, put her at her ease.

'Don't worry. I'm keeping him with me for the moment. He's doing my legwork and he's not a familiar face.'

'Neither are you anymore when you come to think of it.'

'Yeah, well that's not entirely true and in our game absence doesn't make the heart grow fonder. If Connolly or one of his stooges spots me they are likely to get suspicious. Anyway, O'Brien wants this operation kept under wraps which means I don't want to be spotted by any cops, either. The important thing is to get hold of Deare. Then we might know where we stand.'

Nolan said, 'I'll call you back,' and hung up. Orla Farrell frowned. Bernard Nolan was brusque but rarely rude. *Something must have spooked him*, she concluded.

It was the sight of Gerry Heels stomping through the rugby club grounds and directly towards where Toscic stood waiting. Nolan didn't pause when he reached Toscic. He took his left elbow in his right hand and steered the young Sarajevan inspector round the corner and off the main road where he turned his back to the approaching Heels as though the pair of them were engrossed in a deep conversation. As Heels walked right by them he failed to notice the two men. But they took a good look at him, together noticing the sloshing noise as he passed and the trail of wet footsteps he left in his wake.

'A fiver gets you 50, there's your mystery man from behind Deare's house,' Nolan whispered, 'that, my friend, is Gerry Heels, scumbag extraordinaire and a dangerous bastard to boot. We'll follow him but I don't want him to see you with me so we'll stay apart.'

Nolan hung back while Toscic slipped into stride several paces behind the sodden Heels. 'Just stay near him, watch him and don't engage him in conversation,' were Nolan's parting words to Toscic as he dodged across the road at the pedestrian lights.

NOAH

Ivan Toscic measured his desire to stay close to Heels with his need to keep an eye on Deare's neighbour, Sandy Nelson and found a balance was out of the question.

From where he stood though, there was a public phone and with one eye on his quarry he rooted around in his pocket for change. He found a coin and with one last glance across the bar he picked up the receiver and dialled the number he had been given. After three rings his call was answered. 'Speak,' the gruff voice on the other end began. Toscic whispered in a measured tone, 'you've been expecting a call from me. My name is Noah.'

'Noah' was the codename he'd been given. Mossad might be the world's most effective secret service, he thought, but sometimes they lacked subtlety.

'Yeah,' the voice on the other end of the phone said, 'I got your earlier message. I'm on a job right now, keeping an eye on your man. There is no movement so far but you should keep in touch.'

'I will call you again in an hour.' He hung up. Toscic knew his first priority was Sandy Nelson.

Ivan Toscic was recruited as a Mossad agent in 1993

when Sarajevo was in the grip of war.

He wasn't entirely happy with the way things were proceeding. For a start, his departure from Sarajevo was too sudden to put anything in place. To add to his problems his contact in Dublin failed to materialise. His phone was off the hook, out of service or engaged. He left a cryptic message and hoped it was enough to hook them up together.

Ivan hated living a double life. Living a double life in Dublin was going to be even harder. He knew no-one apart from Nolan, O'Brien and Orla Farrell and they could know nothing of his secret mission. The job in Dublin was a rush job and that was all he knew. He had a contact in Dublin but all he had was a phone number.

Ivan Toscic was Jewish through his mother. But Ivan Toscic knew nothing of his Jewish blood until he was in his 20s. His parents were an unorthodox pair who had first met were they were studying archaeology in the University of Istanbul. Neither was overtly religious. Ivan's father was a young academic idealist. He was born and raised in Sarajevo where his family were academics and, strangely for that city, anticlerical and secular even though their cultural and social background was drawn from the tightly knit Bosnian Orthodox community, a tiny minority in the Muslim dominated Bosnian capital.

Ivan's mother was from a devout Sephardic Jewish family that could trace its origins to the 16th century pogroms inspired by the Spanish Inquisition. They had fled from Portugal at the turn of that century and had made their way to Istanbul with the help of friends. They settled and, despite hardships, had prospered.

There had never been contact between Ivan's Jewish family and the Toscics in Sarajevo. Ivan's father met his mother on an archaeological dig in the Negev desert. Both enthusiastic academics, they devoted their time to the countless archaeological sites that dotted the Sinai and Negev. They married during their undergraduate days while living on an Israeli kibbutz, harvesting avocados to finance their desert studies.

Ivan was raised by his paternal grandparents in their Sarajevo apartment close to the University sector of the city. He had little or no memory of his parents. His mother had died in a bomb explosion in the centre of Jerusalem when Ivan was just seven years old. The blast took six lives including his mother and five others travelling to work. His father lost his right arm and his leg below the knee. He retired to an academic post in Sarajevo, secured by his family as a comfortable sinecure. But he never settled and never recovered. He died just two years after the tragedy - of a broken heart, his family said.

Ivan returned to his paternal grandparents in Sarajevo with his father and was raised by them even after the death of his father. He grew up with little information about his parents. What his grandparents said of their death in Israel was limited to some perfunctory information about their dedication to research - the only redeeming quality they could find in a son's willful defiance of their wishes. He could have taken a professor's seat in Sarajevo, such was his academic brilliance. But instead he insisted on taking an international scholarship offered by the American Rockefellar Foundation and had completed his studies in Istanbul and field trips to Israel. Ivan's mother was never discussed and the child never asked about her.

Ivan's grandparents raised him in the Orthodox church. He had no inkling of his mother's Jewish tradition. His memory of the first seven years of his life as a desert rat living in camps with his freewheeling parents, playing rough and tumble games with Bedouin children, was a blur.

But when Yugoslavia fell apart and all the old divisions of family and religion emerged, the violent divisions between Bosnian Serb and Muslim began to appear and before long between Muslim and Christian families in the city that had lived alongside each other peacefully for at least two generations.

Stevie Jackson, the American he met in the second year of his legal studies in Sarajevo was the first real live Jew he ever met. Stevie told him his own family split when his father moved to Israel while his mother retired to Florida.

'He believes it's his duty to live out his days in the birth home of his ancestors. She says it's safer to send them money. Leave the war to the younger generations,' Stevie used to laugh.

He wasn't laughing the day they called him aside and told him his father was dead. A West Bank settler, he was shot by a Palestinian sniper. His friend's grief affected him so profoundly it surprised him, shocked him. Stevie left Sarajevo to bury his father's remains in Israel. It was almost ten years before they would meet again.

Ivan Toscic left his undergraduate studies to join the police, against the wishes of his grandparents. The bitter and prolonged siege of their native city was also Sarajevo's finest hour as many of the city's prominent people, regardless of their birth, risked their lives and the lives of their families to defy the sectarian scourge called ethnic cleansing in favour of a common ground bred by their common citizenship.

The war had been a bizarre introduction to the world

of law and order. The police service had been largely Muslim though there were some Serbs in suburban barracks and a tiny number of Christians like himself in the city but the service had, for all intents and purposes, fallen apart as a security force as the war progressed. Many members left through circumstance or family and joined militia groups on either side of the conflict.

Only a small handful stayed, Ivan included, to fulfill their jobs of protecting and preserving the law, such as it was. In the end all they could do was keep an eye out for snipers, help clear the debris and the carnage caused by suicide bombs and mortars. By the time the war was over Toscic had investigated more suspect deaths than he'd issued parking tickets.

CLOSE TO TOUCH

Sandy Nelson knew the man standing beside her in Kiely's bar had some direct connection with the events unfolding. She knew because the tiny, gingery blonde, hairs on her arms and neck stood on end; because there were alarm bells going off in her head and because the strange young man dressed in black, beside her, his left thigh pressed against her right, was soaking wet.

She didn't know because she had no logical reason to believe it and because the paranoia generated by Garvan and the night's unfolding events had left her nerves frazzled and because none of the evening's events made any sense to her. She didn't know it but she felt it. She believed in coincidence.

Now she needed to gather her thoughts and put her antenna on full alert. She had felt this before and it went back to all those times at home when a car stopped in the road or there was an unexpected knock on the door.

You learned to trust the instinct that told you when you were in danger. Now she was feeling all those things. And she was on a high state of alert. She had no intention of drawing attention to herself by talking to this man but she noted his appearance and demeanour.

'A cup of tea. Black,' he muttered tersely to Colm, the barman. He was dressed completely in black and his long black hair was tied back in a ponytail. He had a Dublin accent, she noted.

The heaving bar gave them little room and they were close enough to touch each other. Sandy realized - though she felt confident about herself - a woman alone is easy prey for a single male on the loose. She strived to become invisible and wished to Christ she'd brought a book or a newspaper with her.

Colm arrived with the cup of tea and, as money and goods were exchanged, Colm nodded in the direction of her near empty glass and asked, 'are y'all right for a refill, Sandy?' Looking up, Sandy smiled and said 'yes', drained her glass, slid off her bar stool and made her way through the throng to the ladies' toilet.

When she got there she marched straight past and around the other side of the half moon bar to a smaller doorway leading into Ciss Madden's. It was even more stuffed than Kiely's. There were a few familiar faces but she ignored them and headed straight through and out the back door, her anger with Garvan Deare rising.

PIGEON

The handwritten manuscript sat in his pocket like a child crying for attention. Garvan Deare nodded to a couple of faces from the RTE newsroom as he collected his pint and sat in a quiet booth under an arch in Madigan's bar.

He wished to be alone while he gathered his thoughts. First things first, he had the Diary to get together before he could even think about finishing the letter. But he knew he disagreed with himself even as he thought it.

He swept his gaze casually but attentively around the room before producing the package. '*If Sandy's suspicions were correct*', he thought, '*this may not be the place to start reading. Sandy, Christ*', he thought, '*I'm forgetting about her and she's on her way here*'.

Sandy Nelson burst through the pub's side entrance on cue. She spotted Deare immediately, despite his efforts to find himself somewhere secluded to sit. *Somehow*, he thought, observing Sandy's demeanour, *that would have been impossible*.

'You've some explaining to do, Garvan,' she began, 'my flat is under siege by anonymous prowlers with wet boots and trousers and cops posing as journalists asking for

218

you….what the fuck is going on?'

'And why all the fucking cloak and dagger, the text messages, the mystery package…who the fuck d'ye think y'are? James Bond? Mine's a vodka and Red Bull, by the way…make it a double.'

Deare's mind was racing. *Where to start, what to tell.* He wasn't sure himself and he certainly couldn't answer half the questions she was asking him and who or what is the prowler with the wet boots and trousers? He got up to buy her drink and avail of some thinking space. Returning to the table, he saw Sandy had calmed down, fixed her makeup, lit a cigarette and crossed her legs. *She's ready to listen*, he thought.

'And, hey, it's good to see you, too, Sandy…' he began.

'Don't fucking start me now, Garvan, I saw you earlier and there was no ingrown hair up your arse then…'

'Ok, ok,' he began, 'first, I want to apologise for getting you mixed up in this…'

'Mixed up in what? That's the real question…I've not felt that scared since I was living at home in Ballymena and I didn't know what I was scared about…at least up there you have some idea of what's going on…'

'And I also want to thank you for all the help you've given me this evening. You didn't have to…'

'And…,' Sandy stopped the rest of her tirade in its tracks. She could see the distress, confusion and even fear in Deare's eyes. She changed tack, touched his hand and said gently, 'just tell me what's going on.'

Placing his head in his hands and rubbing his eyes, Deare began, 'y'know, that's the problem…I'm not sure myself. This all began when I wrote a letter from a pigeon…'

Anticipating her reaction he puts his hand in the air to

command hush and continues, 'it all began in Coogan's…'

Then he told her about Tito and the wounded pigeon, and how a postcard he'd written reached Sarajevo in the pocket of a dead man. He told her about the day he had had since Tito's package was handed to him; about the contents of the diary and the strangers who were looking for him. He told her about Gerry Heels.

'I know who that is,' she interrupted, ' that's Leather Boots…I've just seen that bastard. He's over in Kielys with his trousers soaked from wading across the river behind our building. He's not a nice looking piece of stuff. And I ran into the other two again although this time I was glad to see them…what are they after and why you, for fuck's sake?'

News of Heels' proximity brought a flutter of panic to Deare. His eyes, Sandy noted, had taken on a haunted look. '*He's not cut out for this*'. She thought.

'The other two - the big fella's name is Nolan. He's Irish and he seems alright. The other one's name is Toxic or something. It was foreign, anyway. He didn't say much, Nolan did all the talking. They're cops, for sure, although they claim they're journalists.'

Deare listened and wondered *why*, if Sandy Nelson believed two of his pursuers were cops , *their search was not more official*.

'That's a good question, Garvan, but it's not one I could answer. In my experience, cops can be a law unto themselves and sometimes one arm doesn't know want the other to know what the other is doing, if you catch my drift.'

He didn't but he knew enough about Sandy's background not to question her intuition on these matters.

'Maybe it's best we keep all this to ourselves for the

moment 'til we know who or what we're dealing with?' Sandy suggested .

The lights of the pub dimmed as the barman called for last orders. The new late closing hours were a blessing for those who were fond of a leisurely pint. No rush, no fuss, drink up at your own pace or bugger off somewhere else.

'Look, Sandy,' Deare said, draining his drink and sliding to the edge of the booth 'thanks, again for everything you've done. I don't want to get you involved anymore than you are. I've gotta get out of here…'

'Sit yourself down, ferchrissake, you're not getting away that easy. We'll get another drink because I want to hear more and you look like you could do with it.'

Deare looked at her and as he thought about the day's events a wave of exhaustion swept over him. This shit, he realised, is too big for him and the need to confide in someone had become a painful, hollow ache inside. One more furtive sweep of the room, Deare produced the package addressed to him that had arrived the day before from Tito and planted it on the table before them.

'The answer, as far as I can work out,' he said, 'is in there.'

REDHEAD

'A cup of tea. Black.'

Gerry Heels seethed with anger. There was little chance of finding Deare until later but he was unsure now if he should stake out the journalist's apartment or resume his trawl of the city.

There was a chance Deare would show his face and one of his spies would let him know. *There were enough of them wanting to curry favour with the boss,* he thought. But that could take all night. Deare might have twigged there were people on his trail so he was keeping his head down.

'There's your cup o'tea. And milk n'sugar, that'll be 80 pence, please.'

The barman's arrival disturbed his thoughts. Preoccupied with his own thoughts he handed over the change in his pocket and barely noticed when the barman asked the lone redhead on the stool beside him if she was okay for a refill. She said 'yes' and then got up and walked off through the crowd.

'Sandy', the barman had called her. *'Sandy…Sandy…'*Heels tried to shake the name that had invaded his thoughts. *'Hang on….Sandy…that was the name on the post*

222

box of the basement flat below Deare's…Sandy…Thompson? Henderson? No…Nelson…Christ…nahh, it couldn't be her…too much of a coincidence. No harm in asking.

He'd like to know why she'd pretended to not be at home while he was trying to climb in her window. It wouldn't do any harm to ask her when she gets back. He could pretend to know a friend of hers or something.

But after waiting another ten minutes and watching the ice on Sandy Nelson's drink melt, Heels became convinced she was not coming back and even more convinced he was onto something. He caught Colm the barman's attention and waved him over.

'Yessir, another cup that cheers…?'

'No, thanks…here, that girl who's sitting here,' he gestured with a flick of his thumb, 'she wouldn 't be Sandy Nelson by any chance?'

Heels got his answer from Colm's guarded evasion.

'Who?…eh, I don't know…I don't know her surname… just Sandy…doesn't look like she's coming back anyway… you've lucked out tonight, mate'

Colm swept Sandy's unattended glass from the counter and turned away, 'yessir…what can I get you? Three pints of stout and a pint of rough…coming up…'

Heels didn't care if he was lying; he had his answer. It was Nelson and she must have recognised him to have left so abruptly. Draining his cup of tea he left the bar in the same direction she had gone.

LOST SCENT

The bar, close to closing time, Toscic guessed, reached a frenzy as customers strain to catch the eye of the bar staff. In the throng he could just make out Sandy's head and its lustrous red colour from where he stood near the door.

Heels was standing beside her although there was no apparent recognition.

He watched Sandy rise from her seat and head in the direction of the rear of the bar, where she rounded a corner and he lost sight of her. He presumed she had gone to the toilet and maintained his vigil on Heels who was leaning over chatting to a barman.

Five minutes passed before Heels headed in the same direction as the girl. Ivan hesitated. He had no desire to blow his cover by marching through the bar in pursuit. He felt hamstrung by the conflicting needs to keep an eye on both parties and not lose contact with Nolan who was waiting in the street, a block from the front door of the bar.

The hesitation was enough for him to lose contact with both subjects. Being unfamiliar with the territory, he was unaware of the adjoining bar at the rear and its doorway into an alleyway behind the pub.

Five minutes went by before he decided to squeeze his way through the crush of drinkers. First he checked the 'gents' but there was no sign of Heels. And when he continued through the bar, around the corner where he had lost sight of Sandy Nelson, he realised there was another bar and another way out.

Gerry Heels knew he'd lost his quarry when he stepped into the lane at the back of the pub. *There's at least five directions she could have taken*, he thought, *and it's too much of a long shot to go chasing. Best to get the car and watch Deare's apartment from the street.*

He kicked a can along the lane as he walked. His car was parked on a side street near the rugby grounds.

REGROUP

Sandy Nelson took one look at the disheveled package Deare dropped on the table and right there and then, decided to take control.

'Right, first things first,' she announced, sweeping the folded, crumpled envelope into her handbag, 'we must get this, someplace safe, where we can read it and decide on our plan of action.'

The look of relief in Deare's face told her she'd said the right thing. *He's not cut out for this'*, she thought again.

'Sandy,' he said, 'I don't want to get you involved anymore than you are already and I'm sorry you've been dragged into it this far.'

She could tell what he was saying was not what he meant. 'Away on wi'ye,' she told him, 'sure I'd be sittin' watching shite on the telly or doin' me nails. This is more fun.'

Then, more seriously, 'the one thing is we better not go together in case any of them boyos is still out there. My place is probably the best bet and you know where the spare key is…I'm goin' to the toilet 'cos I'm burstin'…you go on and I'll meet you there. You better take the short cut and get over the wall of the car park. I'll fetch a pint of milk and some biccies.'

Sandy sensed Deare was at breaking point. She turned when she heard him say her name as she opened the toilet door. 'Yeah?' she asked the forlorn figure before her.

'I want you to promise one thing…if anything happens to me you must call Brando.' Then he turned and walked away.

Bernard Nolan was not amused when he heard Ivan Toscic's news. *Still*, he thought, *there's not much point in losing it with him. How was he to know?*

'Stay where you are. I'll come and pick you up outside the pub. I want to call Sgt Farrell and see how she's getting on. We'll have to put a watch on Deare's place and hope we get lucky…time is running out. We may have to blow our cover and bring in the locals…' He hung up.

PEAR SHAPED

Caution and paranoia had taught Garvan Deare only
fools rush in. He poked his head out of the bar and
checked the street in both directions, before stepping out
into the night.

Satisfied the coast was clear, he headed off, slumped
and hunched, in the direction of his apartment. He stared
at his feet and looked at no-one. *It's how they do it in the
movies*, he thought.

He wished it was a different day, that he'd never met
Tito (if that's his real name) and he cursed every fucking
bird in Christendom and the day he was persuaded to
write that postcard.

He worried about the newspaper diary he had yet to
write and didn't see the car emerge from the side street
until he found himself teetering, in mid-stride, from falling
on its gleaming, black bonnet. But his momentum
betrayed him and he pitched forward across the car,
banging his knees along the way. When he turned he
found himself staring into the beshaded eyes of Gerry
Heels.

Sandy Nelson didn't notice how quickly the receding

figure of Garvan Deare had disappeared from view. His hunched figure had been in sight when she entered the local convenience store. But when she emerged from the shop he was nowhere to be seen. It didn't strike her as odd until she reached the door of her own apartment.

Bernard Nolan wasn't happy about losing Sandy Nelson and Heels in the space of the same ten minutes. Things were rapidly going pear shaped and they were no nearer Garvan Deare now than they had been four hours earlier.

'Call Orla Farrell,' Nolan barked at Toscic, 'tell her we'll pick her up at the top of Grafton street in ten minutes.'

LOW SUGAR

Heels pulled into the wire and concrete fenced yard of the disused dockland warehouse, flush with confidence. As he swung the sleek Mercedes into a corner parking spot, he ran through his triumphant arrival in his mind's eye.

He'd give it loads of 'it's-all-in-a-night's-work, boss' as he dropped his human booty at the feet of Joe Connolly. He couldn't suppress the strut as he sprang from the big car's cockpit and strode, keys jangling loudly, to the car's trunk.

Deare will be a pushover, he thought, *after a few slaps he'll be singing and the boss'll soon have this mess behind him..* And it would all be on account of him. *Once more*, he thought, *he delivered for the boss and he'd be well rewarded for it.*

But as he swung open the trunk door and peered at the curled body of the unconscious journalist something about the inert figure gave him cause for alarm.

Garvan Deare felt the first flush of diabetic disorientation while he was sitting in Madigan's with Sandy Nelson.

It was a routine feeling and it came with the same familiar baggage: first, his peripheral vision began to play tricks as though what went on outside his sight line was happening at a different pace. The skin on the back of his hands gave him a pins and needles sensation that spread to his lips, tongue and mouth.

The third stage was unpredictable. It could come half an hour after the first began or might tumble straight after it or worse still, all three stages could happen simultaneously. All he could ever rely on were the first signs and that's when swift action was needed. In the third stage he would lose control of his motor functions, stagger and gibber.

Deare left the pub with the intention of going straight home to gorge on a feed of brown bread, hummous and fresh fruit. The combination had always worked the trick for him, a combination of simple and complex carbohydrates. But all that was academic now.

He hadn't made it home. Instead he woke in the dark, smelly confines of a car boot with a splitting headache and the realization that holding onto a coherent thought had become as tricky as picking up raindrops from a petal. The terror induced by his circumstances, the pain in his blood caked face and the hypoglycaemic symptoms he displayed, were accelerating him towards a full blown diabetic turn. He could neither see to think nor think to see.

He lost horizontal and vertical control as his thoughts flew by like waste in a sewer. On top of that he could feel the approaching dim, envelop him, like a concrete waistcoat. He was only aware of the door opening because of the faint waft of fresh air. His eyesight was clouding, failing.

GOING NOWHERE FAST

Orla Farrell felt the thrill of familiarity as she strolled up Grafton Street on her way to meet Nolan and Toscic on St Stephen's Green.

The night people of downtown Dublin transformed the streets of the city when the day people closed their shops and offices and went home. Street performers vied for attention along Grafton St as revellers, party people and night folk plied their way between the bars and clubs, cinemas, theatres, restaurants, coffee houses and the fast food joints that competed noisily for their custom.

Dublin had changed even in the short time Orla Farrell had been away. Since the Celtic Tiger dug its claws into the remains of a national culture that had begun to show the first signs of rending asunder as early as the turn of that decade, change became a daily event.

By the mid-'90s the new prosperity was showing in the designer clothes, the new cars and the rising property values. It could also be seen in the headlong rush to hedonism as though prosperity had cast off the invisible restraints and a new Ireland emerged, brightly clad and brimful of a confidence bordering on arrogance.

Clubs opened to cater for this new, active society that believed in their inalienable right to party as hard as they worked. Orla remembered it because she had been part of it for almost a year, immersed in the coke 'n' yoke fuelled, alcohol bingeing madness of the Dublin dance culture that embraced hedonism as a misplaced birthright.

In a year, working undercover, she danced and partied with the best and the worst of them and it left her with an appalling void in her being. At the back of her mind she had the job but even with that safety net she sometimes felt, after a long night of excess, that she was freefalling into nothingness.

But she stayed focussed. She tracked and stalked her man, stage managed the slow, deliberative process of evidence gathering, and surveillance while simultaneously working her way to his side, as a trusted aide. There were whispered locker room questions about just how deep she had penetrated the drug dealer she nailed. She dismissed it as professional jealousy.

Strolling the short distance between Coogan's and the top of busy Grafton St, Orla watched a Chinese woman in a red velvet waistcoat dance around a two speaker sound system, oblivious to the drunken ridicule she was generating.

She had time to consider the state of their investigation; going nowhere fast. She dismissed it as soon as she thought it.

She wondered what Ivan Toscic made of it all; what he made of Dublin or what he made of her. She couldn't deny she had feelings for the handsome young Bosnian although what she knew of him was precious little. She was cautious by nature and profession yet she felt attracted to him.

She wondered again about Bernard Nolan and why he had left Dublin. It was a question she often asked herself but had never managed to ask him, even through six months working together in a foreign city.

He was more than a boss and a mentor to her. He was the big brother she'd never had but there was a darker, more secretive side to him she could never penetrate. He was happy in Sarajevo and if he wasn't the copper she knew he was, she figured he'd be happy running Nolan's Bar , where he could carry on his intrigues and be lord of his manor.

The Dublin street life intruded on her thoughts. A half naked black man breathing fire, limbo danced to the clubbed up sounds of Bob Marley, singing '3 O'Clock, Roadblock' for an audience flanked by a band of street urchins, eyes wide open and alert to the pickings. I can see them like no-one else in that small space sees them, she thought.

She already spotted the proliferation of public and private closed circuit surveillance cameras, multiplied since she'd last been here.

From a distance, on the other side of the street, she saw a group spilling from the Michelin star restaurant on the top of the 'Green, flush with rich food and the smug satisfaction that comes from farting through silk.

Sergeant Farrell had time to reflect on all this as she walked the distance to the corner of Harcourt St for her rendezvous with Nolan and Toscic. In between thinking of Dublin and how much she missed it.

WHERE'S DEARE?

Something was wrong and Sandy Nelson was scared. Pausing at the bridge, she craned her neck in a futile attempt to see around the bend in the Dodder, where the contours of its banks, backed up to her apartment building. She shrugged and laughed to rid herself of her paranoia.

I*'m made of sterner stuff than that*, she thought but didn't believe. She felt her legs get weaker and her breathing was strained. She leaned against the wall and closed her eyes to summon some strength. She hadn't felt this way for such a long time and in a very different place.

'*Wise up*,' she scolded herself, '*you silly bitch, get it together*.' And with that she strode purposefully towards the gate of the mock Georgian apartment building, self consciously fingering the manuscript of Tito's letter as she fumbled in her bag for her keys. Then she remembered Garvan was already inside although there was no sign of light or movement.

She tapped her fingernails lightly on the living room window, the same window her previous intruder had rattled earlier. She tapped again when there was no reply and softly whispered Garvan's name. There was no response. A cold chill stabbed her between the shoulders. In the darkness, she groped for the spare key in its hiding place and felt the same stabbing chill when she found it, '*Garvan,*' she thought.

Inside, Sandy turned the Chubb lock on the door of her apartment, checked the windows and curtains, turned off the lights and closed the door of her bedroom. Inside she flopped down on her bed with just her bedside light for illumination.

'*Now the shit has really hit the fan,*' she thought, '*Garvan should have been here holding a steaming, fresh brew for me by now.*' She toyed with the notion of calling Bernard Nolan, the big Irish cop who had called earlier. Then she dismissed it just as quickly. She thought of Garvan's last words to her and for a moment she was tempted to call Brando.

But as she fished in her handbag for her cell phone her eyes fell on the package Garvan said might hold the answer to this unfolding mystery.

She realised that, whatever else she might be dragged into, whatever she might have to deal with, she would go no further without understanding what all this was about. Arriving at a decision, she kicked off her Air Nikes, fished her cigarettes from her purse and lit up. Settled, she pulled out the crumpled package she had taken from Garvan.

HUNGRY

Orla Farrell toyed with the idea of calling Nolan to get an update on what was happening. She couldn't shake the notion there was something amiss.

On the other hand, she thought, *Superintendent O'Brien thought it warranted enough attention and secrecy to bring the three of them all the way from Sarajevo.* She was staring at the cell phone in her hand when it rang, startling her.

'Hello?'

'Sergeant Farrell? Is that you, Orla?'

Tommy O'Brien caught her off guard. She never expected calls from the brass at this hour of the night.

'Yes sir, it's me. Sergeant Farrell, sir.'

'Relax, Orla, I'm just calling to get an update on your investigation…. Is Bernard Nolan with you?'

'No, sir, he's not with me right now but I believe he's on his way to pick me up. I don't know why his phone isn't answering, sir, he called me twenty minutes ago and told me to meet him.'

'Yes, well, never mind Nolan, for now. It's you I want to talk to…where are you, exactly?'

'I'm at the junction of Grafton St and St Stephen's

Green, sir. I'm waiting for Chief Inspector Nolan to pick me up.'

'That can wait. I want to see you, first. Tell Nolan to carry on and he can link up with you later.'

'But sir…'

'No buts, stay where you are. I'll pick you up in two minutes.'

Orla stared at her phone after Tommy O'Brien had hung up. What is that about? she wondered as she dialled Nolan's number.

'Sorry, Orla,' Nolan answered, 'we got delayed …there's still no sign of Deare or his letter and we're not the only one looking for him. We spotted Gerry Heels in Donnybrook…'

'Sir, I've been told to tell you to carry on without me. Superintendent O'Brien is picking me up.'

'What? You can't be serious…when did you hear that?'

'Just before I called you. He told me he had tried calling your phone but you weren't answering…'

'Fuck him. What's his game? Did he say what he wants you for?'

'No, he didn't. He just said he'd pick me up and that you were to carry on and I would link up with you later.'

'If he was trying to contact me I had my phone turned off. Deare has to work tonight, he has to write his diary… now, does that mean he has to visit the newspaper office or does he send it in by email? My bet is email but we better cover all the options. Orla, when you're finished with O'Brien, contact the newspaper office and try to find out how Deare delivers his copy. There's an outside chance he might turn up there. I'll send Ivan back to Coogan's to see if you can get some background on Tito…'

'Yes, sir,' Orla replied, 'where will you be if we want to

contact you?'

'I think I'll pay another visit to Ms Nelson. I've a feeling she knows more than she's letting on…'

Orla couldn't help smiling when she heard Bernard Nolan's plan. This Sandy Nelson must be some woman. She put her phone back in her purse as the Superintendent's car pulled up beside her.

'Are you hungry?' Tommy O'Brien asked her as she slipped into the passenger seat.

Orla realised she hadn't eaten all evening and said as much, she was so surprised at the enquiry.

'Good,' O'Brien said, 'I'm Hank Marvin' myself. There's a late night Chinese on South King St called The Millennium. It's just around the corner and has great Chinese beer. You'll love it.'

Orla Farrell didn't know how to react. This night continued to turn up surprises.

'It sounds great. I'm starving too.' '*For information,*' she thought to herself.

INERT DEARE

Gerry Heels wasn't smiling when he opened the car and found Deare's inert figure. The stench of stale booze reminded him of his father. More gruffly than he intended, he seized the prone body of the stricken journalist and hefted him out of the car, banging his head off the swinging trunk door. The yard was empty but for a wall of stacked pallets and three empty freight containers, locked up and standing in a row. Heels noticed, with relief, that his boss's car hadn't arrived so he had a chance to find out if he'd have to make Mr Deare disappear before he got there. He dumped Deare on his behind with his back to the door while he fumbled in the dark for his key. Deare slid to the ground despite Heels' efforts to keep him upright with his feet while he turned the key in the lock.

'Right, let's get you inside,' he mumbled to himself, hoisting the journalist under his armpits and dragging him with his legs trailing between his own, into the gloom of the cavernous warehouse towards a tiny office in the corner to the left of the door.

Once inside, he nudged the light with his forehead and pulled a chair towards him with his foot and slowly lowered Deare into a sitting position. He recognized the journalist from his picture in the newspapers but only just.

His skin was the pallor of buttermilk with dark rings around his sunken eyes. His teeth were like tiny yellow tombstones against his skin. His lips were colourless and a thin trail of mucus and puke ran from the corner of his mouth to his chin. There was a wet patch of drool on his chest.

TRUST NO-ONE

Sandy Nelson read Tito's letter with growing uneasiness. It had been written in stages. Garvan Deare gave her a ragged outline but nothing prepared her for this.

'I had a freedom while I worked. But I soon realised I was slave like the others. Everyone had job and everyone had boss. In Bosnia people came to Ernesto from everywhere. Many travelled long distances. They were hungry and tired. Some had spent their money already. We took what they had and if they had nothing they were turned away. If they had a daughter, we took her. My first job was collecting that money and housing these people. To go further they needed papers and my boss gave me this job. I found out there details and wrote this information down and gave it to him. He took it away and came back with proper papers, passports and sometimes visas. This could take a couple of days. Sometimes it took weeks. When I worked for Ernesto, he used me to do his work. When the papers arrived those people were assembled for this next stage. We loaded them on trucks and they were driven then to the Croatian border. At each stage a new boss took over so I tried to make myself useful to every one that I met. I had no way of knowing who was big boss because no one else knew. There was chain. In my first year I learned how this worked; first, these people found a smuggler who would bring them to Sarajevo. They were paid by Ernesto for every truckload they delivered. He passed them on to the gangs who would smuggle them further. They were counted and weighed like cattle…

Tito achieved minor status in what was a very hierarchical and independently structured organization. On the smuggling level those being smuggled only ever met the smuggler, the bottom of the ladder. Three more levels followed from those who could liaise between smugglers and organizers to the national organizers and then the criminal masterminds, the big bosses whose identity was often a complete mystery even to those on the second level.

Sandy marveled at the sophistication of the organization Tito described. It was one with access to official documentation, travel papers, visas. No border was closed, no route untravelled. Nothing got in their way.

The entire saga read like an alternative world that existed in the shadows of the world as she knew it, a world that controlled the movements of people across the continent even more effectively than elected Governments and who paid no allegiances nor acknowledged any sovereign state.

' I do not hope to protect myself by writing this letter. But a record must be made. If only for history, Garvin. If I had another chance and I knew how my life would be I wonder would I do this again? I don't know. If I didn't then I would have joined the KLA if a landmine didn't get me. My life was no life and this …well, I got a life and if a life is made of memories then I have found good ones. In Dublin, in Coogan's where I had friends who would talk to me. History, you told me, is always written by the winners and if this is true then we will see who wins…'

Tito's letter came with a list of names of gang leaders, Sandy assumed and a list of addresses and phone numbers of safe houses, warehouses and whorehouses, all the places in every continent where they carried on their activities. The document was neatly typed and the lists ordered in straight lines assigned to names, addresses and phone numbers.

Most of the lists were indecipherable for Sandy but she assumed they would make sense to someone. They would certainly make a lot of sense to the police and the authorities fighting their activities.

The letter, much of it, like the lists, neatly typed, outlined a life of misfortunes and misadventures that might have echoed those of many other refugees and immigrants tossed about by the Balkan turmoil of the past decade were it not for Tito's self confessed involvement.

But what most intrigued her were the hurriedly scrawled notes on the back of the lists. These looked more urgent and less calculated.

She read, '…Garvin, my friend, you must trust no-one…even the police. I have come to Sarajevo to find my sister, Irina. She has become involved with the wrong people and her life is in great danger. I have never been entirely truthful with you, my friend, perhaps because I told so many lies I didn't know the truth myself, anymore. One thing I learned about lying is always mix with the truth and keep as simple as possible. That is easier to say than to do when you come from where I come. It is true I am Albanian but I am a Kosovan Albanian. If that means anything to you then it must mean war. Our family was from Pristina, a city broken by the demands and needs of all who claimed her: Serbs, Croats, Kosovan Muslims, Albanian Kosovans, Bulgarians: take your pick. Our family was split up in the early days of the war of 1998. I left our family home long before that but my sister, when she turned 17 fled to Sarajevo in her wish to reach me somehow in Ireland. Our contact through the years was seldom but I tried to keep in touch with her to let her know where I was. Many of the lies I told for her sake because of my shame for what I became. She thought I was running a bar in Dublin when I was sloshing pints for a wage by night. Irina made her way to Sarajevo and in the way of young girls, alone in a city like that, found work as a 'dancer', she says, in a back street club. In her letters to me she tried to sound hopeful about her life but she could never lie to me. In her last letter she confessed her unhappiness and all the truth spilled out on the pages to make my soul wither with shame. When she told me she had vowed to work against those who employed her, I was beside myself with a helpless fear and despair. Then she told me she feared for her own life and I knew I had to act. She said she was involved with an Irish policeman working undercover in Sarajevo and she believed she had been discovered. I was fit to peel the skin from my own hide. I knew what they do. I felt helpless. Irina wrote about this Pigeon in Dublin and I knew of this man. She wrote of a far darker force behind The Pigeon and his crew but she never told me what she meant. This is why I go to Bosnia. I must find her. She said there was a traitor. She would be betrayed by the very people she thought she was working for. As I've said, if you get this letter then they've found me and I have failed. My life has never amounted to anything but dear sweet Irina believed in her useless, lying brother. Now she is dead, I fear. She wanted for me to meet this Irishman who would help us, she said. But now she's gone. You must help me avenge her. The Pigeon killed her just as sure as he pulled the trigger himself. She knew she was in danger but she warned me 'Trust no-one…'

Sandy Nelson was so engrossed in the story she was reading she barely felt the cigarette ash burn her fingers. She ignored the loud ringing of her doorbell until whoever was there began banging loudly on her living room window.

'Jesus,' she cursed to herself, 'who is it now?' She jumped to her feet, upsetting the ashtray on her thigh, tipping its contents into her lap and on the new multi-coloured throw she'd just bought in the Habitat sales.

'Miss Nelson, it's Bernard Nolan,' a voice called from the other side of the window, 'I know you're home…Miss Nelson, if you can hear me this is important…please open the door.'

A thousand questions and no answers chased each other around Sandy Nelson's mind. She recognized the voice of the big peeler she'd met earlier. Her first instinct was to flatten herself against the wall to the left of the living room window where Bernard Nolan stood on the other side. She held her breath. 'Trust no-one.'

She held Tito's letter tight to her chest, mindful of her need to get it out of sight at all costs. Ducking, she crept back across the living room into her kitchen and grabbing an open packet of cornflakes, stuffed the letter inside.

'Who'd you say you were, again?' she asked, playing for time.

'It's Bernard Nolan, Chief Inspector Bernard Nolan…

if you look through your letter box I can show you my ID...we can't afford to waste any time, Miss Nelson...your friend Deare could be in very real danger.'

Sandy opened the hallway door gingerly and peered through a crack in the letter box at the Garda ID. Everything appeared to be in order. She slid the dead bolt on the door, turned the mortice lock key and snapped the door latch open.

'Have you found Garvan? Who took him? Where is he?'

'No, we haven't found him but we thought you might help us find him...what did you mean 'who took him?' Look, I haven't been entirely honest with you...I am a policeman and we need to find your friend, Deare...he doesn't know the danger he's in...it would help us and him if you told us where he is...'

Sandy Nelson sized up the big Irishman. *Tall and probably handsome once...if he lost a stone or two...eyes brimming with mischief, intelligence, understanding and pain*. She felt herself warm to him which confused her all the more. *Garvan's not here and the letter says 'trust no-one' but suppose he's in real trouble...maybe this big cop can help*?'

Nolan interrupted her thoughts.

'Ms Nelson, did Mr Deare mention anything about a letter he was carrying?'

Her shutters fell again just as soon as he spoke. 'The letter, that's what he's after...?

'What letter?'

'Well, we believe your friend has been sent a letter that might be of interest to some very unsavoury characters. They're after him but we want to get to him first...'

'What's in this letter that's of interest to them or you?'

'We're not so sure what's in it because we haven't seen it but we have good reason to believe there are people out there who would kill for it…'

'Look, Chief Inspector, I don't know where Garvan's gone and he never mentioned any letter but, even if I did know where he was, , you'd be one of the last people I'd tell…you come around here claiming to be someone you aren't, then you won't tell me who you are when you're asked a direct question and now here you are again and this time you're a policeman looking for my help telling me my friend's in trouble…'

Sandy felt herself choking. The fear that had gripped her since she last saw Garvan had grown into a paralysis of funk since he failed to turn up at her flat and then she read the letter. 'Trust no-one,' she thought.

'I've given you plenty of reasons not to trust me, I admit. God knows, I'm not so good at trusting people myself…it's a sort of occupational hazard…in my job, sometimes, I don't know whether I'm coming or going even who I am or supposed to be…but I think I know you. I think I can trust you. If I knew everything all this was about then I'd tell you but I don't and the only way I'll ever find out is by finding your friend…'

She decided. 'I did meet Garvan since I saw you last. He was in Madigan's..well, he was in Ciss Madden's first but he thought I might be followed so he told me to get out of there…'

Nolan cursed quietly under his breath. They had been so close to finding the journalist; he cursed the secrecy that had hamstrung this search.

'…Garvan told me there were people after him but he couldn't tell me why. He said it had something to do with this Tito fella and that everyone thought he had something that Tito had given him that they all wanted…'

'That would be the letter,' Nolan said, 'the problem is,

we haven't seen it and we can't act until we do…we need to find Garvan Deare…do you know where he is?'

'No. I don't. The last I saw of him was when we left Madigan's. He walked ahead of me and I went to the shop to buy fags and milk. We were to meet back here…'

'And he never turned up?'

'No. He didn't…'

Nolan struggled to keep his temper even. He knew she was hiding something, 'Did he give you any indication of where he was going? Do you have any idea where he might have gone? Did he say anything to you before he left you?'

'No, no, no…', Sandy felt herself fighting tears of panic, anger and frustration. She stared back at Nolan defiantly.

'Why did you ask me 'who took him?'

NOAH, AGAIN

Ivan Toscic wasted no time in making contact again. He knew time was of the essence if his mission was to be successful. He found a phone booth and dialed the contact number again. This time the phone was answered after the second ring.

'Speak,' a slow, baritone voice intoned.

'It's Noah. Has our man moved?'

'Not a flicker so far. He won't stay long in Ireland. Things have become too hot for him here. The meeting between himself and Connolly was to happen tonight. My instructions were to get this package to you and after that you're on your own...of course, you understand, our support will be minimal and completely deniable?'

'I understand. I have to go to Coogan's...'

'We won't meet. The package has been delivered to your hotel room.' The phone clicked.

The 'package' was delivered as promised and Ivan Toscic quickly spilled the contents from the yellow padded envelope that had been tossed on his hotel room bed.

Ivan Toscic's work for Mossad, the Israeli secret service agency, began on a small scale. He gathered information.

As a police officer within a fractured state run, for the most part, by a Muslim population, he was ideally situated to gather ground level operational intelligence for Israel. No-one within his own organization in Bosnia was even remotely aware of these ties.

He became aware of his own Jewish background through his encounters with an American friend, Steve Jackson, during his second year at university. Jackson was an exchange student from New York spending two semesters - for overseas credit - studying criminology in Sarajevo.

Stevie's father lived in Israel and he paid him regular visits, he told Ivan. Toscic, in turn, told him of what he could remember of his childhood days on those archaeological digs with his parents.

He lost contact with Jackson until he paid a visit to his mother's grave while on a holiday visit to Jerusalem. Jackson had aroused his interest in what had happened to his parents and their misfortunate death. His grandparents had resisted his questions.

On that holiday in Israel there was a 'chance' encounter with Steve Jackson and his old friend, he told him, had moved and settled in Israel. Jackson wasted little time in probing Ivan on the purpose of his own visit and before long they renewed their old friendship enough for Jackson to probe him about his background.

When Ivan confessed his own suspicions Jackson laid his cards on the table and told him what he knew of his mother's Jewish heritage. Over the final four days of his holiday Jackson opened a new vista in Ivan's background that had long been obscured by half answered questions and evasions.

On his final day Stevie told him of his own work for the

Israeli state. He told him he worked as a recruitment agent for Israeli intelligence and made light of it in the same breezy style he'd made light of everything in their undergraduate days. But he planted a seed in Ivan Toscic, a seed that grew as his interest in his unknown heritage grew.

Less than six months later, Ivan returned to Israel to seek his old friend and offer his services. Jackson wasted no time putting him through a rigorous recruitment process. The people he worked for knew more about Toscic than he could have ever imagined. He was trained in the basics of spycraft, intelligence gathering and counter terrorism. Mossad had watched him since his undergraduate days.

Jackson's arrival in Sarajevo had not been an accident and neither had the 'chance encounter' in Jerusalem. They watched as he set his sights on a career in the Bosnian police and allowed his interest in his heritage to awaken gradually.

During the worst of the war between Bosnian Serbs and Muslims, when there was a complete breakdown of law and order and Sarajevo was under siege, Mossad took Toscic from his Bosnian home to a secret centre in the Negeb, in southern Israel where he underwent intensive training in covert ops, alongside other Mossad agents from all over the world.

The Israeli Secret Service was concerned by the increasing activity of radical Islamic groups in Albania, Kosovo and Bosnia. They traced the training of certain Palestinian extremists to camps in these territories. That awareness had led them to recruit their own independent intelligence sources within the same locations.

Although the investigation of human trafficking and

people smuggling had been shifted into the hands of international police organizations spearheaded by SFOR and the newly formed Europol, Mossad knew the criminal organizations relied on local support for the success of their operations.

The information Ivan could feed back to his handlers was of a low grade, local intelligence nature but just as his recruitment by them had been a long term investment so, they believed, was his value.

When he informed his handlers of the Tito investigation and the Pigeon connection it had lit up as many alert lights for them as it had in European police forces. The Pigeon's trafficking network, they informed him, was financed by those same Islamic terrorist groups who were running training camps in the Balkans and the network was being used to infiltrate terrorist agents into western Europe.

Toscic received specialist training as an assassin. He had already carried out three eliminations within Bosnia.

There was some debate amongst his handlers as to whether he was equipped for his first foreign mission. Those who championed him pointed to his familiarity with the case, his cover as a police officer. In any case, they argued, there would be no interference from their Irish contacts.

His target in Dublin was a roving Middle Eastern diplomat who had a base in the Irish capital. He was The Pigeon's contact with the Islamists as well as a handler for their agents in the west. He was also their fundraiser and banker.

His diplomatic status made him untouchable. Much of their funds were hidden in a network of shell companies under one corporate banner that banked its money and its operations through Ireland's Financial Services Centre. The funds were untraceable and the tax liability was negligible.

The target had successfully evaded intelligence services. His death was sanctioned by Mossad and no-one planned to get in their way. It was a black bag job and completely deniable.

The 'package' contained a loaded Glock 22 pistol, a spare magazine, a silencer attachment, an eight by ten glossy colour photo of a distinguished looking Middle Eastern man in his mid 30s. There was a single sheet of white paper with an address typed on it. He checked the weapon.

The Glock 22 was an improvement on the original Glock 17, a popular handgun, with law enforcement agencies and civilians alike, since it was introduced in 1990. It was a lightweight handgun because of its polymer frame but its .40 caliber Smith & Wesson bullets carried a wallop. The magazine packed 15 rounds and the gun's Safe-Action system made it the fastest, simplest and safest handgun available.

Pocketing the spare magazine, he pushed the gun beneath his belt in the small of his back and put on his overcoat. He picked up the photo of the man whose image was already familiar to him.

He produced a lighter from his pocket and set fire to the corner of the photo, dropping its smouldering remains into the toilet before he flushed. He read the address on the sheet of paper one last time, scrunched it up and threw it into the flushing toilet.

Before he left he took one final glance at the page he'd found in the hotel's A-Z. He gave himself a once over in the bathroom mirror, turned sideways to check his coat for evidence of a giveaway bulge and satisfied, he turned around, flicked off the light and left.

MILLENNIUM

The Millennium was everything the Superintendent promised. The rich aroma of Chinese sauces wafted across the street as they turned the corner into South King St. The restaurant had a plain black front with two glass windows and lacked the ornamentation of the usual stir fry, chop house.

O'Brien was greeted with familiarity when they got inside. He was solicitous and mannerly, introducing Orla as Ms Farrell to the bowing Mr Ho, the manager, as he led them to a secluded, corner table.

Smiling, Mr Ho asked if Mr O'Brien wanted menus or 'the usual.' O'Brien said he'd leave it in Mr Ho's good hands to give them the best the kitchen could offer at this late night. This apparently pleased the smiling, bowing Mr Ho who backed away then turned, barking orders in Cantonese and clapping his hands.

Orla hadn't spoken since they left the car. She hadn't managed to get out a 'hello' to Mr Ho. Instead, she simply bowed, as though nodding was catching. O'Brien behaved as though there was nothing untoward about this assignation. Orla noticed he had stepped behind her chair to help her sit before he took the seat on her right, facing the rest of the room.

'I hope you like Chinese food,' he appeared to state rather than ask. The truth was, the more comfortable he got, the less comfortable Orla felt.

'I do, sir, but…'

'No 'sirs', here, Orla. Please call me Tommy.'

'Yes, sir, er, Tommy. What have you ordered? I don't think I could handle a big meal and I'm still on duty…'

'You've time for a bite to eat. I've only ordered a light meal. I phoned Mr Ho before I got here and he knows what I want. We'll start with Hoisin sauced pork, just thin slices of marinated pork served with hoisin sauce on a bed of lettuce then a bowl of fish and clam soup followed by a dish of chilli beef with rice and fresh vegetables and we'll wash it all down with a few bottles of chilled Tsing Tsao beer.'

Orla was squirming in her seat, wracking her brain for an escape route. He clearly knew what he wanted and she hoped she wasn't the dessert that he left out of the list.

She remembered the conversation she had with him the day before she set off for Sarajevo six months before. Then, she got the impression he intended to pay her a personal visit in Bosnia and he'd spoken, mysteriously, of her being his 'eyes and ears'.

Since then she'd heard nothing from him until he met them in the airport the day before. Now, it appeared as though, his intentions were about to be revealed.

Mr Ho arrived, smiling and bowing, with an ice bucket on a tripod and four bottles of Chinese beer. The interruption gave her some respite as Mr Ho opened the bottles and poured each glass with a flourish before retreating.

'I don't know if I'll be able to eat all that but it sounds wonderful. You certainly know your Chinese,' Orla said, awkwardly.

O'Brien appeared to be enjoying her discomfort as he let the ensuing silence go on before he leaned closer and said,

'I suppose you're wondering why I asked you here?'

Orla inhaled some of her beer and broke into a coughing fit, sending a light spray of Tsing Tsao foam across the table.

He continued, 'you remember the chat we had before you left Dublin, six months ago? My work with Interpol and SFOR brings me all over Europe and I'm a frequent visitor to Sarajevo but I never got a chance to visit Nolan's. It's an important operation for us and Bernard Nolan is one of our most valued operatives. Unfortunately, the results, so far, have not justified the continued expenditure. I sent you out there with a view to getting an independent insight to what was going on. You have been, as I said to you before, 'my eyes and ears' there, Orla. I had intended to pay you a visit but this 'Pigeon' business has put more urgency into the operation…'

He paused as the food arrived. Orla's relief when O'Brien hadn't started professing his love and admiration for her was replaced by dismay when she realised he was, as she had suspected, asking her to spy on Bernard Nolan. Mr Ho stood on the side, watching attentively, as the hors d'oeuvres and soup courses were served. The fragrance of the dishes in front of her made her dizzy with hunger.

Mr Ho clapped his hands, smiled and bowed and he and the two waitresses attending, retreated again. O'Brien carried on as though they hadn't been there.

'You worked with Bernard Nolan in Dublin. You know

how he operates. He trusts you….'

'Yes, but, sir…'

'Tommy'

'Tommy. Are you asking me to spy on Bernard Nolan?'

'Orla, you're an intelligent person and a fine policewoman. You're a sergeant and you're ambitious. Bernard Nolan has been in this game a long time. He has a fine record as a copper, which is why we must ask why there have been no results from his investigations in Sarajevo? We've known this Pigeon fellow has links there for some time but we haven't been able to pin him down.'

'But that's why we're here in Dublin…'

'And what about Deare and his letter?'

'Ah, well, Deare, er, Garvan Deare, sir, appears to have disappeared.'

'Disappeared? What do you mean, 'disappeared' ?'

O'Brien's tone gave her reason to pause in defense of her boss, Bernard Nolan, but everything she could say appeared to land him in deeper trouble.

'Sergeant?'

'Sorry, sir…ah…Chief Inspector Nolan and Inspector Toscic have been at Deare's apartment but there was no sign of him and the neighbours had nothing to report. He's a night owl so we think he might just be out working somewhere.'

A silence followed and Orla imagined the Superintendent was mulling over what she'd just told him.

'And what about the letter, who has the letter?'

It was not the response she expected but she told him there was yet no sign of any letter. She recounted her adventure in Coogan's and the disappearance of the kitchen porter, Viktor.

'Well, we don't have it nor do we know where it is or

who has it until we find Garvan Deare so it looks as though he remains the priority, sir.'

'Clearly, Sergeant Farrell,' he snapped, indicating her cynical tone had not gone unnoticed, 'tell Bernard Nolan to call me before he does anything …'

'Sir, Deare could be in real danger if we don't…' Orla noticed he had stopped asking her to call him 'Tommy.'

'Thank you, Sergeant, I'll be the judge of that…there are other things at play here and you can serve best by doing what you're told instead of questioning my judgement.'

'Yes, sir.'

'It's Tommy, Orla. I'm sorry if this has been sprung on you in a manner that I hadn't planned but circumstances are now dictating our actions that are so far beyond our control. Two people related to this case were murdered last week in Sarajevo and Bernard Nolan and Ivan Toscic were both involved, one way or another. There may have been more deaths since, here in Dublin, and there could be more to come. I must be informed of everything that Nolan and Toscic are up to, is that clear?'

Orla nodded. O'Brien sat back and smiled at the smiling Mr Ho who had appeared with his two servers and salvers of spicy, aromatic chilli beef, jasmine rice and fresh, stir fried vegetables. Orla's appetite was gone. Her mouth was dry. She shifted in her seat and prepared to make her excuses to leave but before she could say anything, O'Brien spoke.

'I'm sure you have things to do, Sergeant. I'm sorry you have to miss the rest of this meal but there'll be another time, I promise. You have my number. Keep in touch.' With that he lifted the lid of the pot carrying the beef and held his nose over it with his eyes shut, ignoring Orla who had already risen to go.

NEED TO KNOW

Orla Farrell caught a taxi to the newspaper offices where Deare worked. She felt it might be more useful, if she put in a personal appearance there, to find out where the journalist might be. On the way there, she called Toscic and arranged to meet later in Coogan's. Orla had noticed the Bosnian's increasing edginess but assumed it had something to do with the unfamiliarity of his surroundings.

Something was not right about this entire operation but she couldn't put the pieces together. She knew O'Brien had a hair in his arse about Nolan but that wasn't a newsflash.

She phoned Nolan as soon as she left the restaurant. He asked her how her meeting with O'Brien had gone and she'd given him an edited version of what he'd said without mentioning the meal. He asked her if she had told them about the urgency of finding Deare and the letter.

'Yes sir, I told him all of that and he told me to do what I was told to do and don't question his judgement.'

She imagined Nolan smiling. 'Fair play to ye, Orla, ye haven't lost it…did he say anything else?'

'No, not really'.

Orla made a decision not to mention O'Brien's concern for the letter or his remark that 'there are other things at play here'.

Keeping the details of her conversation with O'Brien from Nolan went against the grain. *Undercover worked best on a 'need to know' basis but this was taking it to extremes,* she thought, *you can take 'ours not to reason why' so far and then commonsense kicks in. From now on, she vowed to herself, I'll be looking out for myself and watching my back.'*

At the rear entrance to the Evening News' offices Orla flashed her warrant card and asked the bored security man at the rear entrance to page the journalist for her.

'He's not here,' he barked gruffly after giving her credentials a cursory once over and then straightening the newspaper on the desk in front of him, as though to mark the end to their conversation.

Orla didn't budge and the man behind the window put his paper down again with an exaggerated gesture and said, 'he never comes in at night. He sends his copy in by 'phone…'

'Who does he phone? Perhaps I could talk to them…'

This time he heaved a sigh of exasperation.

'He sends it in by, er, electronically…with a computer.'

'Is there anyone from the Evening News working tonight?…this is urgent?'

Abandoning his newspaper, he scanned a list of names and telephone numbers on a time sheet pinned to a notice board on his right. Then he punched a four digit number into console in front of him and held the phone to his ear while keeping a beady eye on Orla Farrell.

The phone must have been answered as he stiffened and straightened visibly.

'Yeah…this is the back office security desk…there's a Sergeant Orla Farrell here looking for Garvan Deare… yeah, I told her that but she says she'd like to speak to someone from…she says it's urgent.' The last phrase dripped with jaded sarcasm.

'Right, right…'

The outcome of the conversation was clearly not to his satisfaction. He handed the phone to Orla through the sliding window, 'he says he'll speak to ye.'

'Hello,' she said, '…I need to find Garvan Deare, the Evening News' diarist…do you know where I might find him?'

'Is this official business, Guard, er, sorry, Sergeant?'

'Yes it is…but it's a private matter. I need to contact Mr Deare in person…do you know where I might find him?'

'He's usually out and about in the nightclubs at this hour…his copy won't be expected for another couple of hours…d'ye have his phone number?'

'Yes, I do but there's no answer and I've tried his home but he wasn't there…is there anywhere he is likely to be?'

'No…I wouldn't be able to help you there…I can try his numbers for you myself and give him a message for you?'

'I can't do that…I have to see him in person…is there anywhere you can think of?'

'Have you tried Coogan's? That's one of his favourite haunts…I'm sorry I can't help ye…now if you'd like to leave your number I can have him call you if I hear from him?'

'No…that's alright,' Orla had decided to cut her losses.

'If I am speaking to him, can I tell him what's it about…?'

Orla smiled and said 'thank you', handing over the phone to the disinterested security man. As she walked away she heard the phone ring again and the bored voice of the security man saying, 'no, she's gone. She never said.'

Calling to the newspaper looking for Deare was a calculated risk. Now she feared it might have backfired. Journalists, in her experience, react only one way when someone starts asking questions: they ask questions too.

As she walked away she was already dialing Bernard Nolan's cell phone number.

COLD FOG

Garvan Deare stands in a crowded room of faceless people. It's a long, wide room, with white walls. The ceiling is very close although from a distance it appears lofty and cavernous, distorting shapes and perspective. People shift about like a shoal of sardines. Deare tries to focus but he can't see their faces. He thinks his sight's failing, or the dull light is playing tricks. Occasionally, in the corner of his eye, he can make out a set of recognisable features, so he scrunches his eyes together and concentrates. Now he notices that for all this movement, he hears nothing. He tries to speak. He tries to reach out and touch someone. Nothing happens. He shuts his eyes and waits. When he opens them again the room is an empty blur.

Light from a street lamp filters through the grime of the skylight window in the ceiling. He's sitting on a swivel desk chair with curved, padded arms that has seen better days. The padding on one arm has burst and someone has idly stripped it back to its wooden base. He tries to apply pressure to his foot, in an effort to move the chair, but soon realizes it has no legs and the heavy metal casters have long since seized with rust. His arms hang, like a discarded puppet, off the sides of the chair. The knuckles of his left hand touch the ground.

The bare walls are painted an institutional, snot green, colour. The desk in front of him is painted two shades of gunmetal grey. It has a smooth, modern top of veneered chipboard.

Occasionally his mind slips into a giddy distraction, flitting about like the reflection of a shiny moving object on a ceiling. He knows the blow to the head has left him groggy but the dizziness comes from hypoglacaemia. He has no means to deal with it. He needs a quick sugar fix, a simple carbohydrate like a finger scoop of sweet jam, a Mars bar or an apple.

Sometimes, when these were not available he devises other means of maintaining his equilibrium and consciousness. One of these is minimal activity and slow but concentrated observation. So he studies the ripped and worn lino floor and notes the upside down coat hook on the back of the office door.

Then he hears a metallic click. He feels a slight breeze on his cheek but doesn't move. He can barely contain his excitement as he feels the recovery of his senses, sensation and sound. Someone's moving about nearby. He dares not open his eyes again. The sound is faint and distant, receding footsteps. He holds his breath.

When there's no further sound and he can feel nothing else apart from that fleeting cold breath of moments earlier, he lets his eyes relax so the light seeps through his eyelids. He can see the room has changed. Or was this the room of his dream? Concentrate. Breathe. He's slumped on a chair in a tiny empty office. The cavern has gone and so have the faceless people.

He doesn't move. He waits while his mind reacquaints him with his body. He's drained and exhausted but relieved he can still wiggle his toes in his shoes. His fingers send him contact signals. He can feel the trail of black, sticky blood on his face and the searing ache where his head has been struck, not once, he thought, but several times.

Disoriented, sore and tired, he sits motionless, struggling to gather his scattered thoughts amid the debris. Gradually, his thoughts return. He remembers walking home and stumbling into a car that appeared from nowhere. He remembers the bumping darkness in the car's boot before he lost consciousness. Every thought struggles to hold a grip as he feels the cold fog descend again.

GULLIVER

Joe Connolly liked to dictate his own pace, which was why his two, heavy shouldered, henchmen usually skipped along before him at a faster clip; one to open and close doors, the other to clear the way for the boss.

Both men were trained for close armed combat, carried concealed weapons and were equally proficient in a variety of martial arts. Each was built as though he'd been carved from granite. They worked out regularly when they weren't on duty and rarely spoke, even to each other.

They were scarily efficient killers and if they lacked the brains for a conscience, at least their, intellectually challenged, condition provided some hint as to the origin of their names. They were known as Bill and Ben, names given to them by their boss in one of his comic interludes that were so seldom, they went unnoticed, except by the attentive Gerry Heels.

Yet even he had missed the reference to the two flowerpot men puppets from an old BBC children's series. So Connolly enjoyed the joke alone and often. He had a fondness for the two lugs that bordered on his love for the late Romulus and Remus.

He was sniggering silently to himself as he watched their hulks skip along in front of him. Then his cell phone rang.

He recognised the coded call sign immediately.

Joe Connolly listened intently to the voice on the other end of the phone. They had known each other for more than half of their lives and for much of that time had been enemies. Then they formed an unlikely alliance that elevated both of them to positions of power and made wealthy men of both of them. Connolly gave the name 'Gulliver' to his secret partner. He liked to call himself a partner but that was an impertinence he would never suggest to the man himself.

Gulliver was the brains behind their organization. Connolly was the public face, the hard man and the operator. Through Gulliver, Connolly built up a network of crime spanning the continent. Connolly always knew his criminal contacts, as useful as they were, would never give him the access and influence he needed. Their success was built on their access to official documentation such as visa and passports. They had influential officials in every country on their payroll. All these were set up and handled by Gulliver.

Connolly had been carefully chosen. He was a successful criminal who built his success on the backs of others. Since those early days, while fortunes in the Dublin underworld were made on shifting quick sands, The Pigeon rose in the ranks through the judicious deployment of his finest skills, stealth and fear.

He betrayed and murdered his way to the top of the stinking heap. People said he was made of teflon. He stayed out of the hands of the law and built himself an empire with drugs, guns and prostitution.

The Pigeon's reach went far beyond Ireland into dockland gangs in Liverpool, old style East End firms in London and the West Indian Yardie gangs of Brixton and West London. He had links to Republican groups in the North of Ireland and through them, a network of quasi-political criminal groups throughout Europe.

In Amsterdam and Rotterdam his own men oversaw his transactions and the transport of goods. He was a hero on the Costa del Sol and had close friends in Naples. He could fly through a shit storm but still smell of roses.

Gulliver brought a new dimension to Connolly's operation. He had evidence of a crime Connolly committed that could put him away, without a chance of of parole, for life. But it wasn't the threat of prison that gripped Connolly most, but the prospect of his own treachery being exposed. He helped put many people away who had considered him a friend and Connolly knew their revenge would be terrible. So long as Gulliver held that, Connolly was obliged to him for life.

Connolly recruited a third 'partner' who provided the money that helped finance their operations but he never revealed its real source to Gulliver. The Arab's contacts in Central Europe among the Moslem smugglers who controlled the supply routes, were a vital part of what made them so powerful.

'And you could never forget the money,' Connolly thought with more hope than conviction. Theirs was a network run by terror fueled by human greed and hunger for profit. 'Everything that makes the world go round', thought Connolly. He meant it, too. For as much as he feared and hated Gulliver, he gloried in the power their association had given him. And it reached into every thread of society from politicians to police, every arm of the Establishment was involved.

Now the Arab was flexing his financial muscle: he wanted a bigger share and more control. Gulliver had only begun to realize how deeply the Arab had dug his talons into Connolly and he wasn't happy.

Tonight Connolly intended to introduce them to each other. Gulliver didn't like the Arab's involvement and would not allow anyone dictate to him. He didn't take risks, he told Connolly, and the Arab was a risk he didn't need.

When it came down to it, it was all about greed as far as Connolly was concerned. There was plenty to go around. He couldn't understand how Gulliver now feigned conscience and wanted to cut the Arab off. He knew such a threat would be dealt with ruthlessly by the Arab. He suspected greed was Gulliver's motive. He's underestimating the Arab, he thought.

Connolly stopped walking, to listen intently. Bill and Ben stopped too. They held their breath while their boss examined the ground in front of him, concentrating. While he nodded assent, he thought: *I have no intention of being the meat in your rage sandwich*.

'You have to meet me tonight so we can sort all this out,' Connolly said to the person at the other end of the phone before he told him the address and time of the meeting.

Connolly winced as he listened to the reply. 'Heels has gone to find Deare,' he answered, 'we'll get the letter and this will end tonight.'

SLICK TALKING

Bernard Nolan knew he had to do some slick talking. Time was running out for Garvan Deare and this entire operation was ready to disappear around the U-bend if he couldn't give Sandy a reason to believe him. She might be tough as nails but something had spooked her.

'Sandy, why did you say 'who took him?' What makes you think he's been taken?'

She was biting the corner of her lower lip and squinting at Bernard Nolan through a thin cloud of blue smoke from the cigarette she had lit with a trembling hand and her second match. She's either fighting back tears or sizing me up, he thought. Or both.

She spat a stray spot of tobacco from her lip and picked at it distractedly, 'Garvan was supposed to meet me here,' she repeated, 'he was only a couple of hundred yards ahead of me. I lost sight of him for half a minute and then he was gone. It's just not like him…he was a bag of nerves in that pub. He knew there were people after him and he was scared. He's a celebrity gossip journalist, for chrissake, this is not his side of the street at all…'

'Sandy, there's something you're not telling me…you're

273

holding something back…I wish I could do or say something that might help you trust me…look, if I level with you about what I'm doing here…'

Sandy shook her head.

'Please, just hear me out…if I had your friend then why would I be back here talking to you about him?'

Nolan noticed her flinch, fearfully. She crossed her arms and stared at the floor. He got an idea.

'Garvan was sent a letter from someone who was murdered in Sarajevo a couple of nights ago. That letter contains vital information about the gang that's chasing him. He gave it to you, didn't he?'

Sandy flinched again then she looked up and her eyes flared with anger. 'If you took him you'd know by now whether he had the letter and when you found out he doesn't, you'd come back here looking for it,' she spat.

'So you do have it?

Sandy didn't reply.

Nolan made a decision. He told her he worked for Europol in Sarajevo. He said he understood her distrust and reluctance to talk. 'When it comes down to it,' Nolan concluded, 'I don't know who to trust anymore either. I don't even know if I can trust you…'

A long silence followed his outburst. Sandy was thinking hard, considering his words. She remembered Garvan had said the only one she could trust was Brando, the cellarman, but she wondered how effective he could be, against the kind of villains Nolan was describing. Three hours before her biggest worry of the day was whether to watch a couple of reruns of 'Friends' or check out two new shows, 'Will and Grace' and 'Scrubs'.

Nolan stared at her intently, silently willing her to relent.

Sandy decided the burden of silence, under the circumstances, was too much.

'OK…Garvan gave me the letter. We were going to come back here to read it to see if we could get to the bottom of all that's going on. He was really pissed off about it and pissed off with Tito that he'd sent it to him and landed him in something he knew absolutely nothing about and could have cared less…'

Bernard Nolan cut her short. 'Sandy, will you show me the letter?'

She went to fetch it from the box of cornflakes.

IRISH CONNECTION

Bernard Nolan read Tito's fantastic tale with horror and fascination. Much of what he revealed was already known by Europol, although not in so much detail. Nolan was horrified to learn how he had inadvertently contributed to the deaths of both Tito and his sister.

He felt little sympathy for Tito who, though he had become a part of this organization through his own instinct for survival, had also been a willing participant.

Only in the final handwritten and hurriedly scrawled pages of Tito's letter could he find any clue to the identity of the figure behind the whole setup.

Tito concluded, '…No-one is who they seem to be. That's why there is no-one you can trust. The Pigeon is the boss but there are others behind him, controlling him.. I never met these peoples. I don't know who they are. I don't know if they know each other. In this world the left hand rarely knows what the right hand is doing. Connolly has connections with Islamic Jihad movement. They have given him the money to set up his network. They control what happens in the Balkans but their reach is long. He has a powerful Irish connection too. I know whoever signed my death warrant, signed Irina's too. This person is powerful in all circles and can move in any, without fear. He controls Connolly because Connolly fears him. Connolly cannot exist without him.'

'Do you know who he means?'

Bernard Nolan had been pondering the answer to that exact question when he realised Sandy Nelson was speaking to him.

'I'm not sure,' he said, stuffing the last two pages of the diary, unread, into his pocket 'well, I don't know. I don't have an answer but I do have a bunch of questions, which is more than I had an hour ago.'

OH DEARE

There wasn't a trace of Garvan Deare, when Gerry Heels returned to the office, where he had dumped the stricken journalist.

He flashed the powerful beam of his torchlight around the bare room, checked under the desk and behind the lone, busted, desk chair. He checked the windows that, apart from a few cracked frames, were locked by paint and rust.

There was only one way out of the room and that was through the door he had entered. He had only been gone ten minutes.

Heels, worried by the worsening state of the journalist, decided to call Joe Connolly for further instructions. But his boss's phone was either out of coverage or he had elected not to answer Heels' calls.

As his anxiety crept to a chilling panic, Heels had sat in his car in the factory yard, pondering whether he should dump Deare's body before things got completely out of hand and he had to deal with a corpse. The boss had told him to get the letter but he hadn't told him to get the journalist. Not in so many words, anyway. And the boss didn't approve of initiative. It was unpredictable, he said.

But Heels didn't have the letter. He only had Deare. An unconscious Deare. *Sandy Nelson,* he thought. He must have met her and given her the fucking letter. He made a decision. He would dump Deare and find Nelson. *And that bitch will hand it over this time,* he thought.

'*First,*' he thought, '*I better check the boot of the car in case he had the letter and dropped it. I can't leave any traces of the fucker in the car either.*' Heels popped the hood of the car's trunk and flashed his powerful keyring MagLite into its interior. There was no sign of the letter but he did find the journalist's cellphone, which he stashed away in an inside pocket of his leather jacket. He made a mental note to dispose of it later.

Anger didn't replace the panic he had felt for Deare's worsening condition when he discovered his disappearance, but it did sharpen his focus. When he was satisfied Deare was nowhere in the empty warehouse he began a methodical search of the walled yard which was littered with abandoned freight crates.

Heels figured the journalist had a five minute headstart, at the very most and, in his condition, hadn't got far from the warehouse yard. The nearest residential housing was, at least, a ten minute walk away and the warehouse was located in a warren of identical streets lined with identical warehouses.

The chances of him finding his way out of the area on foot were slim and in his condition, nigh on impossible. But even the slimmest chance was too much to take. Heels had no option: he had to find him and finish him.

PEDRO

Peter Cahill was surprised to hear the voice of Bernard Nolan on the other end of his phone. Bernard Nolan surprised himself when he called him.

'Pedro, how're ye doing, me ould son? See no long time, eh?'

'Who the fuck is this? Is that you, Bernard? I thought you were in Bosnia…'

'Me bollix, I'd bet my own sainted mother's dentures you knew I was in Dublin, ten minutes before I set foot in the arrivals lounge in Dublin airport…we need to meet, Pedro. Urgently.'

'Alright. How about Coogan's? Ten minutes?'

'I'll be there.'

Peter 'Pedro' Cahill, a burly bear of a man, whose appearance belied his abilities as a sharp witted Special Branch detective, needed no further enticement. The floor of his car was littered with polystyrene coffee cups, kebab wrappers and evening newspapers with the crosswords all completed.

He'd spent the last four hours watching the door of a house where a certain Middle Eastern diplomat lived. He was logging the comings and goings from the building. Except no-one had come or gone from the building in the four hours he'd been there apart from the Arab's occasional gay lover, a young Irish rent boy.

Nolan had known Cahill since their days together as Gardai on the beat in the inner city Store St barracks, one of the roughest and toughest assignments in its day. They had both worked under Tommy O'Brien in the early days and though all three had gone their separate ways, Cahill and Nolan kept their friendship alive.

While Nolan rose in the criminal investigation ranks, Cahill had gone in to Special Branch and murder investigations, their friendship and their respective areas of expertise had occasionally been of mutual benefit.

Nolan knew Cahill's image of a shoddy gambler concealed his skills as a sharp witted investigator with his hand on the pulse of whatever was going on. He thought Cahill was always someone he could trust but 'trust' was in short supply. He remembered someone mentioning Peter Cahill to him in Sarajevo and he had wondered why his old pal hadn't looked him up. 'Unless he was up to no good,' thought Nolan, 'either way he'll know what's going on. It's best to keep your friends close and your enemies, closer. The problem is knowing one from the other…'

When Nolan told her he was going to Coogan's to meet a contact, Sandy Nelson insisted on going with him.

'I'm sorry, Miss Nelson, I can't involve you in a police investigation, you'll have to stay here…'

'That's what you think, mister, my friend is in danger, as you've said, and I've trusted you with something I swore to him I would keep secret. And I'm not the only one with secrets either, am I? I wonder what your Gardai would say if I rang them and reported your activities?'

It was a persuasive argument and he hid a grudging admiration for her gumption. 'Ok,' he agreed, 'but I warn you…keep out of the way and don't get involved. I'll bring you to Coogan's and you can sit with my sergeant, but stay out of my way?'

'Ok.'

'Ok what? I want your word on this.'

'Alright. I give you my word. I'll stay out of your way but you have to let me know anything you hear about Garvan…?'

'I'll keep you informed.'

Nolan was secretly delighted she was coming along for the ride. He liked her, he knew, but he also needed to have her close because he figured whoever had taken Deare would soon work out where to look when they discovered he hadn't got Tito's letter on him. He didn't tell her that.

ESCAPE

Garvan Deare owed his life to the draught of chill night breeze blowing through the broken windowpanes of the bare warehouse office, where he had been dumped. Although he might have succumbed to the fog that threatened to engulf him, something within urged him to stay awake.

The faceless people in the room were gone. The dried sweat that had soaked him earlier, now helped to keep him awake, as it chilled from the night breeze on his skin. He pinched the soft, inner flesh of his upper thigh painfully with his thumb and forefinger until his eyes welled with tears.

With his other hand, he groped in his jacket pockets and discovered three long forgotten hardboiled sweets he sometimes kept for diabetic contingencies. Incongruously, he suppressed an urge to giggle at the absurdity of finding three sweets to help him out of a near death situation.

He flicked the rectangular, citrus flavoured glucose tablets from their wrapper into his mouth with the nail of his thumb and waited while they dissolved.

The sound of approaching footsteps alerted him to shut

his eyes and slump once more in the chair. As the door opened, he could hear heavy footsteps approach. He allowed some of the sodden white glucose spill from the corner of his mouth like drool, sensing his captor recoil, as he rummaged through his pockets and then retreat, cursing, out of the office again.

When he was gone, Deare wasted no time making his move. The instant glucose hit worked like shock pads on a heart patient. The door of the office was ajar by centimetres. He listened intently to the receding footsteps until, through the crack in the door, he sensed his captor had stepped outside the building.

Deare opened the door and in the gloom, groped his way along the wall of the warehouse until he found a toilet in the opposite corner of the building to the exit door. Inside, in the reflected twilight of the street lighting, there was a cracked handbasin and two broken urinals. The door of the toilet cubicle stood propped against the wall.

The handbasin and an empty towel dispenser stood beneath a narrow window with a rusted latch.

Deare eased the latch open, raised himself onto the handbasin and pushed with the padded shoulder of his jacket against the open pane. He held his breath as the pane squeaked and gave way. He eased his head through the gap and, squinting, surveyed the narrow alleyway outside. Pushing himself up, Deare slid one foot out of the window, before twisting his body so he was sitting on the sharp window sill with his torso and head inside.

Hanging precariously, he tilted his body backwards and dragged his other foot through the narrow gap. Now he wiggled his bum outside and twisted his body so he could lower himself through the window and onto the floor of the lane outside. When his feet touched the ground he let go of the windowsill to slide himself into a standing position.

Outside, he didn't have time to dwell on the searing pain in the palms of his hands, he realised, had been caused by his vice like grip on the rusted window pane. He could feel the initial sugar rush from the glucose tablets fading although that had been replaced now by adrenalin and the funk of terror that gripped him.

Luck was on his side when he checked the latch of the narrow side entrance door. It was bolted from the inside but the padlock that held it had rusted and was long broken. Holding his breath he slid the rusted bolt aside, eased the door open and stepped out onto the brightly lit street.

He had little or no idea of his location, but judging by the age and style of the buildings as well as the sharp, oily funk of diesel and salt water, he guessed he was in Dublin's docklands. All he had to do was follow his nose.

IN CHARACTER

Bernard Nolan had his cell phone in his hand when it rang.

'Sergeant Farrell, I was just about to call you…'

Orla Farrell wondered why he was addressing her so formally. She recounted her story about her visit to the newspaper offices. She told him she had drawn a blank on Deare but she feared her queries may have alerted the curiosities of the journalist to whom she'd spoken.

'There's no time to worry about that now. I've seen the letter and read it and I'm on my way to Coogan's to meet a contact. I'll have Miss Nelson with me, so I want you to meet us there.'

'Coogan's? Ivan said he was going there. So am I in character again or do we drop the pretence this time?'

'We're still in character for the moment…since we've both worked in Sarajevo and we're both Irish then there's a strong and likely chance we'd know each other. Anyway I want you to stay with Miss Nelson while I talk to my contact, ok?'

'Got you. See you there in five minutes.'

'We'll be there in ten.

Dermott Hayes

ROCK AND A HARD PLACE

Joe Connolly was pissed off. *Everything's turning to shit*, he thought, '*and I'm stuck between a rock and a hard place.* He was on his way to a meeting that might decide his future.

'*I'm the fucking grafter*,' he thought, '*these cunts wouldn't be anywhere without me. This fucking towelhead is bad fucking news. I can't take him on because they're mad bastards. And if I keep them happy then I'm pissing the other fucker off. He thinks he's cock of the walk. Wanker*.'

'Here's the house, boss. His car's in the driveway…'

Connolly, who had been staring into the distance, focussed his gaze on Bill, the granite faced minder in the passenger seat. He lashed out without warning, punching the half turned Bill square on the left temple. Bill looked surprised but the blow had barely registered.

'Shut the fuck up, I'm trying to think.'

'Yeah, boss but…'

Connolly lashed out again with a vicious fury. This time he smashed the hapless Bill on the bridge of his nose with his cell, shattering the phone in the process. Bill bowed his head and turned around, sheepishly. Ben pulled the car to a quiet halt just short of the driveway entrance.

'Park behind him, you fucking muppet,' Connolly screamed, this time directing his anger at his driver, Ben, 'did I tell you to stop?'

Bill started to object and then, considering what had been meted out to Ben, thought better of it.

'No, boss…is this alright?'

'Shut the fuck up,' Connolly snapped, venting his rage on his two loyal goons, 'you two stay here. Call Heels, he'll be trying to reach me. If you hear from him, ring the doorbell.'

They had pulled into the quiet residential street where his Middle Eastern backer had a home. This was where the rich lived and hid their wealth behind ancient oaks and high walls. *Fifteen years ago I was robbing these fuckers*, he thought.

He wished he knew where Heels was and what he was up to. He didn't like going into the meeting with a loose end hanging in the wind. *How fucking difficult was it to get a letter from a fucking journalist? He'd probably sell it for a monkey*.

The door of the house opened in response to the motion detector lights that illuminated the garden and driveway as they entered. Connolly recognized the swarthy, handsome Arab in the doorway, casually dressed in a silk dressing gown. He climbed out of the car and smiling, extended his arms in greeting.

TWO BIRDS, ONE SHOT

Ivan Toscic stood in the shadow of a tree in the driveway of a house in the secluded suburban street where his target lived. From where he stood, behind a five foot high stone wall, he could view the house.

Moonlight and municipal lighting illuminated the street but there were plenty of mature trees and foliage, as well as high walls and secure gates, to provide adequate shadow for his purposes.

He disliked these jobs because there were too many variables and no groundwork could be done. He should know the comings and goings of all the neighbouring buildings. He should have a ground plan of the target's house and a full briefing of its interior. He had to wait until his subject made his move before he could decide when to strike. The intelligence provided by his Irish contact was sketchy and incomplete. All he knew was his subject was to meet with this criminal, Joe Connolly.

He didn't know the exact time for the meeting and was faced with the dilemma of trying to gain access while his target was alone - impossible, he assumed, because of electronic surveillance cameras in the doorway - or taking him when his visitors arrived. He knew he would have a very narrow window to perform the task efficiently and with minimum risk.

This would happen, he hoped, in the driveway of his subject's home as he climbed into his car. He was also restricted by time since he was expected in Coogan's to meet Sergeant Farrell. *This job*, he thought, *may have to wait for another day*.

Then, for the first time in ten minutes, there was movement on the street. The headlights of a large car lit up the leaves of the trees around him as it swung around the bend into the quiet residential street and purred slowly up to the driveway of his target's home.

Toscic ducked below the wall in the shadows of the trees as the car passed then he raised himself up to observe the new arrivals. Two very big men dressed in heavy, wool overcoats stepped out of the parked vehicle.

One of them, the driver, made a quick check of the garden while the other, who had emerged from the car's rear rubbing the side of his massive head, checked the street to his left and right. He returned to the car, bent down and made a silent signal to the car's other passenger. A short, dapper man with sharp features and a narrow, ugly face climbed out of the car.

Toscic figured this must be the one they call The Pigeon, Joe Connolly. He had an air of authority about him that was apparent from the awkward deference of his two companions.

The door of the house opened as Connolly approached it. He recognized his target, hands extended in greeting. Both men disappeared inside, leaving Connolly's two goons to return to wait for their boss in the car.

Toscic cursed softly. *This is an improv job*, he thought. He had to use what was available and make it up as he went along.

He decided he would dispatch with the bodyguards where they sat and lie quietly waiting for the door to open. Then he would have a clear shot at both Connolly and his target. It was a *'two birds with one shot, special offer,'* he thought, smiling. *Everyone will be happy.'*

FOLLOW THAT CAB

Orla Farrell thought she was meeting Ivan Toscic in Coogan's. She was surprised when she saw him dive in a taxi at the rank on College Green. So surprised, he was gone before she could call him. She decided to follow.

She would have laughed when she heard herself tell the driver to 'follow that cab.' The driver, a Dubliner with that look of amused cynicism that was so much a badge of his being, felt no such reluctance.

'You'll have to pay extra for tha',' he opined, arching his eyebrow in the rearview mirror, 'it's a new charge…like if I had a fiver for everytime sumbuddy asked me to 'folly dat cab,' I'd be living like Bono…people say de strangest things when dey get into taxis, dere was this fella d'udder nigh'…'

'Shut up and drive, for fuck's sake,' Orla snapped.

'Jaysus, I was only sayin'', he replied feebly.

Orla didn't give him another thought. She watched Toscic's taxi take the turn off Westmoreland St, down Fleet St and towards Townsend St. *Where's he going?* she thought, *either that taxi's giving him a run around or he's heading out of town.*

293

Toscic's taxi crossed the Grand Canal at Irishtown before turning towards the plush city suburb of Sandymount.

Orla ordered the driver to hang back as they watched Toscic pay his fare. He paused and looked about before striding purposefully down a side road full of big houses with old trees and driveways. Orla told her driver to turn his vehicle around and wait for her. He gave her a leery look but swallowed his protest when she flashed her warrant card at him.

'What the hell is going on now?' she wondered, *'first O'Brien starts acting weird, Nolan's gone all mysterious and now Toscic.'*

She edged herself to the corner of the cul de sac and found a hiding spot in the tree shadows. She watched Toscic take up a position in the garden of a house with a high stone wall. He was watching something or someone. Orla waited silently. She was in two minds; tell Bernard Nolan or stay and wait.

Her decision was made with the arrival of a large car that drove up slowly and straight into the driveway of the house opposite where Toscic was hiding. Two big men stepped out of the car and looked around them before a third man, short and sharp featured, got out. It was Joe Connolly, The Pigeon. The impatient parping of the waiting taxi around the corner made her mind up. She retreated.

By the time she'd dispatched the driver whose questions were silenced by a forbidding look and 20 Euro, there wasn't a sign of Toscic. Now she had a real dilemma. *What the hell is Ivan doing? Does he know Connolly? Christ, maybe he's involved with these bastards…*, she wondered.

She decided to wait and watch the building before she told anyone what was going on. She settled in to the curve of the low granite wall. It brought back memories of other nights in Dublin, waiting and watching.

She switched off the ringer on her cell phone in case Nolan should decide to call her. The last thing she needed was her phone sounding off in someone's garden.

She knew this neighbourhood. These people valued their privacy and many of them had panic buttons that would bring a circus of security services swarming at the first sign of trouble.

Silence was essential.

PLAN OF ACTION

There was something continental about the atmosphere in Coogan's and the décor, with its national flags hanging from the ceiling and the colourful, ceramic tiled, panels around the walls. A fug of cigarette smoke hung in the air, Kylie Minogue was singing 'Can't Get You Out of my Head' and half the heads in the bar bobbed in rhythm.

Bernard Nolan lumbered through the door at that moment, in the company of an equally robust man, of some six feet plus in height and substantial girth. A tall, slim, redhead stood between them.

The barman, that had served them earlier, was standing on the other side of the bar, waiting. He caught Nolan's eye, 'two pints of Guinness, please and Sandy, eh, what'll you have?'

'Vodka and Red Bull, Bernard,' Sandy Nelson ordered, a glint in her eye.

'Did ye find Garvan?' the barman asked, you were looking for him earlier…'

Bernard Nolan noted how little escaped a Dublin barman, 'No, we didn't,' he replied, 'has he been in since?'

'Haven't seen him all day although I heard he was here

for lunch…before my shift started. He's usually here for a pint before he hits the clubs but he's not been in tonight…'

Their drinks arrived. Bernard Nolan picked up his and placing a hand on Peter Cahill's shoulder, turned to Sandy Nelson and said, 'Sandy, d'ye mind if we step outside for a moment, for a bit of quiet?'

'No, youse go on,' Sandy Nelson piped, 'I'll keep the bar warm and the drinks cool.'

Peter Cahill stepped out of the bar behind Nolan who wheeled and said, 'where's your car?'

'Why? What's up?'

The look of impatience on his old friend's face made him point to his car, parked, illegally, in the taxi rank outside the hotel.

Nolan barked, 'c'mon.'

Cahill was intrigued and tossed his keys to Nolan who slipped into the driver's seat and waited silently for Cahill. In the car, Nolan handed Tito's letter to Peter Cahill. He suspected the 'branch man knew more about his mission to Dublin but he was prepared to play along.

Cahill squinted at the document Nolan gave him. For his part, he didn't wish to betray what he knew already. The letter was like dozens of accounts he had read before. He studied the carefully printed list of names and addresses as Nolan spoke.

'This whole thing began when Ivan Toscic found the postcard and discovered a link between Tito and Connolly…'

Cahill looked up and nodded to indicate he was following.

'Mickey Bradshaw told us about Tito and why he was killed…he was fished out of the river within ten hours of tipping me off…'

Nolan continued, 'Tommy O'Brien told us there was a suspected leak in the force when we arrived in Dublin…'

'And he brought you here in a covert operation?'

'I think you see where this is going…he said he hoped to flush out the inside man. There was a girl who was giving information to me. She's mentioned in the letter. Tito's sister, Irina, went missing the same night Tito's body turned up. Now Tito knew what she was doing but he wouldn't turn over his own sister, would he? Not if he went all the way to Sarajevo to help her…?'

'What's our plan of action then?' Peter Cahill asked Bernard Nolan. Neither of them spelled out their suspicions but both were sure they were on the same wavelength. Nolan didn't answer immediately. They both had things to think about.

Peter Cahill wondered privately about Tommy O'Brien's reasons for conducting the investigation in this style.

O'Brien was a powerful man with almost autonomous jurisdiction in his conduct of the Garda International bureau. He was a dyed in the wool politician too, leap frogging his way through the ranks without ever getting his fingers dirty. He was the opposite of Nolan and before Bernard left for foreign service, he was tipped to fill the role now occupied by O'Brien.

Tommy O'Brien, for all his bonhomie and affability, was a crafty customer and wildly ambitious. His position in the International Bureau had gained greater importance since the Balkan crisis erupted in the '90s and the number of asylum seekers went from a trickle to a deluge.

Of course, O'Brien could have decided to keep their presence in Dublin a secret so he could spring a trap for the spy.

It made sense even if, Cahill thought, '*by my standards, it was a little melodramatic.*' O'Brien's operational squad was very secretive in its movements but that was to be expected. It was a new squad and they would need to establish and prove themselves. They couldn't do that by giving it all away.

He couldn't deny Bernard Nolan's logic that too many signs were pointing in the direction of the head of the International Bureau.

He looked at Nolan, thinking. *Or maybe that's the direction he's pointing me in? O'Brien might have his own reasons. Despite his squad's penchant for cloak and dagger there wasn't much got past his own crew,* Cahill thought, *we'd already picked up on the 'spy in our midst' theory. Trouble is, we're no wiser than he is*.'

Sandy Nelson nursed her drink while surveying her surroundings. She liked the ambience of Coogan's. The music was always banging and there was always some action going on.

She noticed she had the only swivel stool with armrests in the bar and then realised it was the seat where Brando sat. '*It's like a throne,*' she thought. She realised why Brando chose this spot for his daily vigil. He could see everyone in the bar and everyone who came or went through the door. He could even see people coming in the front door. *He's master of all he surveys.*

Thinking of Brando made her think of Garvan - the hapless sap, she thought fondly. 'I hope he's alright,' she heard herself say.

Then she remembered, '*Garvan told me if anything happened to him I should call Brando. His own phone isn't answering*'.

She left her drink on the bar and went to tell Nolan.

TITO'S DEAD

BRANDO

Garvan Deare slapped the red door of the house at the end of the redbrick terrace house with the palm of his hand and his last ounce of strength. He heard a familiar gruff voice from within and approaching footsteps.

'Who is it?'

'Brando…Brando, it's me, Garvan.' The door swung open as he felt his ebbing strength fade to nothing. He fell into the arms of the cellarman.

His luck had held out. He had guessed right about his location and, as he stumbled closer to the riverside, his surroundings became even more familiar.

As he reached the dockside his legs were giving out beneath him and the light began to dance at the corner of his vision. A lone taxi was making its way back towards the city and he summoned the strength to raise his arm. Struggling to remain conscious, he fell into the back seat.

'Where're ye off to?' Deare heard the taxi driver ask.

He mumbled an address close by in the Summerhill district of the inner city.

'Would you have any sweets?'

The taxi driver gave him a quizzical look in the

rearview mirror.

'Sweets? Hey, I know you…you're the fella from the Evening News, whatsisname?'

'Deare'

'Yeah, Deare…Deare Diary…you're Garvan Deare. Jaysus, I love your diary, you have some life…'

'Sweets'

'Oh yeah, sweets…you don't look the Mae West, mate…are y'alright?'

Deare didn't answer.

'I do have some sweets…Eskimo mints, if you like them…I always keep some handy for juiced up Billy Bunters so they don't stink up the cab after a skinful… here.'

He handed the packet to Deare who snatched them from his hand and wrenched the bag apart, spilling the contents all over the rear of the car. The taxi driver observed him, bemused.

Deare ignored him as he unwrapped one of the hardboiled mints and began to suck on it, gaining strength from the sugar. He opened two more in rapid succession and stuffed them into his mouth.

'Jaysus, you'd swear ye hadn't eaten in a week…are ye sure ye're al-ri'?'

'I'm sorry for messing up your taxi…I'm a diabetic…I needed some sugar in a hurry…'

Luckily there was little time for further explanation as the taxi swung into the street he had asked for, 'It's the last house on the right. The one with the red door.' He fished a crumpled ten Euro note from his trousers pocket and tossed it over the seat into the driver's lap. He stumbled out of the car before the driver could respond.

He had taken a risk going to Brando's place but he

knew Brando's love of late night cable over a chicken curry and a few cans of cider before retiring. He didn't trust himself to last as far as home or even Coogan's and Brando was the only man he could trust in a tight situation.

'Jaysus, Garvan, you're in some state…there's been people looking for you all day including that lowlife, Gerry Heels…'

'I know, I know, you told me earlier…Brando, I need something to eat…'

Being familiar with Deare's condition, Brando disappeared into his kitchen and returned with the remains of his chicken curry that Deare devoured, hungrily. Between mouthfuls he recounted the story of his escape from the warehouse.

'Were you followed?'

'I don't know. I could have been. I don't even know who took me but from what you tell me about him, it could've been this Heels geezer.' He didn't know how close he was but he was about to find out.

DIRTY HARRY

Gerry Heels watched as the taxi dropped Garvan Deare at a house on the end of a terrace in Summerhill. He held back from approaching the house. He was too well aware of the likely consequences in this neighbourhood.

Inside the neat red bricked terraced house, Brando made himself busy turning off the lights at the front of the house while he took a long look up and down the street outside through a crack in the window curtains. He knew they were safe, as long as they were in the house, but they couldn't stay there indefinitely.

Garvan Deare's condition had improved since he scoffed the remains of the chicken curry, soaking up the last of the sauce with the remains of the naan bread. He had a swift wash and Brando found some cotton wool and disinfectant to clean the gash on his head. Garvan was plugging in the electric kettle when he re-entered the kitchen.

Cup of tea, Brando?'

'No thanks…I was drinking a can of cider…we're going to have to get you out of here to somewhere safe,' Brando told him, 'maybe we'll go to Coogan's first.'

Deare looked anxiously at the door. 'Do you think we're not safe here?'

'Safer than the Central Bank,' Brando assured, 'you know where I live?'

Garvan did and understood Brando's question was rhetorical. You'd have to walk a long mile before you'd find anyone as straight and honest as Brando but in the three square blocks of houses surrounding them, were generations of crime dynasties.

Brando grew up with them and he could count on them as friends and neighbours. They, in turn, respected Brando as 'one of our own.' And in this neighbourhood, they looked after their own.

'You have your cup of tea. I'm going to make a call.' Brando dialled a number and, turning away, had a brief, whispered conversation with whoever was on the other end of the line.

'Good,' he said, 'we'll have a taxi here in five minutes.'

Garvan Deare poured the boiling water over the teabag in the mug he'd found in the press above the sink. Brando disappeared into the hallway again and began rummaging in a small broom cupboard under his staircase. He groped around blindly for something concealed above the cupboard door lintel and emerged with a heavy item wrapped in cloth. He stepped back into the kitchen and placed it on the table.

As he unwrapped the package Deare whistled at what he saw.

'Brando…Dirty 'fucking Harry, ferchrissakes…'

Inside the package was what appeared to be a gleaming handgun, all chrome with a wooden handle and very long barrel. It was wrapped in thick, plastic and an oily rag.

Brando unwrapped the gun and the air filled with the

smell of gun oil. 'Dirty Harry is right,' said Brando, holding the gun aloft and wiping it with the cloth lovingly, 'this is a .357 magnum Python Elite made of stainless steel with a brushed finish. It has a walnut grip and it holds six rounds of .357 caliber, enough firepower to stop two tons of baby elephant in its tracks. It weighs slightly less than three pounds, has a six inch barrel and is just half an inch less than a foot in overall length…'

'Do you know how to use it?'

'Do I what? I could field strip and reassemble this in less than 30 seconds. You don't think I was scratching my arse in the army, do ye?'

There was no time to answer as the front doorbell rang. 'That's our taxi,' said Brando, 'look sharp.'

FOLLY THAT CAB

Brando's phone rang at the same time the door was kicked open with force, knocking Deare straight back into him. The former soldier had no time to react as Heels caught him square on the throat with a karate punch that made him crumple like a sack of spuds. Another kick followed to the temple of the prone cellarman. He was out.

In the same movement Heels grabbed the dazed journalist by the lapels and issued two swift slaps with the inside and the back of his right hand. Brando didn't hear the cell phone he'd dropped beside him and the voice of Sandy Nelson asking, 'Brando?…Garvan, is that you? Brando? Another kick splintered the phone.

Sandy Nelson didn't like what she'd heard - or didn't hear. Someone answered the phone then the signal went dead. She had a bad feeling about it, '*Garvan's at Brando's and they're in trouble*', she thought.

She turned to the bar man and demanded the cellarman's address as she grabbed her coat and rushed out the door. Outside she collared a taxi dropping a fare at the nearby Westbury Hotel. She wondered where Nolan and Peter Cahill had gone. She had intended to tell Nolan what she suspected but that could wait.

'Summerhill,' she barked, 'Egerton Terrace. And don't dally.'

The driver couldn't believe his luck. 'Jaysus,' he began to say, you're the second ballsy woman to get into this cab in the space of half an hour. There must be sumpin' in the air t'night…' The look of cold fury in Sandy Nelson's eyes cut him short.

'Fasten your seat belt', he said as he slapped the car into gear and sped off, tyres squealing in a fury of burning rubber, straight across Grafton St, south Ann St and swung left into Dawson St. 'That's more like it,' Sandy Nelson said, as she struggled to clunk the seat belt into place.

They had swung into Nassau St by the time she could straighten herself. The driver gunned the cab through the gears, as he swallowed Nassau St, Westland Row and lost a hub cap careening into Pearse St, horn blaring and against the lights.

'I picked up another girl earlier who asked me to 'folly that cab', the driver ventured.

'Shut the fuck up and drive,' Sandy barked without looking at him. She was busy texting a message to Bernard Nolan; ' Found Deare. With Brando. Trouble. 15 Egerton Terrace, S'Hill.' She worked the phone's keys with her texting thumb. Holding on with one hand to steady herself she pressed 'send' as the cab swung into Tara St and thundered towards Butt bridge and the river Liffey.

Fuck me,' the driver thought, 'they're probably sisters… the ballbreaker sisters.' Still, he thought, 'it breaks the boredom. This is better than a movie…'

Dropping a gear, he gunned the engine for extra thrust through the junction of Talbot and Gardener, barely slowing as he flung the vehicle into a right turn down the backstreets of Summerhill. There wasn't a soul on the streets.

Egerton Terrace was narrow, one way and lined with neat, two storey, redbrick cottages. The cab screeched to a halt, at an angle to the path and right outside the door of number 15. Sandy Nelson tossed a 20 Euro note at the driver and was out of the passenger side before the car had come to a stop.

She rang the doorbell, banged on the door with the palms of her hands and shaded her eyes as she tried to see through the thick living room curtain.

The house was as quiet as the street at 1.30am. There was no sign of life and when she strained to hear, not a sound.

Sandy dialled a number on her phone. Garvan Deare's Hammer House of Horror ringtone could be heard clearly on the other side of the darkened door. She resumed her hammering and called out, 'Brando, Garvan…open the door.

TAKING CARE OF BUSINESS

Ivan decided it was time to act. The motion detector in the driveway of his target's house had given him cause to worry but he figured a direct approach, as long as it was fast, was the only solution.

The lights sprang on in the driveway as soon as he stepped through the gateway. Connolly's driver glanced at him through the car's side mirror. The window was already being lowered when Ivan arrived alongside. The driver never had a chance to react.

Toscic leaned into the car and gripping the driver's throat, shut off his cry of alarm. With the silencer fitted handgun in his other hand he shot the car's passenger dead with a clean, round wound between the eyes that was only marred by a thin trickle of blood and the look of complete surprise on his victim's face.

Before he could react, he trained the gun on the driver and whispered to him to get out of the car and walk to the door of the house. Keeping the gun jabbed into the small of his back, Toscic used the bodyguard's body as a shield and told him to ring the doorbell. He expected there to be some exchange on the intercom, but instead the door swung open and both Connolly and his target stood in the doorway.

'It's you,' Connolly said, 'what the…?'

He never finished the sentence as he fell beneath the lumbering weight of the bodyguard whose dead weight pinned him to the ground. Toscic had no margin for error.

The target reacted first, fleeing down the hall corridor, but Ivan wasted no time. With cool detachment, he took aim and fired. His target fell just as they heard the coughing thud of his weapon.

He shot him square between the shoulder blades, stepped over the wriggling Connolly and walked to the fallen target, a steady aim on his prone figure. He pointed the gun to the back of the man's skull and fired another round at almost point blank range. Toscic turned over the body of the man he'd shot, to make sure of his identity.

He didn't notice Connolly wiggle free until he heard a car door slam and the sound of screeching tires as the car reversed from the garden, beyond. By then it was too late. Connolly can wait, he thought. My job is done.

He quickly gathered the shell cases and slipped them into his jacket pocket. He gave the scene one last going over before retreating to the doorway in the hall corridor where his target had tried to escape. He stood in the gap, gun poised and listening. Then he slipped into the shadows.

FIREBRAND

Gerry Heels wasted no time venting his anger on Garvan Deare, the man who had caused him no end of hassle all day.

'I don't know how you fucken got away from me but you're going nowhere now, bud. I'm going to knock ten shades of shite out of ye just 'cuz you've fucked me off and I want to…'

Deare didn't know what hit him when Brando's front door whacked him square on the chest and forehead, knocking him back, winded, into the flailing arms of the cellarman. He had only begun to gather his thoughts when Heels manhandled him, apparently bent on serious damage. His face smarted from the slapping he'd already got. Now Heels had him slouched in a chair, his hands tied with gaffer tape. The unfortunate Brando hadn't stirred. Deare felt something warm and sticky run through his right eyebrow. He tried to blow it away and only when he licked it and tasted its thick, saltiness, did he realise it was his own blood.

'My boss wants that fucken letter so you're going to phone that redheaded bitch friend of yours and tell her to bring it here or else.' Heels patted the pockets of his jacket for his cell phone when he heard the screech of brakes and car doors slamming. The last thing Garvan Deare remembered was the misspelt tattoo of 'PEAC' on the knuckle of Heels' right fist.

Heels held his breath as Sandy hammered the door and slapped the windows. Garvan Deare's cell phone rang in his pocket and the person outside resumed their hammering on the door. This time when he heard the voice of the person shouting at the door, he smiled. He recognised the voice of Sandy Nelson from Kiely's bar in Donnybrook.

'There's a stroke of luck,' he thought, 'the bitch has found me.'

Sandy hurtled through the open space where Brando's door had been and crashed headlong into the wooden post at the foot of the stairs.

'Glad you dropped in,' she heard Heels say behind her, 'we were just about to call you.'

Tears welled up in Sandy's eyes as Heels grabbed a handful of hair and, with one arm pinned behind her, hauled her to her feet and frogmarched her into the front room where the inert body of Brando lay curled on the floor. Sandy took in the slumped and bloodied form of Garvan Deare strapped to a kitchen chair.

'Garvan?' she called, struggling against Heels' grip, 'if you've hurt him, I'll fucken kill ye, ye bastard,' she spat.

'Jaysus, you're some firebrand,' Heels taunted, "your boyfriend'll be fine, if you behave. He's only had a few slaps.'

Heels threw the struggling Sandy into another chair beside Deare who began to revive, a drool of blood and mucus falling from his battered face. Heels secured Sandy with the same roll of gaffer tape he'd used to bind Deare.

'You'll find a little co-operation will go a long way. You and Mr Deare have been giving me the runaround. I want that fucken package he got…'

CARNAGE

While she wondered where Ivan Toscic had gone, Orla was startled by Joe Connolly's swift departure. First she heard the roar of a car engine. The gangster left in such a hurry the car door swung open as he reversed into the road and sped away. There was no sign, from where she stood, of his two bodyguards.

She decided to slip across the road to get a better view of the building. From her new position she could see the hallway door of the house was ajar. She decided to get a closer look. Crouching, she darted across the street and into the house's driveway.

She didn't notice another car turn into the quiet suburban street. She had other things on her mind. The driver of the car was in no hurry and turned off his lights as he approached the walled garden of the Arab's house. The car slowed to a crawl as it edged past the open gateway then slowly rolled away.

Orla armed herself when she spotted the corpse of the bodyguard lying in the driveway. At first he looked like a discarded refuse sack but when she got closer she saw it was a body. Crouching in the shadow of the hedge that lined the driveway, she drew her weapon and kept it trained on the front door of the house as she felt the man's neck for signs of life. Her mind was racing - should I withdraw and call for back up? But what if Ivan's inside and he needs assistance? Maybe I should go in? She decided to go in.

With her weapon aimed, she edged closer to the open hallway door and pushed it with her free hand, keeping her gun hand trained on the entrance. The door resisted and she stepped back, hesitating. She lunged at the door with her shoulder but there was little give. There was a weight against the door, she concluded.

She listened intently but could hear no movement inside. She stepped back from the door and rang the doorbell as she called out, 'Gardai, open the door… GARDAI, OPEN THE DOOR…' She got no response.

She tried to open the door again by leaning all her weight against it and edging her arm through the doorway to try to gain some leverage or dislodge whatever was blocking it. It didn't budge.

Using a powerful Maglite she kept in her purse, she made her way around the back of the house to look for another way in. There was an arched wooden gate at the side of the house that was bordered by a gravel pathway. She eased the latch on the gate, hoping it wasn't bolt locked from the other side. She was in luck and the gate swung open. She tried the kitchen entrance but that door was locked. Then she found a French window, wide open, in the tiny rear garden. The house was deathly still.

Orla scanned the room with her torch, picking out the interior of an expensively furnished drawing room. It was a deep room with a baby grand piano to the left of the French window. In the centre were two settees, arranged in an 'L' shape around a low, glass topped coffee table that was covered in magazines.

Two doors led from the room, the nearest of which, she guessed, led to the kitchen. The other, she believed, would open into the house's front hallway.

That door was ajar and a crack of light broke though from the hallway that stretched like a thin beam across the width of the drawing room.

She leaned against the wall to the right of the kitchen door and, with her gun poised in her right hand, took a deep breath, yanked it open and stepped inside. Crouching in a shooting stance, her eyes swept the room. It was empty.

She wasted no time repeating her action on the door of the kitchen that led to the hallway. The scene of carnage she found, surprised her.

On the other side of the door in the narrow corridor, between the stairwell to the left and another doorway to what she presumed was a dining room, a man's body lay stretched on the floor. The carpet around him was wet and sticky with his blood. The back of the man's skull was a mess of blood and brain tissue.

She stepped over the body, wincing as she felt his blood envelop her shoes in the carpet's pile.

At the end of the corridor, slumped against the outer front door, was the heavyset body of Connolly's other bodyguard. The thick, dark pool of blood around his head told her there was little chance of his being alive.

When she had checked every room in the house she decided it was time to call for assistance.

CRIME SCENE

Peter Cahill weighed his options as Nolan approached the entrance to the road where he knew 'Noah', the Mossad assassin, was busy dispatching the Arab financier.

Just two hours earlier he had been sitting in his own car on this same street. Nolan slid the car into a parking spot under the bare canopy of a tall oak tree, right across the street where Toscic had been hiding.

'Bernard…' Cahill began, but was hushed by Nolan who was reading the text message he'd just received.

'That's Sandy Nelson. She's found Deare but there's trouble, she says.'

'Where is he?' Cahill asked.

'Brando's house in Summerhill.' Nolan bit his lower lip. He was in a quandary.

'Let's go,' Peter Cahill coaxed urgently, seizing his chance to divert the hesitant Nolan.

'No,' he said. He had made his decision. 'It can wait. I want to find Orla Farrell. She's a good cop. I'll call Store street and ask them to send a couple of cars around to Brando's house. They'd get there sooner than us anyway. Toscic is my responsibility and I want to know what the

318

hell he's up to.'

'You go back. Let me sort this out.'

Nolan stared at Peter Cahill as though he was looking at a stranger. He dialled the Store St number and asked for the detective on duty. He told him there was a kidnapping and serious assault in progress on Egerton Terrace and requested backup as soon as possible. Peter Cahill listened but didn't interrupt.

Peter Cahill managed to hiss a warning to Nolan as he stepped from the car.

'Bernard …be careful…'

Orla Farrell was a whisper away from discharging her weapon when Nolan walked through the front door, pushing the big bodyguard aside. She hadn't heard him approach and the first thing she saw was the body moving. Her phone rang at the same time.

Nolan ducked in fright as he caught sight of Orla pointing a weapon at his head.

'Christ.'

'Mother of Jesus.'

'Hello? Yes sir. Hang on, the DI's just arrived. I'm sorry, sir…we have a situation here. I'm going to have to call you back.' She hung up and her arm flopped to her side. Now she held a gun in one hand and a phone in the other. She looked drained.

Bernard Nolan and Peter Cahill had both stepped into the hallway and were staring soundlessly at the scene.

'Sergeant? Orla? What in fuck's name is going on?'

'That was Superintendent O'Brien. I have to call him back…'

Peter Cahill noted Ivan Toscic had done his job. He wasn't sure how much Nolan's partner knew and he wasn't about to offer any help.

'Sergeant Farrell? My name's Peter Cahill, Sergeant? Peter Cahill…are you alright?'

Orla Farrell stared blankly at the man speaking to her.

'Sorry, Orla, you remember me talking 'bout Pedro Cahill?'

Orla shook herself, closed her eyes and opened them again.

'Yes, yes, of course. Weren't you in Sarajevo last month?'

She wasn't sure where the question had come from but it was the first thing that came into her head. Peter Cahill's face bore no expression though she thought she saw his eyes open a fraction wider then relax again.

'There's enough trouble for me here,' Cahill said as his hand swept their surroundings.

'What happened here. Orla?' Nolan asked again.

'I don't know,' Orla answered, 'I followed Ivan Toscic here. He was watching this house when Joe Connolly arrived with his two goons and was greeted by this man here.' She pointed at the body

'So where's Toscic?'

'I don't know. He disappeared. I took my eye off him for a minute…'

'Did you speak to him? what the fuck was he doing here…following Connolly?'

'I don't think he was …he got here before him…'

Peter Cahill spoke. 'Look, there'll be time for post mortems later. We better call this in…'

'Peter's right. Let's get a crime scene team out here… we'll find Ivan Toscic later…where is Connolly?'

The three of them exchanged soundless glances but no answers. Orla Farrell pressed redial on her phone.

Tommy O'Brien answered the phone on the first ring.

'What the fuck was that about, Sergeant?' he barked.

She apologised and gave a brief explanation for hanging up on him earlier.

O'Brien listened without comment and asked to speak to Nolan. Orla handed over the phone, mouthing 'O'Brien' while she held her hand over the mouthpiece.

'Bernard, you have this letter? Good. Keep what's going on down there, contained, until I get there. I want a minimum of involvement by anyone other than a crime scene unit and yourself and Farrell, is that clear? What? who? What the hell is he doing there? Who brought him into it? I don't give a flying fuck, you had no right to involve…I gave you strict instructions…we'll see. Keep him out of it. That's an order. I'll be there in five minutes.'

Bernard Nolan didn't mention Ivan Toscic to O'Brien who hadn't asked about him either. Nolan was puzzled about his Bosnian sidekick and why he had fetched up in a Dublin suburb after a Dublin gangster.

Even more intriguing was the identity of the unknown Arab lying dead in the hallway of his own house, apparently the victim of an assassination. This is Pedro Cahill's area of expertise, he thought, and he's not giving much away.

KRAV MAGA

Sandy Nelson figured all she needed to do was delay Heels long enough for Bernard Nolan to respond to her call. He needed the letter but she no longer had it and she wasn't going to tell Heels that in a hurry.

'I don't have the package,' she told Heels, 'Garvan does. He hid it.'

Heels looked unconvinced. He lifted the lolling head of Deare, whose eyes rolled around in their sockets, and slapped him a vicious uppercut with the back of his closed fist. Deare's head and neck jerked backwards, spraying blood and mucus over Sandy.

'Leave him alone, for fuck's sake,' she pleaded, 'slapping him about won't get you anywhere. I'm telling you, he has the package. He knows where it's hidden but you won't find anything out until he gets some help. Surely you can see he's sick.'

Heels paused.

'What's wrong with him?' he asked.

'He's a diabetic. He needs his medicine because his blood sugar level has fallen. He could lapse into a coma if he doesn't get help.' Sandy hoped Heels didn't know too much about diabetes.

Joe Connolly shook and his teeth chattered. He knew he had had a very lucky escape. He knew whoever killed the Arab would have finished him off next. He also knew who he could thank for this outrage. He had underestimated Gulliver.

'The bastard figured he could get rid of both of us in one stroke and take over himself. This is fucken war...I'll have that fucker's balls for this, he fumed.

First, he thought, *I need to find Heels.*

He cursed when he realised he'd broken his phone over Bill's head. He cursed Bill and Ben for fucking up and not watching his back. He felt nothing more for his two loyal bodyguards. He made his way to the the Velvet Slipper where he could shower, get a change of clothes and a new phone. *I might find Heels there, too, the pervy fucker,* he thought.

He mulled over the events of the evening. It was clear the shooter was a hitman intent on getting himself and the Arab. Only one other person knew about that meeting and that was Gulliver. *The lying bastard set me up and I'll fucken do him for that...*

He pulled up outside the club and tossed the keys of the car at Armand, the tuxedoed maitre'd who flipped them in turn to one of the beefy doormen and snapped his fingers.

Armand held the door of the club ajar for Connolly, making no comment on his boss's dishevelled appearance or the bloodstains on his shirt and jacket. Connolly strode ahead through a doorway marked 'staff only' behind a beaded curtain to the rear.

'ARMAND', he barked.

'Oui, M'sieur Connolly,' the Algerian whispered dutifully, following his boss through the door.

Connolly threw another door open into a spacious office with large desk, a bank of phones and two large television screens. He went straight to a private bar set in a tiny recess and poured a hefty measure of Jameson into a heavy crystal tumbler. He didn't speak again until he downed the lot and poured another.

'Is Heels here?'

'Non, m'sieur Connolly…'

'Where the fuck is he?'

The Algerian wasn't entirely sure how to answer so he threw his boss a Gallic shrug.

'Don't fucken pout at me, ye black poof…get me Heels' fucken number and run the fucken shower…'

Armand was relieved to have something to do. The boss in this mood, he knew, was unpredictable and very dangerous. He switched on the water jets in the shower and adjusted the temperature with one hand while he searched for Heels' number on his own phone.

"ere is 'is number, boss…is there anything else?'

'No. Fuck off,' Connolly snapped, tapping the number proffered by the Algerian into the phone on his desk. Armand noticed he had poured himself another drink and opened his shirt to his waist. He retreated from the office, holding his breath until he got outside the door.

As he waited impatiently for Heels to respond, Connolly opened a drawer with a key and pulled out a Browning nine millimetre pistol, spare clips and a box of ammunition, which he tossed on the desk. For someone who'd built a career on treachery, being betrayed was beyond business, it was personal.

Gerry Heels wasn't sure what to do with Deare and he knew his time was running out. He figured if Nelson was able to track him down then it was only a matter of time before the cops got there too. *Or the fucking journalist snuffed it.*

'Where's his fucken medicine? he asked Sandy Nelson, 'Are you yanking my chain, you fucken bitch.'

'No, no...I'm not. Look, all he needs is something sweet. Like jam. Shove some jam in his mouth and give him a drink to wash it down. All he needs is a sugar hit.'

Heels' phone rang as he pushed his way past her into the kitchen where Sandy could hear him talking as he rummaged through cupboards in search of a pot of jam. She used the respite to split an acrylic nail to saw through the tape that bound her.

'How're ye, boss? Guess what...?' Fuck, yeah, right, right away...but, boss...I have Deare. I found him. No, he doesn't have it on him but his girlfriend says he has it. Wha? Yeah, I have her as well. I'm in Summerhill...where are you? The club? I can be there in five minutes, yeah. Right now. OK boss, see ya then.'

Sandy could feel the plastic adhesive give way as Heels returned with a pot of jam and spooned it roughly with his fingers into Deare's gaping mouth. When he'd stuffed some into him, he tilted the senseless journalist's head back and poured water into his open mouth. Deare coughed and spluttered as water and jam bubbled from him and ran down his chest. Sandy felt the tape give as she sawed.

Heels was too preoccupied with Deare to notice Brando waking. The ex-soldier had been awake since Sandy Nelson had arrived but had bided his time to regain his strength and pick his moment to act.

He rolled over and yanked the foot long cannon he'd been hiding, from his waistband. Heels caught the movement and lashed out, the heel of his boot catching the former soldier just below his left eye, smashing his cheek bone. Brando fired off a round into the ceiling that brought a shower of plaster down on them both and left a hole the size of a football, as a crescendo of loud bells began ringing in his head.

Sandy Nelson seized her moment, delivering a sharp kick with the heel of her boot to the inside of Heels' left leg knocking him off balance. Leaping from the chair, she followed it with a straight arm choking smash to his throat with her right and, stepping aside nimbly as he fell, finished him off with an elbow blow to the top of his spine, between his shoulder blades. Heels hardly knew what hit him. He was out cold.

'Jesus, what was that?', the reviving Garvan Deare asked in amazement.

'Krav Maga,' Sandy Nelson said, helping to release him from his restraints, ' …I knew those night classes would come in useful.'

Then all hell broke loose outside as police cars and emergency services began to arrive, alerted by Bernard Nolan.

TABLE FOR ONE

Ivan Toscic had no problem gaining entrance to the club where he'd seen The Pigeon go. *It had been easy to follow him as the gangster had driven slowly, perhaps unaccustomed to driving himself about*, Ivan thought.

Connolly had surprised him with his agility. He had managed to wriggle free from under a man who was twice his size and a dead weight. It had all happened in seconds and Ivan had made sure of his kill before turning his attention to the gangster. He didn't follow him through the front entrance either, opting instead, to make his escape through the rear garden. He scaled an adjoining wall into the car park of a small apartment complex at the back and quickly picked a vehicle.

The bouncers found nothing untoward about the smartly dressed foreign man who sought entrance. He looked like he had money and he was handsome. The girls would chew him up.

Ivan handed over the 20 Euro entrance fee and was offered a table by the obsequious, French speaking man in the dark suit. The club was low ceilinged and dark. Amidst the fug of smoke and stale alcohol, there was a faint mustiness of damp and cheap perfume. Ivan gestured at a small corner table that commanded a good view of the club's main room and all the doors that led from it. There were two of these apart from the front entrance. Both doors were behind beaded curtains. One was marked 'private' and had a half lit sign that read 'xit' above it. The other was marked 'staff only.' Ivan guessed that was where Connolly had gone to ground.

'What would m'sieur like to drink?' Armand asked the new guest as he wiped the table, arranging the ashtray and the blue lamp without moving them. Ivan asked for a vodka with ice and a bottle of water, Armand snapped his fingers and the drink appeared. Ivan noticed the tall black man hadn't moved.

'Thank you,' he said. Armand didn't move.

'Would m'sieur like to run a tab?' he asked.

'Yes. Thank you.' Ivan repeated, dismissively.

The man paused. Then he was gone, before Ivan noticed him going. There were a handful of patrons in the club. They were surrounded by scantily clad girls in too much makeup and high shoes. The men looked bleary and buzzed. They were watching one of the girls as she gyrated round a pole on a low dais to Madonna's 'Like a Virgin.'

The absurdity of his own situation occurred to him but he dismissed the thought as swiftly. He knew the dangers and this job was outside his experience. Keeping his two identities separate had never been a problem before. Now they were too close and there were friendships involved.

As a cop he had sought to keep his humanity as a defence against the bloody horror of war. As a killer, he kept himself detached. With both sides walking the same path, he felt confused. Dismissing these thoughts, he sipped his drink and waited.

HISTORY

Connolly tried Heels' phone again, but there was no answer. He was sure he said he'd be here within five minutes, but ten minutes had elapsed since they'd spoken and he was getting anxious.

He checked the bolt on his weapon again, snapped the clip from its chamber and looked at the ammunition, as though something might have changed in the two minutes since he'd done it before.

He decided he'd phone Gulliver to find out why he hadn't turned up at their meeting. His call was answered on the third ring. The voice on the other end sounded calm.

'You didn't turn up for the meeting,' Connolly said.

'No, I got hung up with something else and by the time I did get around there the place was crawling with cops… what happened?'

Connolly realised he hadn't thought out his answers and had to think quick about how much he was prepared to reveal.

'Nothing,' as far as I knew…I was there on time but left when you didn't show. Cops? I didn't see any but the Arab was pissed off about being stood up. He took it personally.'

'There were cops there alright and I wasn't going to wade in asking questions...we can't meet now until we find out what's going on...I told you this Arab was a risk...'

'Our biggest risk is Deare and that fucken letter...' he paused to let that sink in, then he said, 'but I think we've cracked that nut...Heels is on his way here with Deare and he says he has the letter...'

Connolly thought he heard a faint hiss of breath intake. 'At last, a result,' the voice on the other end said, 'what will you do with Deare?'

'Well, he's read the letter and he's seen Heels. I think he's history. Meet me here in fifteen minutes and we'll sort this out for once and for all.'

'I'll be there in ten minutes.'

BIG FISH

Superintendent Tommy O'Brien pulled up outside the Oakdene Close house in the leafy suburb whose tranquillity had been completely shattered by the events of the past hour and the arrival of the crime scene investigation circus. Telescoped lighting rigs illuminated the driveway of the house and a tunnel of white canvas covered the entrance. None of the bodies had been moved and the first corpse lay undisturbed apart from a drab grey blanket that covered it.

Forensic investigators in disposable white bodysuits milled about, some hefting clear plastic evidence bags, some with evidence kits and a few with digital cameras snapping every inch of the crime scene.

Bernard Nolan stood in a huddle with Orla Farrell and two of the investigation team. O'Brien noticed Peter Cahill hovering in the background, a cell phone to his ear. He motioned for Nolan to join him, apart from this group.

'What in fuck's name is he still doing here, Bernard? I told you to get rid of him. I don't want those fucken spooks sticking their nose in where it's not wanted. This is our investigation, the International Bureau…'

'I think it's more complicated than that now, Tommy. One of the dead men carries an Arab passport and he's a diplomat of some sort. That makes it in Peter Cahill's business and he's made that very clear to me…'

'Fuck him, the other two are associates of Connolly and this is directly related to our ongoing investigation…how much does Cahill know about what's going on? You know secrecy is vital in this case as we have a traitor on the inside…I can't stress to you enough…' O'Brien stopped talking as Cahill approached.

'Superintendent O'Brien…it appears as though we have a big fish here…'

'I don't give a flying fuck what you think you have, Cahill. This is an ongoing 'Bureau investigation and I want you to keep your size 14s out of it…so fuck off back to whatever rock you crawled out from under. We'll take this from here…'

Peter Cahill grinned at O'Brien, unfazed by his outburst and clearly enjoying the discomfort he was causing.

'No can do, I'm afraid…this house belongs to someone we've been watching for some time…he's a big wheel in the 'hawala' system. He organises credit financing for Islamic Jihad groups all over the world under the cover of his diplomatic passport. We think he's been working with criminal groups too, which might explain why the other bodies belong to associates of this gangster you've been chasing…'

O'Brien exchanged sharp looks with Bernard Nolan and, ignoring Cahill, grabbed him and pulled him aside.

'Where's this fucken letter you've been chasing? I want to see it now.'

Bernard Nolan fished Tito's missive and its neatly typed lists of contacts and figures from his pocket and handed them to O'Brien. His superior stuffed them into his pocket without examining them.

'So you found this Deare person? Where is he now?'

'We're not sure…he was snatched by Gerry Heels who works for Connolly…'

'We must lift Connolly tonight before he bolts,' O'Brien interrupted, 'you come with me. Sergeant Farrell can look after this…'

Nolan exchanged shrugs with Cahill and followed O'Brien to his vehicle.

TRAITOR

Connolly considered clearing the club before the arrival of Gulliver but thought better of it when he figured his partner might get suspicious if the club was quiet and empty, on what should have been a busy night.

Things had begun to pick up outside. Every table in the club was full and there were more punters outside, waiting to get in. All the girls were up and working, the tills were jingling.

He checked his weapon for the umpteenth time and thought better of pouring himself another drink. He pushed the weapon into his waistband and pulled on his suit jacket, when he heard Armand rap on the door.

'Come,' he barked.

The door opened and the Algerian tumbled inside, followed quickly by O'Brien and Nolan.

Connolly stood, but said nothing.

Nolan spoke. 'Mr Connolly, where were you between the midnight and 1.30 this morning?'

'Who the fuck are you? What's this about?'

'I'm Inspector Bernard Nolan of the Garda International Bureau and this is Superintendent

O'Brien…'

'I know who youse are,…how're ye, Tommy? Superintendent? Jaysus, you've come up in the world…'

'We have reason to believe you were involved in an incident at a house in Sandymount this morning, Connolly, where were you…'

'I was here, Inspector, looking after business…ask anyone…Armand?'

Armand was nodding earnestly. Nolan noticed Connolly was staring and grinning at O'Brien.

'Two of your goons are lying dead in a house in Sandymount and you were seen leaving there in a hurry… you're coming with us, Connolly…'

'And,' O'Brien piped in, 'we have this,' as he slapped Tito's letter down on the desk.

Connolly reacted with rage, 'You fucken traitorous bastard,' he roared as he yanked the gun from his waistband and started blazing.

DOWN AT HEELS

Orla Farrell caught Peter Cahill's attention as O'Brien and Nolan drove off.

'What was all that about?' Orla asked.

'It was a question of territory, grown men, pissing in the snow,' Cahill told her before adding, 'look, Orla, I have to go. Bernard asked me to check on this Garvan Deare and his friend, Sandy Nelson. Apparently they've been found and are now in Store St along with one of Connolly's henchmen, who's been arrested. You'll be able to handle this show yourself, won't you?'

He didn't wait for her reply before marching out the gate and commandeering a police car and driver and speeding off. In Store St, he didn't ask for Deare and his companion, but went straight to the cell where Heels was being held.

The custody sergeant opened the cell door, knowing better than to ask any questions of the man flashing a Special Branch warrant card.

Heels had lost his cockiness. He'd been bested by a woman and the street cops in the station hadn't wasted any time letting him know about it. Cahill wasted no time either, finding out what he needed to know.

'You're in big trouble, Gerry, boy. You'll get a good stretch for kidnapping and assault, if not attempted murder...you can help yourself right now by answering one question for me...'

'Fuck off, copper. I'm saying nothing.'

Cahill guessed there was little he could get from Heels so he left. Outside he sought out Deare and Nelson. The journalist and another man were receiving medical attention. Cahill brought Sandy Nelson into the hallway.

'Sandy, did Heels indicate where he might bring you? Or where his boss was?'

'No...he didn't. No, wait a minute. He did get a call and he said he'd be there in five minutes. That's when we jumped him.'

'We?'

'Myself and Brando...he said something about 'the club' but he never said the name of it.'

Cahill didn't wait for her to finish. He knew where Nolan and O'Brien had gone.

CLUB NIGHT

Ivan Toscic was growing concerned as the crowd in the club grew. His view of the door, where he believed Connolly had his office, was partially obscured by revellers and half naked dancers. He knew he had only one course of action; he had to kill Connolly because the gangster had seen him.

He was figuring his next move when Superintendent O'Brien and Bernard Nolan entered the club, pushing the Algerian ahead of them through the door. They didn't see Ivan because they were obviously preoccupied and the club was too densely packed by now to see much further than the person in front of them.

Ivan made his way across the room and followed them through the door. He had to force the lock with a sharp shoulder and elbow punch but it went unnoticed in the drunken melee outside.

Once through the door, he paused to get his bearings. The 'thump...thump' of the sound system was duller but no less loud. He took a second to breathe and as his ears adjusted to the stillness, he caught the faint sound of raised voices on the other side of the door at the end of the corridor.

When he heard gunshots, he drew his weapon and charged through the door. The air was thick with the smell of gunpowder and Ivan didn't hesitate before taking out the startled gangster behind the desk in front of him.

Connolly took the first bullet through his open mouth as shards of teeth and blood sprayed from his shattered jaw. The second bullet his his throat while the third hit him in the chest as he fell and knocked him sitting in his chair.

Ivan swept the room in a crouch. Superintendent O'Brien lay slumped to his left clutching his stomach and a spreading dark patch on his shirtfront. Armand cowered behind an armchair in the corner, his hands around his head, whimpering. Only Bernard Nolan remained standing and unharmed.

Ivan Toscic waved his hand in front of Nolan's face.

'Holy God,' was all Nolan could say.

It was all over by the time Peter Cahill came crashing through the door with reinforcements. Bernard Nolan sat in a corner with a glazed expression. Cahill took Ivan Toscic aside for a huddled discussion, while Gardai and emergency service personnel attended to O'Brien and Connolly. Armand was led away, handcuffed. No-one noticed as Cahill led Toscic outside to a waiting car.

RACING CHANCE

Three weeks later, Bernard Nolan met Peter Cahill for a quiet pint in the seclusion of Coogan's. Nolan had become a minor celebrity. He knew he could kiss his career as an undercover cop goodbye and there was a lingering whiff of unanswered questions in all the media speculation that followed.

What rankled Bernard Nolan most was his failure to fill in the gaps. He couldn't shed the persistent feeling of having been manipulated in a much bigger scheme and he was certain his old friend, Peter Cahill, was the one with the key to unravel the mystery.

'Well, here's to Ivan Toscic whoever he was? and wherever he is, Pedro?' Nolan toasted, raising his pint to clink glasses. Peter Cahill raised his glass too, avoiding Nolan's questioning look.

'Have you heard from him?' Cahill asked.

'I was about to ask you the same question,' Nolan rejoined.

'Sure how would I hear from him? I barely knew him ten minutes before he was gone…'

'That may be true, Pedro and it may not. I may be the

shadowy figure in the murky twilight of undercover investigation, according to the hacks, but there are people lurking in deeper shadows than me and I wouldn't have to travel far to find one.' He paused.

'Orla Farrell has heard from him. I hear she's taken her annual leave soon for a holiday in the sun, somewhere in the Adriatic..'

Nolan watched his old friend closely for reaction but there was none. Cahill remained impassive, a study in detached nonchalance, thought Nolan.

'It occurred to me that if there was one common thread in all these events of the past month, it's you. I never took any notice when someone told me they'd spotted you in Sarajevo. And that was only last week. Then Garvan Deare told me how you knew Tito and how you'd been there when he'd written the letter…'

Pedro Cahill made a show of flicking open the folded Racing Post he had produced from his jacket pocket and he proceeded to study it with determination, scrolling a bookie's pencil down the column of runners in the 3.15pm at Leopardstown that afternoon. The flesh between his eyes furrowed in studied concentration as though 'the form' was his sole concern.

He fixed Bernard Nolan with a steady, penetrating gaze and paused.

Nolan ignored him and carried on. 'As far fetched as it might seem,' he said, 'at least eight people were now dead…and for what? So some shady bunch of spymasters could nail one fucking dodgy Jihadist?'

Cahill held his hand up to silence him.

'Tito's letter helped you shut down a gang of criminals. It helped put a crooked cop out of business. We got rid of a terrorist too …and if you ever made any wild allegations about anyone?' he smirked, 'Well, it would be easy to dismiss them as the jealous rantings of an overweight cop with a grudge…'

The silence between them was deafening before Cahill said, 'Fuck all that, Bernard, let's have a flutter for old time's sake. Here's one with little or no form, but you never know, it might be worth a risk and he's been lucky for me before?'

Aghast at Cahill's studied nonchalance, Bernard Nolan picked up the paper and scanned the runners in the race Peter had picked. He didn't see it immediately, then there it was…

The sixth horse in the 4.30 was 'postcardfromapigeon.'

THE END

Made in the USA
Charleston, SC
08 September 2014